The Joshua Tree

Robert Cabot

THE JOSHUA TREE

North Atlantic Books, Berkeley, California

The Joshua Tree

Copyright © 1970, 1988 by Robert Cabot

ISBN 1-55643-023-X cloth
ISBN 1-55643-039-6 paperback

Published by North Atlantic Books
2320 Blake Street
Berkeley, California 94704

Revised Second Edition

First edition published by Atheneum, New York, 1970

Designed by Harry Ford
Cover designed by James and Ruth McCrea

The Joshua Tree is sponsored by the Society for the Study of Native Arts and Sciences, a nonprofit educational corporation whose goals are to develop an ecological and crosscultural perspective linking various scientific, social, and artistic fields; to nurture a holistic view of arts, sciences, humanities, and healing; and to publish and distribute literature on the relationship of mind, body, and nature.

To Bill Keys

Foreword

When I first saw the manuscript of *The Joshua Tree* twenty years ago,
I wrote:

"There are few genuine prose-poets around these days, and fewer still
with anything to say. Cabot's first book is a fantastic exception. He is
a poet and a damned good one, and he has words for us of love, and hope.

"He also has a warning, a gentle one, which is heard in the beating
and the dying hearts of men, women, and beasts—and the Joshua Tree.
I don't know when I have read such evocative and truly lovely writing,
nor heard a man speak so truly of the curse that lies upon us all."

Much time has passed since *The Joshua Tree* first moved me. Through-
out the world, animate creation is in worse jeopardy than ever before.
But there is a bright spot. There are those amongst us who recognize the
extraordinary danger to which our world is currently exposed and they
are evoking a response from people of goodwill which may just possibly
be our salvation.

The message which Robert Cabot gives us in *The Joshua Tree* is as fresh
and vital as ever it was. Now that the book is being reissued, I am convinced that it will fill an enormous need and be as moving to the people
of today as it was to those of an earlier generation.

Farley Mowat
Port Hope, Ontario
March 5, 1988

The Joshua Tree

Paiute Pinenut Prayer

When we come to a pinenut place
We talk to the ground, the mountain, everything.
We ask to feel good, strong;
We ask for cool breezes that we may sleep at night.

The pinenuts belong to the mountain.
We ask the mountain that we may have of its pinenuts.
We would eat.

I, Joshua tree

Sigh, the wind of time.

Cycles, wheels — the sand blows thin over my roots. This is my time, passive, there is no end. My flower, my honey, gentle moth strokes, my seed.

Reaching down, cool, moist; reaching up, breathing, suckling the sun. Out, balancing on the sand, wrapped in hot blue. Air that flows through me, I cut the air with pointed blades. Blunted on joints and limbs, sighing in hollows, air with the dust-puffs from the raindrops, with desert scents, the sage, the piñon, the freshness of hot granite lichens.

To be. Rooted. Bending, a leaf torn; returning, the seasons. Accepting. Tear at me, burn me, ice me over, gnaw, burrow; I flower again. Bees trembling white petals, oriole swinging in the spikes, woodpecker hollowing, nesting wood-rat and lizard.

We are the desert. We are its dust, its scent, its stone and sand and washed soil, its echoes and motion and life, the gold of its veins, the flower of its flesh. We drink in its earth, we stretch in its air, its sun, we spread our seed. We are.

You are of the desert too, old Will. You learned, you leave your engines now to melt into the sand, you have silenced them and have left their scarrings to grow over, your hungers are stilled. You accept now and give back as did the dark ones, the soft feet, before you.

3

I feel the slow halting pressures as you pass into my thin shade. When you are gone my roots will sprout again through the sand, I shall feel the multiplication, the new life.

Your weight stretches over, stirring, breathing; quiet.

The piñon sings beside us, splinters the sun, dusts yellow. Our roots entwine.

Another joins you, as you joined the silent ones before they left. The dancing step, the presence. Your Lily.

The others, the danger. The shifting of the moon, the dirtying of the sun, the stink these new ones bring. Show them, O friend. The balance, the essential balance.

The moth, my gentle lover; without him I should die.

You breathe my breath, I yours, Will.

My black bones, peeled layers: your shelter, your warmth, nourish the earth.

My hollows: honey.

My silence to soak your noises. The silent conversation.

In the drought, one flower, my lily to you.

I, old Will

Old Will, old Willy. My mattress fits me — a wife, a lizard in the sunny sand — with my old saddle frame under the head. Curled, my knees bent to ease the beating pains. My walking sticks in the afternoon dust beside me, one splinted like a bone: snapped in a ground-squirrel hole carrying copybooks from the school cabin. Half-sun under the piñon and the Joshua tree, old friends, the dry rustling and the sighing.

There's kick left, though, a lot of kick. When I've rested a bit, when the bees go 'way, buzzing in my ears, itching so fearful under my cap, under my pate. When the banks untie that money (worked, always, a day's work; most, they don't know what it means now). I'll be going: this once-promised land to another promised land, like to follow again the wild bees to their honey. East, east, east, back and beyond across the steppes of Russia, four thousand miles in the Rand-McNally Atlas, from Volga windmills and the white beards and the clots of fresh cream and the starched kindergarten collars.

So they twist the moon from its orbit; so my mountains dry and the wild hay grows no more; so the

dyas

I listen —

my

Inner
Voice

5

mountain quail have left and the valley quail come, getting their water from the mistletoe berries, and that neither's not enough and their eggs are sterile this year and they cry now as never before, out in the sage. So they drove me to prison once more, a last time: their taunts and thievings, stole my cattle . . . *O my wife, my Mana, left alone* . . . so they take my land and close my mines and send the revenooers out. So their smog comes closer, in from L.A. now, a hundred and twenty miles, flowing over the San Gorgonio, you'd see it this year on the high Mohave Springs desert where the grass was like the golden Caspian and the antelope ranged in thousands. So they prepare for Armageddon and their blasts explode double from the sky and we are beaten in our desert like ore in a stamp mill. So they drag their sub-homes here behind them, foul and trample the desert and steal away those bits about me, rusting; so they scorn my gift of all this for a museum (no money, but they blast at the moon) — I'll sell it, bit by bit, an auction, and it will be lost, but it will take me out there, the banks cannot hold me then.

And to India where they have no Christian soldiers and they know about the soul and love, and to the promised land. Virgin for a thousand miles. I've read about it, I have it in my albums. Colin, he'll take me, like he said. North of the Gobi where the dinosaur eggs hatched: lay out there and hatch, make a dinosaur. Lots of things grew more then, there, when the earth stood straight up and down on end and there was no night.

Another gopher, Walter cat, good, wildcat half-blood—tufted ears, the hoarse purr—I'll trap no more

may

the setting

be

the rising

6

rats for you under the Joshua tree.

They'll not keep me in and there's always another Jericho. Where Joshua stood looking down from the hills, his spear stretched out in his fist, and demanded all their blood. And the Mormons came and they saw these cabbage trees with their arms out to the valley and they called them the Joshua trees — the promised land, the slaughter, the chosen people.

The innocent tree, protector. Where the yellow-black oriole nests. Where the giant sloth stood twenty feet tall to feed on the new growth until he was brought down by Indian spears and made into jerky forever. Where the yucca moth puts her eggs in the flower and brings them pollen and fertilizes the peaceful lily tree. Where the desert rat finds the spiked leaves with their spiny fringes to protect his nest amongst the fallen trucks. Where the yucca borers and the ants tunnel and she petrifies her wood to protect herself. Where the hawk rests and the buzzard retreats, the night lizard lives under the bark. Where the woodpecker and the flicker dig insects from the trunk, the red-tailed hawk nests in his creosote twigs, the Chemehuevi found fibers for their sandals and the red root to decorate their baskets.

It gives life, it does not take.

my

Cosmic Tree

cross

on the

immortal

path

Canaan. Spear's Ranch.

SERRANO PALMS STAGE   1921

LEEV MAIL HERE PLEAS

I retouched it with green paint left over, for posterity. Another rusted bit made from a Banning biscuit box, brought here to my collection, beyond the pile of ore-car rails where the black sage grows, where the apples

7

and peaches and lettuce once grew, where the arrastra still stands with its cartwheel and mule harness on the end of the sweep, its stone circle where the rocks dragged, crushed the ore before I got my first stamp mill. My promised land.

It'll be cool, Lily girl, draw it up on the pulley. Dug that well deeper nineteen oh nine. The Missis planted the bamboo—never could get rid of it since. Pardon that I don't help you. Knees, the knees.

Sit down here, girl. There's shade some. A heavy load for a girl, that pack, a long way. Colin, he sat there, first time, dust white on his eyebrows, pack stuck to him where the sweat had dried. Walking away from something, Mexico to Canady he'd do. Maybe nineteen and sixty-four, three four years back. Come up on old Will here in the shade, shade like you'd not find down on the Sonora.

You learn it from him, Lily girl, this traipsing off alone?

Alone, like I'd never had time like that. Only looking for cattle or gold, and I'd get the Missis on a horse to follow the wild bees to their honey in the hollow piñons and oaks and Joshuas.

Sit down, be with Will.

lie softly,
Robin
little son

8

I, Lily

Lily girl, little Lily.

Enough, though, to make the milk crate creak, little Lily — my bottoms are so tired, where the muscles run under, climbing muscles. Bottoms that fit so cool in my Colin's warm strong hands — here old Will all cracked and gnarled.

I listen,

Blessings from my thighs, calves — I'd hike the desert again just for that.

White House Evaporated Milk.

I'd die, I'd cry, I'd shudder right through to my toes for Colin's milk that dries flaky in the morning on my belly — poor Will, he can only touch a little, I suppose, but it's all relative, relative.

I
draw
it
in
deep

Oh! but my heart explodes. Does Will know, can he know?

Colors explode, sharp shadows — a black window shattered by the desert sun, jagged blacks, jittering whites and yellows, greens. The scarlet flower of the beaver-tail cactus, it burns inside, in my tummy. Spiked leaves blue-green pick at my nerves. Plop! a lizard gray on my pack, stunned, scuttles — fell from the piñon — a twitching bit of tail left, scratching o's

my
Treasure

in the dust: I will not think of the first trout, me only seven, that cried cruel! cruel! and writhed o's in the four-leafed clover.

No! because I cannot stop singing, and because my skin, because I have found my skin, dry, hot, the dust and salt, feel it crying to be free again under the shirt, under the soft old faded (finally, finally — Clorox) jeans. Would I have thought of it? Colin hiked naked for a month, he told me. Kind of sexy at first, and then I'm an animal. Boots and a hat, the pack that rides on my hips and straps just at the dark hair and makes my belly stuff out, hat with the leather thong and the slider Colin made so it won't blow off down some canyon. But nothing hiding, nothing between me and the desert sun, and they bobbed sexily and then they were me like everything else. Tightened skin, hot, cool, feeling the air. (Grumbling organs with limbs and a head, that's clothing.) Unity, one me, I'm all me.

And the tender air, love me, we embrace.

I shall just sit here for a bit, just: "Knees?" and: "Willow Hole dried up, you told me 'bout, found it; coyote wells too."

And he'll know. Cicada silence, long, long; no, you don't measure it, you let it rest till it's ready to wake up by itself. (Always they want to talk, even if the words are beautiful, and the bells on their elbows and their flowers, and the music can lift you right to the snowy edge of the volcano, crush you.) And when it wakes (can I wait, oh! can I?) maybe he'll "Yuh."

Then, quietly; no, all in a rush, I'll tell him. Oh! my bighorn, my wild wild desert ram, your proud free eye, and mine. I could have touched you with my nolina-stalk walking-stick, I could have leaped to

Air

the

Male

your back, and your muscles so smooth, so male, your cock and your dark bag (how much my Colin has taught me, how beautiful!) so strong. Your great horns curling back and full around — stone roots to the cliffs. To see them lowered, thrust up, up, thrusting head strained, exploding, dissolving in white light.

come
up me
up me

You sprang so swift to the boulder, scorning the scrubby oak and yucca, alert, the wonder, the pride, naked we were one. The eternity of curiosity, the never-ending moment where we met and understood.

And you scaled the cliff in an instant and stood in the sky, looked down on me, invited me. And you wheeled and were gone with the hawks.

You took me with you. I rode with you, hanging to your horns, elbows flying, heels tight against your thighs. Up, away, springing over the pink rock, the burning sand, the black sage, leaping the cholla silver in the early sun. Forgive me that first fear; you will know now I am you and shall never leave you. You are my trip, through the flowers, through the ringing of the bells, to the sun.

Aries, my

Creator

Your flight, the flight of the Joshua tree. Racing through the clouds, through the driven sand, through time. Joshua tree, stretched in your strange angles out over the piñon pine, over old Will propped on his mattress, hurtling through time. Roots of the desert reaching deep into the sky. Your single green flower white against the sailing moon, you run in the wind. How many voices has your silence? The giant lily, the praying tree, praying over us, for us, for the promised land. I join you too, you carry me on, you lift me clear of that sucking and cloying and jingling and numbing. And it is the strength of your limbs, of your will, that

my

Shaman's

Rope

tied

11

bears me, not some arcanum to be distilled from your corpse, juices drawn from your wounds, elixirs from your flowers.

Their sad delusions. The trapped ones, trapped in their freedoms, caught by the easy trip, the new convention, the "Grass, man, grass." Weeds for the spirit, weeds of the spirit. The collective and the external; substitutes for the true exploration, the true voyage inward . . . *Our journey, O Colin, out of space and time. The Pacific to the Mediterranean, but really an inner sea. Weave your web of poetry, my Colin, I'll be the woof. Together we love, to the sheep bells and the wind in the plane trees and the brook rushing down the village street, hanging so high above the sea.*

Sky

"Peyote from the mescal, belladonna from the lily, desert Indians, the Shoshones, with their visions, their grasp of the soul. Don't you see, Lily? The giant lily may be their secret. Ask while you're there, look around, bring us some, Lily, be our girl of the flower again."

Interlude—between mountains of Calabria, deserts of Mohave. Empty day—fog blowing through the rhododendrons, Golden Gate Park, Drive Slow— vacant eyes, vacant friends.

Vacant asking.

Will humphed and was angry, he was right. And he almost discarded me there and then.

"A corruption of man's nature, Lily girl, like fornicating when the female's out of season, no other animal would do that. Yuh, heading for the end."

Pa would talk like that too. Not about the fornication, he'd have been embarrassed, wouldn't have believed it either, but about the corruption, the decline, the regression, the progress to extinction, yes. Often in these last years. Before no, though. Then he perhaps didn't think much, and perhaps it wasn't so clear, and life was more of a desperate season-to-season business, I guess, though he didn't let us see that side then.

Yesterday, my boots crunching in the sand, so happy watching the hummingbird in the mesquite, tripped bang on an enormous turtle (how clumsy, humiliating! no one to see), I'd just stripped off everything, tied to my pack. My skin, oh! my miraculous skin, shouting to the wind, my hat . . . *"That's a hat that never was new," they said of Colin's; five months he'd hiked, alone* . . . tugging at my jaw, and who would have thought there would have been any of man's structures here, beehives where no man had been since the wild hay dried up and the black sage took over . . . *Do they choke my Valley Hope? So far to the north, where California climbs into Oregon* . . . and the Indians left ollas hidden in caves, arrowheads after a rain, drawings of their sagas under overhangs, metate grinding-stones in the sand or hollowed (how many generations stretched back?) in a granite ledge convenient to the site? But there it was, so familiar, oh Pa! the bleached gray wooden box (only with different initials, J & M) on its rock above the buckwheat.

Valley Hope. Rows of white beehives stacked neatly in our Model A truck (its round eye of a gas gauge, floating like a compass; they still write Ford that way), rows of white beehives. It meant he would go now, he would leave me, his Lily of Valley Hope, Ma is crying too. Initials carved deep, JT, Joe Tocca,

wings

on the

Turtle;

soar, the

heavy

Earth

O

Divine

Eye,

13

Giuseppe Toccacielo. Your little Liliana, your flower, how could you leave me behind to fade? For days, for weeks, forever, and my tummy turns cold and hard, I shiver, my nerves are aspen leaves. Hate, I hate you, you are bad, I will die right now and that will show you.

Oh! I love you so, Pa.

You said it was no life for me, Valley Hope, and you were damned if you'd buy me a husband when the time came the way the others tried. With honey and the hunters now, and city uncles, you'd send me off, to the south, an education, a profession. San Valentino, Los Angeles.

You drag me onto the bus and the world turns ice-blue bleak behind their hateful glass. San Valentino State — agriculture in steel mills, education in the super-everythings, regulated lust and greed and numbness in the country clubs. And the desert out beyond. Seven hundred miles you sent me, you turned the world upside down. I called you and called you, I cried for seven years. Never, never, shall I tell you what they did to me for your PhD that I never got. How I've lied to you! but that was what you wanted of me. How many lifetimes have I lain alone in my flaming grief? How often did I, in despair, crush the flowers and paint my face, your face, jiggle and consume and waste and turn hollow with the others? But I couldn't, oh how could I? forget forever my smile and how I love you. Then, one after another, they would reach out for me, and, untouching, turn away in their grief or bitterness or anger or humiliation or hate or even perhaps in love.

Do you know why I left, why you had to let me go,

may

you

live

the

Shadow,

14

why I cut my beautiful hair, that death could have had me, what led me to San Francisco?

Saint Francis with your birds and soft animals, your flowers, your bees and honey. Broken hearts, their rat race still, their rules, their noses stuck high. But there were other worlds and other hearts, there were quests. And I found my love, my eternal flowering tree where the lily can grow full, my Colin.

Ah! Joshua tree, Will (a lizard crawls on your swollen knee), Liliana who reaches for heaven, we have so much to say. Here, take my hand, I kiss your bark, your beard, the weathered aeons.

may

you

live

the

Light.

Me, Will Spear: little Jerry Dan once – windmills on the Volga, bottles dancing bright on the Elbe

Your face is dim, girl. Your lips, I shiver and bristle. Sure, if you like. Go ahead. I'll come along. No, no, I'm all right, just get these sticks under me. Get around pretty good. Keep working, day's work, never missed. Don't know this nowadays, something for nothing. Chilling up anyhow, now, with the sun sunk. Just split this oak, kindling. Came from up there near where you must' seen that bighorn. Used to be lots, big ones, oaks and mesquite and piñons. Bring them in on the wagon.

Set a fire. Joshua, petrified, best there is, burns all day.

Can of corn, coffee, still working on that watermelon you and Colin brought, out back. Saltines.

Old black Majestic, The Great. Fifty years ago we hauled you in. Got sanded in the draw. Screwed on your lion's feet and the oven door with its flowers and leaves and newfangled thermometer.

The Missis, Helen, my Mana—"it's Mama, Robin boy." Her sourdough cooling on the shelf. Shoulder roast, potatoes dug with a mining pick when my shovel broke, gravy and cabbage and applesauce. Well

I look –
dark
signs

jungle

fire
outside
the cave

sabertooth

16

water. Them fellows with the still, they'll kill old Jamie yet, weak and cheating and alone, they'll kill him with that liquor.

Just sit here now. I'll get the albums and the lamp.

By damn! must open that damper, night air sets like death in the knees. Still comes in, wind pushes it up through the floor. Weather, heat, time, drawn the cracks open; tight when I laid it, sixty years. Termites, mice, our house a piece of cheese . . . *Twenty-five-pound cheese chunk, up from Banning in the wagon, spring and fall, in the cooler with the burlap wicks, outside the window over the sink. "But it'll make it dark in here, Willy, can't you?"*

uncrowning

me

Where'd I put that other album? So dim and dusty in here, cold, closed off from the kitchen. But the pink sunset lies on my writing table, my pens, my poetry. Pink like a birthday card I made for my Mana in 'forty-five up at San Quentin, out of silk.

> And never would I see your face
> In God's sweet world again.

Breathe, old Will, breathe deep, or the heart will strangle. Distance, Will, from way back, from way up ahead. The upright piano is covered with her bed throw, guitar's dried out. They're propped along the top, smiling out. She's sitting by the window, her arm on the sill, the winter sun coming in on her white hair.

ghost fingers

playing

> Now she looks down upon me here
> Through her window in the sky

Distance, Will, let it stretch out.

Do you think the Volga flows into the Elbe, Jerry

boy? Do you think these Protestant towers hear the chants from the scruffy beards? The black hulls come sliding in, the cranes as high as the stars swing back and forth. Look out across the river, covered with dancing bottles, shining ice. German shouts up from the street, cursing the dogs pulling his cart piled high with bottles. But it's not your German. Catherine the Great, Elizabeth Petrovna, Hunsinger (the Huns, the monstrous raping Huns), Danziger who married your mother, Hewlett she was (her soft round face, so grossly fat, ten children do that natural to some women). All your people, shipped from Prussia to the Volga across the marshes and the thousand miles of wheat, but they kept their language if not their religion. It was going home after all those centuries, though they laughed at the way you spoke. The world was so small back home, you were such a little boy, but here you start school and you walk alone. Look out for the dog-carts! But you are born not to fear anything, your mother told you. And you saved pennies and bought such delights at the food bars.

Or was that when you'd moved on to Cornwall and the hot tarts? Jerry Dan, born on September seventh, eighteen seventy-seven, Kov on the Volga, so you're eight years old and the best school is to go down in the mines with your father, a thousand feet down and out under the sea . . . *They sold me a piece of a mine, the dividends come on ever since . . . Don't worry, Helen Jane, there's always the mine money and the warden thinks we'll get a pardon . . .* here where England's tied to the Ruhr, and the fossils make you so small and nothing. Tropical England, before it became an island. America, tied too through Siberia. Still, it's the other side of the world,

black

figures

line

on the

snow

comfort
wrapping,
a
Mother

it's the new world. Always they're talking, arguing, writing, reading the maps, and Father was learning to be a miller too and he'd come home powdered every night.

And I hear you ask, Jerry, "But when will we go home?"

the ancient

Home to the windmills dusted with flour, the voice of the great river, the smell of haying, the work

Tales

horses, you squat for hours on their flat backs hanging to their harness. Here, ponies for the mines and they won't let you ride them hardly ever. But there's Dangler who's much older and can do everything and takes you rabbit-hunting with slingshots and wouldn't kill them except to eat, wouldn't be right. Roast them, right there in our cave on a green willow stick over an elder fire, and you suck at the bones and be hun-

Hare

gry even if you aren't. Dangler, who'd cuff you, who shoved his slingshot at you on the gangplank. "I'm

Cow

too old for it," and the cattle bawled back.

Prize Herefords for America. And you. You were all jammed into one room, slept in three shifts, and

moon
beasts

learned to vomit to leeward. He wouldn't pay for steam. You cried into your stomach, Russian tears, German tears, even English tears. It was no good. Kov was there before, trains came and went, connected,

dark

and your language hadn't changed. But now: The waves were yellow or black or flaming and the dis-

lunar

tance sank and sank. The Atlantic gurgled by through the bilges, rushed in the scuppers, washed and washed.

way

Here, girl, photos, I've got them all. Jumbled though, can't keep them straight. Don't see so good, and then they'll slip a few out now and then, get them copied for *The*

19

Wild West and *Frontiersman* and palm them back wherever, or maybe not at all, some's missing. Jumbled. Poke the fire, comes in cold with the dark, though the wind drops. Wick needs trimming, get to it tomorrow. Used to have a power plant, outside there, beyond the ore samples. Didn't seem worth the trouble and devil's noise after the Missis went. Shoo any visitors away before sunset, except you. You stay right here, keep old Will company. Can't eat a whole can of corn alone.

George Dan — Danziger too foreign — that's him, my father. It's my face, and the bald dome. Set on the photographer's chair, his belly bulges down on his crotch, pushes his thighs apart, pushes his fat hands out to his knees — what's left of his lap. I'm hard and slim, though twisted now: old Will. Miller George, there was more room then on that lap for a thrashing. Nebraska ("flat" that meant to the Omahas, Flat River, Platte River) near where the Frenchman and Republican rivers join. The mill sluice where we boys'd float sticks down to their end in splashing paddles. The mill that bought him land and cattle, and sometimes we'd work on the buffalo ranch at Palisades until Buffalo Jones ran them all up to Yellowstone at government expense in 'ninety. No, I never liked it, buffalo meat. Stinking Creek Ranch, stank 'cause the buffaloes wallowed there. Between the North Platte and the Frenchman.

There's Mother standing behind him, beside him, her hand on his shoulder heavy. Her gray skirt set firm on the floor, rising up over her enormous hips, up over her stomach, until finally finding a waist under her bagging breasts, almost up to her armpits. And the gray shirt buttoned

fairy Tales

cold Volga

Dragon

that

swallows

the

Hero

up to her chin. And her hair pulled tight to keep out of the cooking. Childbearing does it, some women . . . *A cow colicked—blew one with my knife once, in the Big Horns, and she lived; horse wouldn't have though, different kind of stomach* . . . Always had her hands in something, fat red hands with their smell of the soap she made, hands that nagged at me and wiped at me and kept closing doors and turning down lamps and hushing things and scrubbing and scrubbing, purity, purity. Did I ever know her? Those hands couldn't keep me. The others, some of the others, yes. Eleven of us, they're all gone now. Just old Will, Jerry Dan, who took off after the buffaloes and the cows and salvation, found his gold and another name.

my

Dragon

slain, the

Treasure

That's Jamie Pope. Doesn't look like much, does he, girl? Wasn't either. You seen his grave that I put up where we found him.

JAMES POPE

DIED HERE

FOUND AND

BURIED BY WILL

SPEAR, JOE

WILEY, GRANT

REAGAN. MAR

23 1925

IN LIFE AND DEATH

I LIE ALONE

That's it. Maybe I'll find my poetry to him later too. Wasn't often, I'll tell you, that he wore a stiff collar like that, and a jacket with button pockets. Not when we found him, not now either, his mustache half loose from his rotting face. Forty days.

Forty days. The wind like a coyote through the yuccas and the Joshuas. Will Spear. They'll name this place for you when you get the road made and the Buicks and the Packards and the Hudsons and the Fords come dusty by. Spear's Outlook—over the Smoke Tree Desert and the Santa Claras and Serrano Palms where they've come from. She said they would.

me

Will Spear

Desert

King

The coyote wind. Your legs freezing in those overalls, your toes pinched to ice in those roping boots, your ears still cold where you have your hat tied down with that scarf. That's quite a rig you worked out there, that brush rake on the back of your wagon, Joe at the mules, you and Grant working the rig. Kind of fresno scraper . . . *When my knees are working again, I could still do it, though's work, plenty. Might, too; need a road to get back into the high country, show it to the city folk, find the wild honey too. Ninety, but I still could . . .* Young fellow then, you were, not fifty. Raking brush up along each track of the wagon, make the ruts, make the road, to Spear's Outlook. By damn! but that's a wind. Do you feel your rifle back there, the one with the silver and turquoise the Walapais did for you, hung on the wagon post? Never can tell, lots of folks want what you got with your wells and tanks and good land, good with the wild hay, and twelve hundred head of cows and the mules and horses and the high grade in sacks by old McQuillen's adobe barn (may he rest well at Serrano Palms) ready for the five-stamp mill.

Pull that Joshua trunk to the side a bit, pick it up for the Missis' stove on the way back. Hold up! There's something there behind that buckthorn. Tarpaulin, back pack, rocks rolled in against the down yucca,

22

ashes, a boot sticking from under. Death in the coyote wind, and you know it's Jamie Pope. Curled up, rotting between the freezes. Barricade against the cold and the coyotes and the cats and the buzzards. But nothing would work against death and the rotting and the bugs to take you away, Jamie, alone and in despair like you always were. Even your last mule you ate years ago, and your brand disappeared twenty years back and whenever you found cattle in a lonely spot not too far from your cabin you'd shoot and pack off the meat for jerky. More than once your friend, your friend Will Spear, would find the carcass and maybe even his brand still visible, and he'd have gone after anyone else with his rifle, but not you, Jamie, you were too alone. And when your sight gave out and you couldn't find cattle, one by one you tied a mule to a stake and killed it for meat. And there weren't any left.

Remember, Will, in 'sixteen, winter too, out pulling a slip with the mule team, grading down below the windmill, before you married your Mana, your Helen Jane? He came crawling up your road in the dust and puddles. Somehow he'd come those miles from his shack in the canyon under Ram Mountain. Thirty days, he said, with just a case of milk, and too weak to get out of bed, and feared of the hydrophobia skunks gnawing around him, attacking him in his sleep. Somehow he got there—did he crawl just that last stretch for effect, could you even question that of a decent man, you who nursed him back for more than a month? Jerky from your best steers, and gravy and potatoes and lettuce and fruit you'd put up, and the fire always red in the stove. Until one day he danced a jig with the liquor in him again which he couldn't take for those weeks, from those fellows' still, a jig with the jug on the kitchen table, such as it was, and said he thought it was time to be going.

You were the only friend he had, and you couldn't say much for him, nothing. A worthless old man who'd cast himself out from the world. Worked with him for a time, you had, digging in that mine he'd started on the back side of Two Skull Mountain. Ore was poor, though, you both quit and he moved over across Juniper Flats to where he'd found water, Jamie Pope Canyon it became. And before that he'd worked the night shift for years for Clem Toole's Two Skull Mine, and Clem had told you how the weight was often short, measured against the day shift. Must have hid the amalgam near his cabin he had up there by the mine. Kept showing up till the end with gold for you to sell for him, though there was nothing up there on Ram where he said he got it — damn, didn't even have mules for years to work the arrastra he'd set up as a front. Cross-country it wasn't more than nine ten miles from his shack back to Two Skull, abandoned long before, where he could dig up his amalgam till his pockets bulged. And he was heading back, coming out across the valley, when the coyote wind caught him, worst of the year, remember?

And still they want to dig him up and look in his pockets. Buried him as we found him, pushed him in pieces with sticks into the hole we'd dug right there, and we'd had no stomach or heart to touch a thing.

That's what you say still, isn't it, Will? Worthless, a disgrace, no one'd live his life alone like that if he weren't a black disgrace, like you said in your poetry. Don't know, though, don't know. He could dance a

sun
man's
heart

gold
earth's
heart

wind
death's
heart

24

jig, and maybe did my take on the gold make up for the cattle he took? Remember his eyes? Those same eyes there, a little light, lot of sadness. Kind of a beauty, hanging on to aloneness, shouldn't I know this by now? Why'd you go up there, young Will, that spring after he'd died? Weren't nothing there, you'd known. But Jamie, Jamie was there and it's the prettiest canyon in these parts. His cabin in the yucca and his well all stoned in, with its bucket rig, his pride. There's Jamie, there, in that heap of rusting cans and broken stone whiskey jugs and bottles out his door. And he's there each time you passed, on your way up to the head of the canyon, working on the sulfide bismuth mine. Hundred-foot shaft, two-hundred-foot tunnel. Japs would like it, even if Kaiser dropped it 'cause too much sulfur, killing all the trees round where they worked it at Fontana. In Jerome there was that sulfur and arsenic in the ore and the tuberc'lars came from all over, gosh yes, killed the TB, yuh, killed the TB. Each time you pass there's Jamie, there, not under that tarp and those rocks we rolled in so's the coyotes wouldn't dig him up.

Hard to see in the yellow photo, the black pages with their torn gaps, they soak up all the light. White turns to ragged orange to black streaks: trim it tomorrow. Turn it down, see less. The eyes, bees scratch inside behind them. Touch o' Heaven, orange bees on the yellow label, Joe Tocca, Valley Hope. Peace, Jamie, I wrote the poetry day after we shoved you underground, I've learned, by looking back at you.

And there's me above and they'd got the beard off sure. Beard better'n Colin's it was. Got it off me, womenfolks. He be keeping his, trimmed up some for

kings

all

and

deep

the

golden

sulfur

purifier

his Lily, though, since he came through here that other time. Half the Sonora on it then. Me, I dumped a bucket over his head — must' liked it, stayed a week. Or'd trimmed up for his Dad? Yuh, I see you smiling, girl . . . *Juney, little daughter, here, we got that copy-book to do* . . . crying, girl, but he'll be back, few days. Denver's no place, not for Colin.

Yuh, that's me, all posed and slicked up. Didn't get the mustache, not that time, bushy too to make up, the hat to hide the bald.

Kov

men

kiss

on the

lips

Me, Lily; touch your heaven, little Lily

Propped against the honey can—Pa's honey sent to Colin and me—the first album. Time tipped unsteady in the dim light. You're there, so many of you.

Will Speare, dropped the "e" when the fellow in Serrano Palms got all your mail (why you?). With your finger propping up your cheek and your thumb hooked in a jacket pocket, pocket they don't have nowadays.

And Jamie Pope, the crack in the gloss rotting your skull.

Here Buck Brown, high on the covered wagon, like you'd always sat on that bench with your foot on the board and that loop of a whip and the waterfall of a brown beard (did you make the name or the name make you?) with its white spray in the center, framed by the front hoop with the canvas shoved back to the second, water barrel strapped to the side, black oxen looking amused under their yoke.

And your Indian girl straight like a poplar, the band on her forehead, the black braids in front of her shoulders down as far as her crotch, bits of colored cloth woven in, and the cougar-claw necklace, and the doe-

Honey

birth

from

death

27

skin dress to her ankles and wrists. Standing beside the front wheel. Squaw walks.

You-without-names in the willows and the sage, your boots and blacks and whites, kerchiefs, you on that great roan white-stockings-and-star with the rifle slid under your knee. No leather chaps in that country — no brush, no cactus, no rain. One-Man Canyon, leading down from the east into Death Valley. Down from his Golden Girl Mine.

All that, propped against the honey can.

He's put a can in my duffel bag. The bus leans down on top of us. His arms are so strong and warm, and I shan't! I shan't go! O dearest Pa, do not let me go, don't make me go, like all those other times. The duffel shoved into its roaring stomach, like all those other times. It's terror and can't you hear me cry, or don't you dare? All that I would do is love you and stay with you always, and instead you push me off into the dark, into all that metal and black glass and vomit and gasoline. How could you take my arms from around you? And you are crying too, I am sure.

love's weight

is

hate

Your pride, you want something better for me, you say, but it's really your pride; what you've done, not what I've done. Your PhD.

The door bangs shut behind me. A cop, he seems, with his uniform, that thing on his belt, his badge, his manner. And the cells down the dark corridor. I look back tight against the glass. The pickup's lights swing off into the dust, up the line of poplars, gone behind the hay barn. Forever.

He sank me into forever.

Up that line of poplars. Little Lily, driving the

Percherons, leaning against the oak tubs with your little bottom for support, feet spread out in their new boots. Proud, as your Pa watches you bring the sloshing grapes up to the cellar door.

Black grapes and their thick smell and the bees hurrying to drink the juice before it's dumped into the tun.

Black scowls from over at the silent house, for "That's not proper girl's work."

"Give me a son then."

Black cellar as Pa and the neighbors come and go with the tubs. Loud and cheery and sweating against sunset, the more so for the black disapproval from over there, "But you know this is not wine country and all that fretting for no more than we can drink and give away to Padre John and you could be working more bees and hauling in more firewood."

Your alliance, how you love him, how you spring straight from his temple. And she slapped you and screamed in a whisper because you leaped up, your arms around his neck, your legs around his waist, all crumpling the dress, and kissed him and kissed him . . . *Years later to learn from Bella next door that Valley Hope, your people, gossiped of incest. Stunted, stupid, and I don't care, let them, they can't hurt anything.*

Your braids tug when they're tucked into your blue jeans, but they don't get into trouble there. Your hands stick to the harness and to Sun's sweaty rump when you slap him off into the corral. Purple from the juice, black from the vine mildew, aching from the millions and millions of bunches you snipped into your basket, from dawn.

Purple stains on the linen, bread crumbs strewn

black Crow

white Dove

white

white

white!

white Knight

black Troll

29

about, chicken bones, and still there is venison sa-
lami—oh, don't shoot, don't shoot!—on a chunk of
bread and they didn't water your wine this time at all.
It's just planks on those sawhorses, stools, benches
from the tack room and the honey room, and it's still
warm in the night air.

It's not, though, it's not, it's not! . . . The lords and
ladies, down from the castle with their wolfhounds,
reds and blacks and billowing skirts, tambourines to
the tarantella, a hundred flasks on a table from here
to there, the donkeys screeching and screeching for
attention, the sleeping pigeons fussy about all the
commotion, black-frock blessings, and meats that you
never had, and cakes and fruit and holy wine and
coffee thick as an egg yolk.

fairy

princess

Lily

And Miele Toccacielo, il Nettare d'Italia, they say
Garibaldi lived on it for a week and afterwards they
would bring him a jar whenever they could. From the
oranges and the almonds and the wild flowers of the
hills.

Pa smuggled them in, when he was three months
old, remember? They'd brought a swarm over all the
way, in steerage, fed on rock candy. Drugged them
with smoke from the bark they'd brought, before they
got to Ellis Island, and with ice from the galley. Sewed
them into little Beppe's mattress and hoped the wet
wouldn't wake them up. The buzzing baby.

Bee

royal

Right across the country too. And they flourished
and swarmed and divided and divided until Tocca
honey reached all over the West. And those Tocca
Italians with their four dark yellow bands, so diligent
and gentle and hardy. Pa, he raises queens now.

And buys bus tickets.

30

Oh Lily, you were so happy! Even when you had to go off to high school every morning, Fort Badly. Not that other bus; this came back every afternoon, and you'd hardly missed a thing.

Like packing in the hives, high into the mountains for the summer sage and the mahogany and the late wild flowers and the fir honeydew. Like the grape harvest on the last day of September. Like working the old centrifuge before he hitched it to a motor. Like honey tastes—lined up in little plates with numbers, and still you close your eyes so as not to see even the color and know how much the sample has ripened in the comb.

spinning

colors

figures

Like our Saint's Day with the procession and the Dodg'ems and the Cracker Jack surprises and the spaghetti-eating race. Like being a little girl and pinning all those black skirts one to the next as they knelt in a row during mass and watching one after another tug and trip and turn livid and not being able to swallow your laugh and being spanked on your bare bottom as the tears ran down his face and you loved him so. Like kissing the little cross Pa takes with him whenever he's up in the mountains.

racing

tumbling

glorious

skelter

Ma's Madonna, over the olive-oil flame—how she can yell when you leave the front door open and the valley wind snuffs it out! But you don't care, and he just looks severe. And there she sits, flicking the shuttle back and forth with her thin wrists, up and down on the treadles, knotting in her colors, counting rows against her pattern pinned to the frame. High heels and a permanent now that summer's here and the mountain road is open and she could find time to get over to Alturas. The dresses she brings you girls,

31

and'll make you wear to school in the fall!

"Remember your position, girls. We're not just anybody. And I won't have you running around with those Mexicans."

But she'll work away on your trousseaus year after year though what's the matter with the bedspreads at McFadden's? But don't say it, Lily. Her eyes are so tired and you've crossed her enough and she just isn't like you, that's all.

Pa's: "Tomorrow I head for heaven. Who's with me?"

You leap on him, screaming. How can you help it? They all know you'll do that, and they'd be embarrassed, and they'd think it sentimental, and they'd think it unbalanced. But don't you listen and don't you think, Lily. You will go and none of the others would dare go too, even if they wanted to.

With her dearest father, that little girl, bouncing on air, flinging about like a tumbleweed or a horse's mane, or really like only that little Lily can. Two miles straight up, there's the touch o' heaven, the home of the gods, the food of the gods.

free!

straight up

from the

And you're already there. Every step is a skip . . . *Oh! walk with joy; remember London in the fog, my Liliana, London on your way together to Calabria, on Birdcage Walk when your Colin could hardly keep you from floating off into the treetops?* . . . every word is a shout of double joy, and you throw your arms about your mother and even she laughs and smiles and kisses you as she grumbles. And you pinch your sisters' eyes and bite their ears until they become quite cross — but I love you, I love you, can't I love you? are you all so boiled in propriety that you just

heart

soar

up

can't move? I *won't* say I'm sorry.

Oh! but there's nothing, nothing, nothing else but now, this only moment, this explosion which is you, Lily. Look around you, there's nothing but the sun, the mountain air, you touch heaven. And do they know it, these sitting here just like before, looking away, looking busy, looking untouched? All except for him. He's watching you, and he's dancing with you, and he loves you. It's just that he has to sparkle mostly inward. You have to watch him carefully to see it, his way of sort of storing it up for later. But you can see it, his way of playing with his wedding ring, his oh-so-solemnness, and he turns all gruff and delicate.

wed

The hives to carry tomorrow must be closed, now that it's dark and all the bees are in, and screened so they won't suffocate. And the grub lined up and packed in a pannier, our duffel, bedrolls, and tarp packed in another to balance, with extra horseshoes and nails, bells and hobbles, some oats to keep them close to camp, hive tools, extra combs to be cached up there, smoker and greasy waste, the rifle and ammunition.

to

me

wed

to

How can you sleep, the way the night sings: crickets, your friendly owl, coyotes out on the desert, the moon spinning and spinning?

the

The earth presses up against the sky, you have no weight between them, you dance naked in the ring of a snake with his tail in his mouth.

undivided

Whole

Tiptoe clattering, you are awake, pulling on this and that with sisters rolling over to grumble, and it doesn't really matter that much. Almost you fall back into the sheets.

Splash water from the pump, milk and honey, pack

saddled tightened, heaving on the hives, three to a horse, upset buzzing in the dark. Oh but it's black! The moon's no good. One bulb near the hitching rail but you do it mostly by feel, with the leather slippery and stiff in the cold, morning pisses splattering in the dust. And you're still asleep as Stella flinches to the saddle blanket and rolls her eye and acts offended when you know she's dying to go.

my

Moon

You climb on, sit there dumbly, all pulled together to hold out the cold. Shadows become shapes. From the saddle you can see the desert hills against a lesser darkness. Pa hands you the lead rope of the least experienced packhorse. Lost Horse Canyon. Stella jigs sideways—none of that for the packhorses. Easy walk. He looses the other ten, ties their leads with a slip knot back onto their diamond hitches, drives them after me—strain around, count them in the dawn, don't get far ahead, slow till they're all in line.

mother

Owls fly down into the brush, the stars are going one by one.

A million birds are singing, a million cicadas come to life as the sun touches pink on Eagle Peak, spreads down, quite suddenly reaches orange in through your Levi jacket, shivers the warmth.

Sun

Your're leading, hours now. He hasn't said a single word, just, "Lost Horse Canyon" and sometimes hissing "Assalà!" when a packhorse strays, reaches for grass forgetting its muzzle. And hummed snatches of "La Donna è Mobile" when the heating air carries it up the canyon. How could he love you more, how could you love him more? He forgives you every-thing—your impatience with the bees, and how you can't abide being orderly and organized, and how you

father

ride Ma so because she just can't understand, and how you fly into their bed at any hour and maybe bring your sisters too.

Pa's beautiful hands, strong, containing. To quiet my sobs, to shut off difficults, protecting, warming.

Dive into his bed when the others have gone, deep under the covers, curled like a baby pink mouse by the cold, his hands to hold me. Moving, warm circles on my back and thighs, the nightie bunching. So gentle and generous — to cure his little Lily. The sun shines hot through the sheets, my honey hair where it lies across my arm — like our ancient ancestors, Pa would say, shaking his black hair with his funny wry look — dark honey.

light

I hide from mirrors — would it be another me? — yet curled in here I see — I don't, I don't! — my silly pointed things and the black ringlets below. Tight, tight close my eyes: all's a shining white. His hand comes to hide me there, to comfort me, to explain the mysteries — his low voice — and it hurts too but he says it's all right and I love him so.

means

He takes my hand to him: soft, a great nubbly hard. "Like horses," giggle with relief, his voice so far and strange. He moves away, and why is he trembling so?

Touch him, kiss his shoulder, tell him my last-night's dream.

And you have nothing nothing nothing to forgive him for.

Yet you weep.

Cry on, Lily. The mountains and the sky see your tears. They hear your heart, they are your heart. Let earth and air drink your tears. He left you — how can you forgive? — Ma, you, the girls, and Luis to help with

shadow

the bees. How could he leave you? To drain the last tear, heedless of the last breath, the long unstirring dying pain. He killed you, stabbed to the heart of your warm dark unimaginable sweetness—his two-edged uncapping knife, steel-hard, sweet with new honey from slicing the comb.

And it would be you they'd send, you whom he always loved best, you who hate him so, who see him as the black monster of your dreams, stabbing, stabbing at him. The bus, lurching and stinking and imprisoning. Fort Badly, where she lives, where they say he's staying with the Servadios, she with her clicking orphan high heels—and he bought them for her, I know it, I know it—her head tossing, her nose held high and her mouth stretched as if she had bird shit on her upper lip (it was you, Pa, who told us that, from Grandpa, talking of the girls of Palermo, how could you?), her low-class airs. You to beg him to come home, you to hear his anger, his reasons: Ma driving him to it; just taking pity on an orphan; no one will tell him what he can't do. So proud and sure and strong. And he doesn't even kiss you. You weep and hate him and crush your face to his shirt.

You love him so. And on Twelfth-night he came back.

Dividing, sundering, when all should be one. To embrace means to unembrace, to couple to uncouple. Only death is unity. So Colin would say. But it's best not to use the formulae, Lily. Best to let the wind blow through you, the sun burn through you, the darkness take in the light, and the light receive the dark. And anyhow you didn't know Colin then, or anyone like him.

shadow

means

light

"Vai su, ciuco!"

Would a horse know he's being called an ass? Pa's voice touches you, you reach back. The salt pulls on your cheeks, rubbed off with the back of your wrist.

"Ho! Lily! Right fork. There's water there. Water 'em, and we'll go on up to the plateau, the Landing Place."

Stella picks her way across the slippery ledges of the dry creek bed. A marmot, a yellow-belly, whistles at you. Whinnies, they smell the water, though it's still a quarter mile. Steep into the fir leaving the willows behind. How the world closes in, how sounds are given their own life, how thick is the air with earth! Fairy birds in every tuft of grass, a crashing in an alder thicket—a mule deer who won't be seen. Hang to a tuft of Stella's mane up the rise to help her balance and the slipping saddle—you're always too gentle on the girth when she groans so. Hold her down, she wants to run it. But this is where the waterfall was from the pond above, last spring—now it's twigs and needles and dry dry leaves. And the pond? it's silver trunks lying in the giant ferns. Three dead firs stand guard, naked white, blackened arms into the blue, clutching the sky. But Stella goes on—you would have too, oh yes!—confidently through all that green.

cut stream

cut love

More than beech leaves splashing in the breeze, more, it's the rustling of water. Chuckling a bit, winking, then diving underground for good, never reaching the pond bed.

Rumps jostling, water muddied. First you, then Pa, flat down in cold moss, sucking at the icy water. Then back a bit to piss, we all do.

"Never claim to be romantic," Colin would say.

"Romanticism never got to Southern Italy, I guess. Meno male."

On to Landing Place, little Lily. Were you born there, Lily, there where a great round sky-ship set down: Japs spying in a balloon, or the blimp from Moffett missing forever, or Martians, or God? Same winter, 'forty-two. Left a gouge, they say and lots of scuff marks, but it was gone when they'd climbed up those hours on snowshoes to see, nothing else — except maybe you? Seems like it must be so. Fate and reunion await you there, and it's only Colin you can tell. Only children dream, the others say, and who, but the flowers, would be children?

Stars

slide
down
to
the

Earth

Your high plateau. Where flowers tilt up to the top of the world, stretching out from the fir and the ponderosa pine and the cedar. Here you will set up the hives. Here your lovely Tocca Italians will drink of the blue sage, the only patch in these mountains; a clear white honey so stiff you can tip a jar upside down and it won't run and it won't candy even in the snow. The specialty honey, Touch o' Heaven, twice the price, flavored too with the wild flowers: the snowbrush if it has not already passed, the ground sage, chokecherries, the wild peppermint.

And here in August your bees will turn to the honeydew of the white fir, the droplets from the scale lice sucking the sap so wastefully that, when they've had their fill and their young and the ants that tend them so fondly and will build little houses for them of mud and will carry them from bud to bud and tend their eggs, still there will be hundreds of pounds for the bees. A brown honey, for the bakeries . . . *J & M, Will, what's that for?*

While there's sun and warmth, with the hives set on rocks, firm against the mountain winds, you'll open them, let the workers have a look around, orient themselves, learn where their hives are, each with its bee color so they won't stray into the wrong hives: zinc white and lead white for the bees see ultra-violet, then blue, yellow, and black; they don't know greens and reds and any-old whites. And you'll set the traps — oh! stay away, little skunks, you clever ones who will come to a hive at night when the bees are all in and will scratch on it till the guards start out in alarm and in defense, and will calmly eat them all, finish the best part of the worker population, they say. Honeydewers in the Trinity Alps put up electric fences against the bears, or give them lead poisoning with the thirty 'ought six, or keep dogs around. How lucky you have no bears!

And the horses to hobble, three to bell, saddles and bridles and muzzles to hang from deadwood stubs in the ponderosas against the rats and porcupines. Firewood. Water where it flows out of the ledges at the edge of the plateau. Ground to smooth and gouge for hips and shoulders before it gets dark.

Last! please, every moment, as it rushes on you, you beg it to last. But it's gone, so you try to grab whole groups of moments, like cooking-and-eating-and-coffee-which-Ma-won't-let-you-have-around-the-fire. But Pa whistles "La Donna Ricca," shifts under a branch to avoid the dew, and the black presses in on your back. There's something waiting for you, you've known it all along. Out there.

Fires make the blackness. Opposites. Before fire, before the severing. Before, or beyond, night and day,

Honey

the

divine

rebirth

39

good and evil. Oh! you confusions, you resistings, you ignorant blind knowings. It can be so simple, accept, let the dark come and it will contain the light.

Out of the pines with your bedroll, out where the moon sparkles in the quartz of the ledges rolling in the sage. Strip to naked you in the moon, wriggle into your roll, legs and bottom cushioned in the grasses, back against the inclining granite, warm, so warming you. And the dew cools on your face, your body finds such pleasure stirring in its womb, warming you, sliding down you and up you and lying softly on your breasts, caressing ever so lightly. Oh! that lovely flowering secret where your fingers lie, where your heart lies, where all comes together.

No, no, but you haven't found that yet, little Lily. Your tingles spread outward, your gaiety is for all, your heart fills every cell of your body and bursts out all over creation.

You lie there in the crickets' song, wanting not to sleep, knowing you won't right through the night. Their song spins round and round you in cool golden threads, your raggedy old bedroll that you've banged around in all these years, it's lamé of the ancient moonbeams, nesting you in splendor. The coyotes, peak after peak, one to another to the moon, soft, distant, to the roots of every hair on your downy body, sending the tingle in swirls; how they love you! And as the voices run ever so gently over your skin and enter into your flesh, as you raise your arms, silver in the night, out of your warmth and up into the shining sky, turning slowly like shadows of the owl's call, your love is so strong for your own being that it flows out over the whole expanse, honey-cream,

shadows

in the

cave

my

infinite

40

Little Mother, Great Mother.

You feel it all. Flowing in and in; you and all are filled and one. Up here on the outstretched slowly turning limb of the earth, here under the flood of the golden night sky. Where night joins with day, where the moon is the light of the sun. Where your bees touch heaven, join the seed and the egg, the air and the earth one, and they take the nectar of the flower of the earth, ripen it in the thin air, and give a honey as rich as the food of the gods. Where the black sage springs from the dark earth and opens its blue flower to the sun — sage, with the power to make you wise, brings down the sky. Where fawns are born and rabbits die screeching to the eagle.

Here, here where They chose to touch the earth, and the earth received, and They marked the place and They left.

The stabbing sky, the reaching enfolding earth, they are one, joined, a snake biting its tail in the great self-destroying self-creating round, beginning and end of all.

You shiver, Lily, draw your arms back into your bed. Your hair, bleached in the moonlight, falls over your plain and peaceful face. You curl in the grass and the night flowers, open to heaven, touching.

So, little Lily, so you were, so you are. Come up the years, come to me, slip into me. Me, the Lily that sits here licking saltines and honey from her fingers. Fill me and we'll leave no room for the numbness so many have wanted of me.

Listen as the night wind stirs under the floor, rattles the stovepipe, sucks at the burning Joshua

filled with

All One

so

  nothing

so

  all

tree logs sending orange flames dancing through the chinks, scratches the piñon on the tin roofing. Smell the desert dust and the sweet pollens, the smoke backing up and puffing through the damper, the faint mustiness of his old body, not scrubbed bare to modern stinks by baths. Neglected curtains . . . *"Four years now she's been passed away, girl; and our little Robin long before; then our Juney; they'll not be coming"* . . . Curtains that stir in the currents. Walter's tail twitches and even I can hear a mouse under the sink. The oil light glowing on his glob of gold, a thousand dollars milled out last spring from some of his high grade which still lies about in sacks. Watch, his old hands turn the pages, his lips sucked to his gums jumble the past, his eyes are the flame.

Lily

hold

the now

42

Rooted, the sky

The desert stars are flames: when the night wind blows through you and the coyote juggles the moon, when the cold rises from where your feet are buried in the ground, when the dew lies shining on your outstretched arms, flames that burn time. Where before and after mean nothing, where time is a spiral. Position, presence, faith. Roots, the continuum, for they hold the past, they collect the present, they bear tomorrow's sprout.

And now old Will he takes his warmth from the burning roots dug free for him by the winter winds.

You, young Willy, cut loose

Two canes, short shuffling steps, the warped linoleum. The lid slid off, hot red where the cheeks are thin over the bone. Twisted root chunks, petrified against the borer. Sparks that dive into the eyes. And the thin oil flame dazzles through the rheum, shines white on her face under the green hat, blacks out the treacherous floor—the poking cane, the hollow linoleum wave popping.

A buffalo hide, that a miller from the Volga and a Cornish miner wouldn't know how to cure—soft like that Sioux girl's skin; hard, bulging, popping when you roll on it. Roll to escape the swinging cuffing hand, flour-specked from the milling or the baking, it didn't matter which. That was you, young Jerry Dan—was it Willy then, changed to Willy, Jerry washed clean away?

seek

soft

comfort

Did you know you'd be popping the linoleum in eighty years, hurrying to be back by a pretty face, keeping her eyes wide round with tales of the old days and philosophies of the new?

mother

Mother

Hickok County, Nebraska, Wild Bill, shot in the back by Jack McCall in Deadwood, Dakota Territory,

44

the year before you were born. They'd still talk of him, though, when they came in with their wagons for their flour and you'd be hoisting up the bags. And the cuffs would likely be for getting caught shooting down by the river where the mill dam hides you, a gun borrowed while they waited the weighing and paying. Caught and she'd drag you by the ear, growling German . . . *Hamburg for a few months, I'll get it back, bitte sehr, schönes Fräulein* . . . A bear pregnant, always pregnant. Or he'd have you by the arm, tight, and you're just a shaver, so's the tears run.

through

time

Those Herefords in the boat with their wild great bawling; the bricks of Ellis Island pressing on you to make you scream; the train clipping along like a horse loping in shale, out into America, prairies, rivers, the buffalo herds, the wild western hills of Nebraska; the Omahas camping along the right-of-way; the cattle driving across the tracks in a cloud of pink dust, cowboys sidesaddling and ignoring our yells.

But those two, they'd just sit there, like they'd be still in Kov. Even their walking was a kind of sitting, solid, squat. And the heavy hand ready to smash you.

You're on the range now, Willy, and it won't be often they'll know where you're at. Wyoming, Nebraska, Dakota, Montana, the little Big Horns, the new states. Before you could grow a beard, before the lice were much interested. But your rifle speaks and you take your cattle where you will. Till the sun drops into the wild grass, and the cattle bunch for the night, and you blacken the dark with your fire and your talk with the others.

moving

out

And in a silence, with even the prairie owl still,

45

you hear the distant shuffle of a herd. They're sneaking
in to claim your range; Grady, he tried it once before.
Circle and lie waiting on the bluff with your horse
tied down wind. Outlined against the silver grass.
You yell, and "Like hell I will!"

tribe's

territory

He wheels but your rifle's on him.

root

You find him head down in the gully at sunup when
you've driven the rest well off. And the sheriff finds
you.

club

This judge, he's got no gavel. His ham hand slams
down on the bench, though he'd like it to be on you.
As if his law were better, who's never been west of
the saloon and wouldn't know a range war from a
church picnic. This time you can't roll away though,
Willy, and they'll have you in jail for a couple of
years . . . *San Quentin? No, Will boy; fifty years to
wait for that hospitality* . . . But they treat you well
and bring you tobacco and you learn to read and
write a bit. And your beard begins to grow.

No, the term's not so bad, sitting around easy like,
taken care of, and going to get out. Like those cuffing
hands, it's not the hurt, it's the fact, the law slamming
down on you from some authority you'd nothing to
do with. Somebody else's rules, what do they have to
do with you?

Leave it, boy, get clear away. You've a horse still
they're keeping for you, and a saddle and a rifle. And
you know which direction's southwest. Off where
there aren't no fences, where Arizona Territory
means you're what you want.

You're out, all legal. They come to take you home,
smelling of flour and their hands so pink and pudgy,
and they'd be thinking of cuffs and school and kissing

46

their icons and the three-fingered crossing. Wayward, but what do they know of the horizon? Tobacco or incense, Nebraska, eighteen ninety or was it ninety-two? The mill to grind and grind away at you, and he'd even fenced his few cattle too on his bottom land. Slamming down on you, the silence, flour-dusted crust, crackling bearskin worn thin on the humps.

Dragons

Ai! Willy boy, you've rolled inside a grizzly hide soft like her skin, soft as your chin was then, warm so you shivered, cool from the sweat when she'd showed you. The pine smoke to keep off the no-see-'ems, horses stamping in their sleep, her crooning like you was a baby, stars dropped right down in the branches. And again she'd do it, like throwing a handful of salt in the embers.

Or just the soft rub of your saddle jogging the seat of your pants and the rifle barrel fitting under your knee and the horsehair hackamore she'd braided for you so light in your fingers.

How'd they think they'd have you back there, make brown flour of you, make numbers and wheels and The Word of you, sieved and bleached and prosperous? Clear out, Willy, clean away, and it's easy. No one'd be interested in chasing a kid just on account of miller Dan and the schoolmarm.

the Hero

slaying

So you've done it, Willy Dan. And you've beat the moon so's the dogs won't see you or scent you downwind and raise a ruckus and a clicking hoof's no more than they'd expect in a pasture. Careful though, slow, no more'n a walk or the saddlebags'll start slapping and the saddle creaking like no bare horse would and a dog can tell; or they, for that, with an ear for thieves.

Great Mother

Great Father

You've got beyond the hill, Willy, and the moon's
on the east now, a Crimean orange, rotting. Put it
over your left shoulder, let out to a jog — you'll learn,
walk or run, jogging's tiring — let the prairie slide by
now, boy, distance. Stay clear of the telegraph towns
till your beard and your hair fill out long, trade horses
soon's you can. For the rest, isn't much to identify,
nor worth it.

Polestar back over the right, let her hang there.
There's snow still on the north slopes, the air comes
in cold from ahead. Hunch well into your winter
buckskin, fur out for the rains. Lost your fishskin
slicker. A scarf to tie your hat down over your ears.
Hands so soft from jail, one or the other slid into
armpit or crotch to keep warm. The moon's hard   warm cave
silver in your left eye. Howling, the yips and the long
cry, hill to hill. The shadow form, the thin voice, and   outside
the answering, answering. They'll lift you, with
their calling, high into the night air, and you'll hang   black
there even when it dies. Reaching for something,   monsters
you and they, but will you ever know what or why?
Origins, something way way back that ties us, or the
fearful unknown, or hunger, or song?

Watch the sky rise, Willy, the stars fade, the
prairie flatten without shadows. But then it's time for
cover, for the first days, for you wouldn't have them
sending out after you and finding you under the sun.
A draw, down out of sight; that'll hold the sun, grass
for tethering, too close to home for hobbles and
he could wander up onto the skyline, doesn't take
long to tell a hobbled horse even from miles off.   rising
And runoff water, and dry willow wood, dry so's not
to smoke, and the side of bacon you borrowed with a   sap
pot which will make coffee too. Sugar you've brought,

48

and the salt, a shirt too, and the other bag's mostly ammunition—best eating there is. Pick off a spring-fat hare, roast him on a green willow spit, and you'll be gnawing him each time you wake to piss and change the tether in the new grass.

And the sky drops and rises, drops and rises, the sun slides higher, the moon dies and comes back a sliver, and always the polestar back over the right shoulder. Your hands are hard, the hair's worn off now in the inside of your legs. You can drape the chaps behind except when you're cross-country in the brush.

You ride through Denver at noon and spit on the sidewalk in front of the Brown Palace, for your beard's filled out, your hair's long now, bleached, and Jerry Dan is somebody else.

Down the dry edge of the Rockies. Your third horse now; not for hiding, you're beyond them now, Willy, forever, but because the second one lamed and you had to work in the stockyard a week to pay the difference. Where the thunderheads pile up every afternoon and break on you if you're in too close to the foothills. Head into them, Willy, your first mountains, leave the roads and the trails. Let them have you, these great black afternoon shadows. Your saddlebags are full, you're fleshed, the two of you, your boots and the clicking shoes are new again from Canon City.

Where the black turkeys race through the dark forests and you've missed them more than once. Where the antelope won't come, for their safety is the open distance. Where the deer slips through the aspen stands and the green spring ponds backed up by the beaver. Where the wolf has full voice and the elk

Russian

Polestar

hole

to escape

from time

from space

49

swings his antlers on the skyline, roots into the sky. Where the white goat and the bighorn drop rocks from cliff faces that lean down on you till you've slid clear out of the saddle. Where a rifle shot isn't once and maybe a splat of dust in the thin grass, but comes back at you, closed in, angles and halves.

And where finally the spruce and the juniper cripple and can climb no further. The air is light like whiskey, and what are you doing here, Willy? Here where the grass and the flowers quit and it's all a pile of rock set like a bear trap to let loose on you. Here in a wind that turns you back-to and whips your tail to your belly.

Back to the timber, Willy, follow the game trails and you'll find a pass over.

Round cat tracks big as your hand, in the soft earth, crushing the flowers, with the claws drawn in. Here the moss and violets are still moving, straightening. The brook is loud and he's up-wind. Easy now, tie the mare in the thick spruce stand. You've heard of them, cougar, two hundred pounds. You could use the meat, jerky in this dry weather so you won't have to bother with small game, and the skin'd come in useful, saddle blanket, a jacket, the claws for ornaments. Must be hunting up ahead or already set on a ledge above this deer trail ready to drop. Careful, Willy, it could be you. Here, where the big center pad pressed into the humus, a rock bug is just getting free. Rifle on your hip, Willy, it's quickest there. No ledges here, though, no trees big enough to climb out on for the drop; must be moving on ahead on a scent, concentrating, less likely to pick you up.

let me

be the

one, the

first me

club

so still

in the

giant ferns

50

Black-flies swarm, eyes, nose — swallow it, swallow it, wouldn't do to loose a hand or sneeze or cuss the critters. Or piss or loosen your shirt or have tobacco on your breath or fart in your gut or mineral oil on your rifle (just animal grease) or soap or a glued felt hat or the stink of man-fear. Or walk on your heels or shine the whites of your eyes or your palms or the city-shine of your rifle or wear spurs, rodeo boys, or have a scarf-end flutter in the wind. It'll come, boy, it'll come and there'll be no thinking about it.

Better to catch him before he's found a ledge. Slide along, Willy. Here you can see ahead through the trees, he'll be beyond by now and perhaps heading up the side of the open draw. Slide along as fast as you pick up his tracks. His stride is spread now, running, why? There are no other tracks he could be on, and would he suddenly run a scent or a sound? Or is it to spring over this fallen trunk? But he'd need no run for that. Mind that drop of fear, Willy, mind it well, down, with the rifle light and free, no breathing, your knife hangs loose at your hip. A ground squirrel on the trunk, back and forth.

hands at

his throat

No! Willy, it's his tail, flick before the leap, up, ready at your hip, he springs, you fire and throw yourself to the left. He twists in the air, falls on his shoulder, you have your knife in his brain.

slice

You're on your hands and knees and you drop to the damp earth and your vomit gurgles and stings in your nose.

your flesh

Jerky, Willy, and a hide and fresh steaks, but most, you're breathing and it's his blood, and you'll know how and how not to press game close. It's then they'll turn on you. The three-fingered cross before you know it, and perhaps it's the last time ever.

Jerky, Will Spear, but Willy Dan sits here in your skin, hefting your albums—Danziger, Dan, Speare, to Spear 'cause the feller over in Serrano Palms kept getting my mail, nineteen ten that was when I'd moved into the ranch a piece. Left the last sack for the Missis when they took me off to San Quentin, 'forty-three that was. Beef jerky, but it'd be good from the wild-cat's white meat or the cougar or the desert bighorn or badger or horse, and Jamie Pope would jerk mule meat. Coyote stinks. Any time of year here in the desert. Strips of raw steaks, dipped in hot tallow boiled out of the bones, and salt and chilies for flavor and to keep the flies off. Hang'em just before dark, when the flies bed down, on a rope like a clothesline so's the flies have no place to lay their eggs. Turn'em over the next morning and they'd be ready in perhaps five days. Keep'em in a gunny sack to let the air get through. Indians they wove sacks of grasses.

Few whites, least of all these parts, jerked meat. Prospectors'd buy from the Indians. Omahas taught me, I taught Jamie. Eat it dry or boil it or the Missis'd grind it up and make it into a good gravy on potatoes. Well water, put-up peaches and barrel-cactus candy dipped in lime water the way the Walapais taught me. She's gone now, Will, gone now, gone now. Looks at old Will, her window in the sky, at the canned corn and the rice and the saltines and jam.

the pit below

hold on
hold on

onward

Jerky, Willy Dan, wrapped loose in the skin, tied on the back of the saddle. No chilies, but you tried a bit of wild onion, gives it an edge. Not bad,

52

boy, and you've found your way over one range, and you slide the talus 'most on your hocks—tallow, you've kept it in the bladder, on the fetlock cuts, lamed-up would be bad. Bark-slab lean-to for the rains the mountains catch from the westerlies on this side, fire reflecting in to dry things some.

Through the flames—freeze your gut, Willy, get your rifle back together, Willy—that form, moving at you. Don't know bears, but would he come at you upright? Fool! to come at a campfire, silent like that, would've dropped him if your rifle hadn't been knocked down. Old-timer, come up from downstream when saw the fire. Hungry more'n company, prospectors don't look for company. Can't find time, for the fever, to hunt vittles. Jerky, Willy, but you'll make him pay well. Stay with him a bit, feed him, get more game and jerk it for his cache swinging 'bove bear reach. And learn all you can—gold, the panning and the sluicing and the dry-washing, that's all he's got for you and you'll be waiting till Prescott and Death Valley and Kern County for the rest of your education. And something about silver and sampling and how to make something good look bad and vicy versy. And how to live alone with your fever . . . *Jamie Pope.*

That bag of dust looks good, does it Willy? Hefts and shines and should pay well for the jerky, should it Willy? Yellow Jacket Pass and down to Durango and you'll learn different. Worth salt, ammunition, postage to Nebraska (you'll be long gone in the Territories by then), and then the drinks, that's all, Willy.

Whiskey and the fever, corruptions.

gold

Sun's

threads

spun

'round

Earth

53

They're beat now: only a drop for company when the old fellers come up with a flask and the Seven-Up out under the Joshua tree, and gold is just to keep the stamp mill going in the spring, use up those bags of high grade. Corruptions, man against his nature, like when he ruts when the woman's out of season, or gives himself to machines, or fouls the air and the water and the land with his wastes, or rips up the desert or the jungle or his brothers with his explo-sions — Armageddon. Quiet, old Will, the bees are stinging in your brain, itch and itch on the pate, buzz, millions in your ears. Files for your corns, sticks for your knees, pills and quiet, old Will, for the bees — but you'll be moving on soon, yes, you'll get there. Hamburg for the bottles shining on the Elbe, and the dog-carts, and to get your tongue oiled up. Kov for the windmills and the men dancing in the dust, and Elizabeth Petrovna saved us, and the mists caught in the reeds along the Volga. And on. To Siberia, fruit and forests, Eden all around, radium in the earth to suck out the pains and the bees. India where they understand. You'll be moving soon, Will.

Weaver

tying

threads

Durango, between the San Juans and the La Platas, two whiskeys and it lets you go, and by night you are well over the border. Navajos and Utes, down along the San Juan River. The country stretches out. Game is scarce and distant, hard to hit in the heat.

Dust cloud hanging, a moving herd of cattle. Lope over, Willy, in clear view, though, and not against the sun. Could they use a hand? Heading west, they are, and that's your direction, clear to Kern County, California, to the gold towns, pay fancy for any meat, though it'll have come a long way without fattening.

54

The nights are long and hungry, Willy, the coyotes bark in close, the dogies cry, the herd is restless. Talk to them, Willy, sing to them, let them know you're there. And keep your girth tight, for they've come a long way, makes them edgy, and the wind hot and dry and nervous. Sing the steppe songs, the river songs, the German harvest songs your mother would sometimes sing. Soft, the slow ones, the low ones, the sad ones of lost love. Move around them, slow, show against the night sky, and keep looking, Willy, out across the bottom land, up to the hills behind camp, and don't look into the fire. Open country, rustling country, Indian country. Where to start them running and cut out a few would be so easy, and they'd skin you, Willy, and you'd be shamed wherever the story went. Show 'em, Willy, show 'em how they ride the herd in Nebraska, but don't go over your time, don't let the Dipper swing too low before you wake Black Jim. Slide off your saddle, hobble up, curl under your cougar, used to the stink from not knowing to cure it quite right though it's soft, but not like hers. Dawn'll be on you before you can roll over.

Lady Brahma

melodious

Cow

So they give you the down-wind side every day. You're the new one and they see some through the scraggly beard and the long half-blond hair. Pray for rain to lay the dust, for untracked grassland, or a change of the wind to come in from behind so no one need eat dust. But the east wind is scarce and fitful. Pray, but still it billows up, and it lays on you like hoarfrost on the juniper.

Bawling, shaking the air, shaking the earth with a thousand hooves. Jostling, noses on the rumps,

white eyes, and the young bulls mounting, lurching
up, stupid, desperate for a plug they'll never get.
Watching and your pants are tight, Willy, and you'd
be doing that . . . *Black Jim and the bent cock from a
heifer's kick* . . . Throw your knee over the horn,
sidesaddle, that'll ease it a bit, ease the heat in your
eyes and cheeks, the twisting of shame in your
heart . . . *Mother, hogshead with the hair pulled
tight; she with the dark waves of hair and the lips
waiting* . . . Saved.

unmanning

Monster

Hunting day, they send you off with your stories
of the white-tailed deer of Nebraska. But you know
the antelope too, the pronghorn. Ride up ahead, fast,
Willy, watch for the herds as you come over the rises,
the high bouncing and the sentries. Circle wide on the
down-wind side. Beyond the shoulder, on their line
of browsing; tether, crouch to the top, slide over on
your belly. Toward you, half a mile. Scarf tied to the
muzzle, raise it, wave it slowly. They gaze and can't
resist. One then another then all start carefully toward
you, picking their way, tugging mouthfuls of grass
as if to hide their unbearable curiosity. The wind keeps
up so they'll not get your scent. Pick the fattest young
one, careful, lower, aim for the heart. They'll spring
and fly like pigeons, but yours will fall.

desired

fought

They'll offer you a whiskey tonight.

slain

That was New Mexico Territory. By Arizona you've
earned enough.

*O Jenny, Jenny, come ride with me down to the
river again; is this you Jenny now, with your golden
honey hair and the eyes that smile at me and don't
turn away, come to bring youth to old Will, come to
ride with me off for the wild honey? Helen, my Mana,*

from your window in the sky. Arizona, like the sweetest fruit of Eden in your heart, melting, singing in your blood. But she'll see these tears that drop on the splotched twisted hand, hear the breath sob in you, your shoulders shaking. Grief, Lily girl—O Jenny by the river, O Helen under the stone with your name in turquoise from the Walapais.

Willy

Arizona. Jerome. The Fashion Saloon. The girl with a red ribbon in her hair playing waltzes on the piano. Pulled into herself, high on her platform over the sweating hairy faces, looking for someone in her hands. Your glass stays full, the voices are like rain on a lean-to, and it's not their laughter that makes your ears sting under your hair. How many years working cattle here, working in the mines, prospecting, rodeoing on the Fourth? How many saloons without feeling the sweat, the dust, the grease in your hair, the rips in the buckskin?

to win

the
Maiden

the
Treasure

Dollars, nuggets, a bit of gold dust. Mustache waxed, your hair like silk, long almost to the collar so's Jim Roberts—the sheriff, come down from Montana—asks "You Billy the Kid?" A hat from that old cougar skin, new suit of duds from the General Store, pistol belt polished, and a big cigar which'll make you sick if you don't mind. Bit of silence when you enter this time, except for a few who don't see you, and the piano— gentle and soft, a love song must be.

"William, just William, M'am, and I'd like to buy you a drink, if you'd be caring."

Before the last chord dies.

O Jenny, Jenny, long since gone, by now, I'd know, or are your eyes still full of those candles and lips still getting set to speak to Willy boy, the kid?

57

"Jenny, William, and I wouldn't be caring, for all your kindness."

"I'm not much for drinking myself, M'am, Jenny, for the truth of it. Would you mind for me to sit here for a spell to watch you play?"

"As you'd like. What would you hear, or watch?"

"Whatever comes, M'am, I'm sure will do just as well."

And she sings too, like a hermit thrush in the moon. *Annie Laurie,* and you'd like to cry, astraddle back-to on your chair with your chin on your fist to hold in the trembles.

"You won't clap for me, William?"

"No M'am, Jenny, it would not do justice to you. I'd like for you to try my mare, though. Tomorrow morning, perhaps? She's the most beautiful creature alive; barring you, that is of course. For me I'll get one of Clark's horses, W. A. Clark, you know, he owns the mine. Will you come, M'am?"

"Oh! but I'd love to. But is she mild, will you show me how, and we won't go too far?"

O Jenny, Jenny! You'd hold the stirrup for her and she'd swing up so light, and she'd laugh like a mourning dove if you touched her, turn all over red. And soon she'd be riding like an Indian, college education and all, and you'd teach her bareback with a hackamore and she'd ride low, bent forward with her hands so steady, like a boy, her dark hair flying behind. Scandal, the other women, buckboards or sidesaddles in their great dresses. Mornings: you'd got put on the night shift at the stamp mill. And you'd get her a pretty little rifle all laid in silver by the Wala-pais, and you'd take her out for antelope one long day,

sacred

Dance

too

night side

dark side

desert

shadows

58

and you'd wave them down till they were right up on you, and she'd pick well and catch him nice and be so scared and trembling and delighted. And she'd leap to you and throw your hat away and kiss you so strong on the forehead.

But it's down by the river bank like as not you'd end up, after the long ride down and a run in the desert, or climbing up into the Tuzigoot pueblo. The Verde River, at the foot of Cleopatra Mountain. And maybe a bit of bread and antelope sausage and beer. The river bank in the reeds and the willows with the cotton flying in the spring air. Never did touch her, didn't even know how, except with your eyes when she wasn't looking and sometimes when she was. She'd laugh and she'd ask about the Omahas or the cougar or the bottles on the Elbe. Or she'd be lost, all turned into herself, her eyes with a distant inner look, sad and a thousand miles from you.

Take her hand, Willy, tell her who you are, not who you wish you were. Be you, Willy, or you'll just be her image, to disappear who knows when in the desert sunlight. Or you'll lose her—the fear sits cold in your stomach—to search again in her hands on the keyboard, to look for another paper cowboy, Boston scrapbook. It's untamed she'd want you, it's your world she'd go to, but solid, not an image.

O

sucking

heart

How would you know all that, she not showing you, you who'd thought you'd spat on Denver's Brown Palace because they wouldn't let you in?

Say it, Willy.

"You'll soon be knowing all there is, Jenny, of horses, and hunting, and this hick life. When I've experted my mine, my Breyfogled claim—night-shift-

ing with Clark so's they won't suspect—a bonanza, no
mistaking. I'll give a ball for you in your Boston,
Young's Hotel you say? and the Governor'll call on
me to beg for an invitation."

"A ball's one thing, and the Governor will probably
be Irish. But a cowboy on Beacon Street . . . !"

And of course she laughs and laughs, the wind
moves through her hair, her eyes put you in a cage, on
view. If you'd crush the laughs from her . . . but the
sky closes down on you like a hood, closes in til! all
you see is her long dirty fingernail poking at an ant in
the weeds. Her hand stops quite suddenly, reaches
behind to her saddle she's been leaning against, takes
her little rifle from her saddleboot. Sitting still, with
her ankles crossed and her knees spread wide in her
long split skirt . . . *O Willy! why weren't you there?* . . .
she cocks her elbows on the insides of her thighs —
the ache and the loathing—and before you know it
she's got the rifle up against her cheek, her lips on
the silver, her finger curled in, white with the pressing.
Look up, Willy, along the black barrel, out across the
river, to the sage beyond, to a lone buck pronghorn—
springtime, and the bucks separate. Oh no, Jenny! He
leaps high with the explosion, twists, falls kicking on
his back, screaming as the dust rises.

"Now you'll take me home, Willy." While the sage
still shudders around him.

"I'll be fording over to pack him up first, M'am."

"I'm sick of antelope and I must be getting back.
Saddle and take me now."

"Then you'll not have learned, and it's not something you learn, got to grow up with it. Beacon Street
in the desert."

Mother

Monster

still

unslain

60

But you can't laugh. Ford over, high to your stirrups, spring thawing in the mountains. Heave him, more'n a hundred pounds, onto the haunches, tie two hoofs under the belly with a thong. Back and she's silent as ice.

Her songs that evening are gay, from the music halls of New York. The mill would crush your skull.

Or again, Willy, other days, high on Cleopatra, out over the Coconino Plateau. Pancho Villa'd be packing water in soon, with the spring waters drying up, that'd be his trail along the shoulder. The black teeth of the Superstitions. Lost Dutchman's Mine. Go, Willy, better a pack burro than ladies' rifles, up into the mountains where no one returns.

"I'll be going soon, Jenny. Be getting along. You'd be going too. I've saved up some, can help on your fare."

"I'd come, Willy, if you'd but ask me. I know where you think I belong. Oh, forgive me forgive me, dear Willy. I've to learn, I know now . . . How could I leave the desert? Where's the choice? Can't you see the courage it takes? To stay and go on with my cowboy?"

"The courage is in going back, like in me not buying Beacon Street . . . And I'm not your cowboy, I'm Willy."

Willy who, though, Willy who?

You'll sit no longer by her side up on the platform of the Fashion Saloon; no longer watch her ahead, flat to the mare's neck with only a blanket and a hackamore, or jogging straight in her little saddle with her elbows in and her hands so high. And always her hair moving, flowing like dark brook water. Or hear her

my

Hecate

hungering

for

sacrifice

61

laugh so controlled, turning from your eyes, or tell you of the romance of freedom and space. This is who you are, she says, with your buckskins and your cougar hat and your shooting eye and your pistol draw and your hair bleached blond to your shoulders and your beard trimmed like the scouts. No longer, Willy.

She'll not know. Better. Swing through the doors once more, quietly, behind heavy boots and voices. Sit in the shadows of the afternoon sun coming through the blue smoke and falling at her feet. And she's playing the waltzes again. Are those tears on her cheeks, does she know? But she never looks up, and you stay back. Your skin is dry and hot, your stomach is filled with sand, your throat blocks your breath.

Move on, Willy, you'll find out. When you've walked down Beacon Street and they've held a ball for you at Young's Hotel. When you're back again on the desert and the sun burns in your blood and your water cache's stolen and you may not make it to the coyote well you know in the purple shadow at the foot of the mountains. When you've been with them famous people at Scotty's, been honored at the Desert Inn, inspected the Tank Corps with General Patton. When you've been behind bars, year after year, or when you've worn still another pick down to a nub on the desert rock . . . The cold bites in on you, your boy lies dying on his cot . . . When you're back from a day of moving the herds, castrating, branding, Helen with the hot water on and the copper tub, the steaks charring and the fresh corn and the cherries from your own trees. Your Eden in the desert mountains. When the sun lowers in the simmering, the cool sets in, the earth tips back and back, and from high among the 'olinas

too

joy

down by
the
river bank

never

to

forget

62

on the side of a granite pinnacle shines the ancient Indian light, steady, silver. When you're curled in the lizard's sun by the Joshua tree with the breeze talking softly to you in the piñon.

You'll know, Willy.

Now, without knowing, you must go. No burro, no grubstake, no lone figure winding up into the No-Come-Back Mountains. Her ticket took it all. Your mare, saddlebags full, your rifle — like when you took off from Nebraska to see them never again. Never to see you again, Jenny? Choices, dammit! And they leave you bleeding

Out into the sun. Unwind the same horsehair hackamore, the bridle for working cattle tied to the saddle, swing up. Through the swinging door the music stops. Lift her with your heels and your hand straight into a run. Do you hear those hooves in the dust, Jenny, that would set you flying by the river, that would lead up Cleopatra into the sky? Fading into the afternoon sun, Jenny. Rickety Jerome left lonely in the desert.

White line of sky on the dark horizon, mare's ears turned forward, expecting.

Faded line of oilcloth, canes hooked on the edge to dangle into the dark between my knees, against the white line, turned forward; the black of my lap, crotch, fly buttons shiny. Ai! but my neck is broken. Close your eyes, old Will, your neck will be numb.

spirals

spiraling

time

Two soft white fingers, still against the shiny black wood cover turned down over the keys, closed on the waltzes. Turn back, Willy, take the hand that would wait for you still. Soft and warm. Pressing lightly, her thumb caressing on your knuckles, moist, old Will,

63

and you feel the tears drying, tightening, on your cheeks. Colin's girl, she has come to be with you: Beacon Street and the Fashion Saloon, the telegraph office in Los Angeles, the window in the sky. Here with old Will.

Lily girl, must forgive an old man, dozing a bit, eyes kind of water. Yuh, that's me, Coso Springs, hadn't cut my hair yet. I'll show you, got a lock of it in another book. Nope, before I met the Missis — that's what you were thinking, I'd guess. Do you mind bats? *Fledermaus,* eighty-five years ago. Get in the hair, they'd say. Not true, sonar to sort of see in the dark, won't touch you. Little feller lives here with me, now that I don't trouble with the electric plant, in the corner there over the sink. Cloth there's to shade the light so's he'll know when it's time to go bug-hunting. Still, night too he'll often come in, chink under the eaves, perhaps to check on old Will.

climb up

Willy

up the

years

Presences

Hooked on the rafter, squeaking squeaking, how much can you hear? Familiar, the vague light, the nodding shadow. New for the night another shadow, jiggling, still. Hot smells, cool smells, bugs drawn by the light to scoop up now and then in the tail pouch, munch on later. Peace and feeling and why not? Rejected there, accepted here. The part, the whole. Sleepy in the warm air, swinging in the currents in and out the chink, bat sounds outside hunting in the night air, creaking branches, flapping paper in the wind. The rasping of the Joshua tree where the owl lives — dangerous, however musky the bat, when other food is scarce.

Lights and shadows, comings and goings, dozing waking. Familiarity; no danger smells, even with the new presence.

Innocences, Lily, in your heart

Flowers, Lily, in your hair, pinned to your breast. Never mind that they're supermarket left-overs.

In the parks, jonquils and pansies, organized and neat. Along the dunes by the ocean, fat rubbery leaves, pinks, pressed down by the sea spray, the sand, the driving wind. Yellow poppies in the valley, laurel in the forests, silver sage clinging to the summits like and old woman's hand, so small.

passing

passing

Flowers turned sour in the airless pads of Haight Street.

Or flowers of the desert, your first desert, low beyond the Santa Claras. Brought there by Perry.

O Lily! Finally may you breathe deep the thin singing air, faint perfumes trembling in the heat? May you embrace the sun, let it penetrate to the heart, purify every cell, join, give life, bring forth the flower? Put your cheek down in the sand, Lily girl, into the enormous world of the tiny blue gilia with its yellow throat. Look up the purple beaver-tail, creased and spiked, to its flaming banner, a solitary desert bee, stuffing her leg sacks with pollen to feed to the brood. Higher, against the pink granite wall, the slender green fingers, giant feelers, specked with a million scarlet blossoms, the ocotillo. And against the sky the great shaggy arms of the Joshua tree holding out to the sun, over all, their handfuls of white lilies.

rape

Yet what holds you, Lily, why are you not dancing free in that air? Behind do you feel the shadow of the mountains reaching out in the afternoon sun, out onto the desert? Black and infinite against the light, a veil of mist hung on the sun's rays. And in the pass, wedged down into the range, is the brown air, spilling over, flooding out onto the sand. Wherever you look, how can it matter? The corruption, the saturation.

the Lily

the Lion

This is not the Nevada desert, with the north California mountains, touching heaven, hanging to the west, and beyond the great grasslands, pierced by volcanoes. Here the desert, the Mohave, is richer, its secrets deeper. It rises to the west in strange unfriendly peaks and shoulders, low passes, failing against the human blight behind. But it stretches east, up and forever.

Behind, a death-in-life sentence, the creeping, the all-invading, the putrid breath of that vile man. How can you cleanse yourself? The foulness reaches even here, and do you carry it with you, is that your sentence?

Lost Grail

wasteland

O why, Pa, why did you send her away, drive her from you and her dear mountains, her own country?

Lily, crouching in that desert, the weight pressing on your back, your heart cold in the sun, your breath hardly stirring as the tears flow into the dust. Remember, try to remember.

Emancipating you, Pa called it, freeing you. The tight ties of Valley Hope, its proper ways, its proper marriages, its proper poverties, its proper hopelessness. Opportunities, professions; agricultural economics and you'll be someone, San Valentino Agricultural College. Little Liliana Tocca.

The tears drop on your books, each evening, staring at the meaningless words and formulae. Temple Street with its Mormons at one end, its Aggies at the other, you in the middle. Second floor, one window, on the street. Always the clamor, still battering in your skull, from the milk and drunks and the meat in the black early hours, to the buses belching at you, the genteel shoppers with their Buicks, the great trucks endlessly hauling, the sports with their cutouts blasting. Always the miasma of the fumes, rising up into your window—closed and you faint of the heat or the stale smells.

O flowers

of the

sun

Tears shuddering in your heart, fevered, nerves jerking with pep pills. The poster photo of your mountains whirling on the wall, *Swan Lake* spinning in the clogged air. The bright patterns of your bed cover—Pugliese, woven by Ma winter nights—shimmer and ache behind your eyes. Your very floor bounces with the jukebox bass drum of the Ice Cream Parlor below.

Tears, the sunshine dripping from you, left dry like the fragile skull of a fawn pulled down by the coyotes. The passions weeping from you. Alone, driven away to suffer for your gaiety. Each step you try is a trap to kill your heart: a smile or a touch of friendship or a word for his handsome eyes turns monstrous, an invitation to press hard on you till you vomit green from the pain in your soul. The kind and the good and the beautiful, they all turn to dust when you approach them.

femme
d'homme

my

.
innocence

68

Three days ago, four or five maybe — how can you count time under the smog and the roar and the sodium lights and with only a can of Pa's honey, O dearest, dearest Pa!, to keep you from death? — their foods that cake in your belly and pound behind your temples and tear from you bloody spoor — countless days back. Slowly up the spitty chewing-gummed concrete steps into the smog-black brick. Late for your appointment, late, O why could it not be never? A groomed and glossy frog, with his charts and tables and built-in twitching leer for the classroom, his trembling hands and shifting eyes and voice like the dirty white cardboard Office Hours. How envied, to have as adviser the professor himself, how easy, the gut, the set-up, toady up and you're in!

my

prince

The long hall, disappearing in the gloom beyond the water cooler, woodwork, dirty brown plaster, transoms projecting yellow light and typewriter clatter and hollow voices onto the ceiling. Your footsteps are another's, for it is not possible that you are here, you whose footsteps are always horse gaits, who laugh in whinnies. Walking into the vanishing point down that unending corridor.

Blonde and perfumed, her made-up voice, "The professor has been waiting for you."

Frosted glass, the clammy doorknob. In the fluorescent desk light the white face, flushed pink when he looks up. "Ah! please sit down, Miss Tocca."

my

Anywhere, look anywhere but at that gasping mouth, those eyes bulging under the fatty brows, those fingers, swollen, shuffling. The stuffed buzzard, hunched enormous on the radiator. The productivity graphs, the chart of the bugs and the poisons, the

tender

Colin

ribboned diploma with the college seal that always
looks like a fox. And you know you must look now,
just over his head, at the prize bull, great things
dangling between his knees, the sheath like a fin on
his belly. And from the right-hand desk drawer, those
hands — you've smelt them sour when they've tried
to touch your cheek — bring it forth.

Flicking, flicking, flicking, black forked flame,
black eye of fear, body twisting steel, tail hissing. In
the hot dust, rasping on the rock, still in the sun,
straight, swelling to split the skin. Eye a drop of
poison oil. Wake up, Lily, wake before it coils to
strike!

Brown, leathery, freshly oiled in his yellow hands,
so cruelly huge and long, pointed, ripping inward.
Once he said, the first time, when he brought it forth,
"I do not show this in class, Miss Tocca, for perhaps
some would not understand, but it is, as I know you —
how exceptional you are, Miss Tocca! — will recognize,
a most noble specimen of the forces of life, the phallus
of a prize bull."

Phallus, what did he mean? The dry tremor of his
voice, some stink in the airless dark room, some spasm
tightening in your belly. You knew.

Even now, the sharp pain of that tightening. Now
as you sit in the clatter of the wind in the tin roof,
the squeak of the bat, Will's sighs as he stares through
the darkness into the oil flame — longing, for past
and future.

Tightening as you watch again the hands taking
forth that . . . try the words, will it help?, but you
cannot. Somewhere, far in the distance, you would
laugh, high, shrilly, at this obsessed creature, this

tempt

you

take

innocence

in the

brothel

laughter

lightly

70

pig, nasty with the foreign lisp. Not here. Somewhere you would feel pity for this grotesquery. But you cannot.

I am alone, O my dearest Pa!, why why did you drive me away, down into the infernal dark? Why do you leave me? Alone, the cursed diploma, this wanting and wanting and wanting of men which leaves no place for being. Alone in the black, me, who would look for but a slit of pure sunlight as the greatest joy. O come to me, my cleansing sun! Alone midst these mad thirsts—facts and facts and facts and the reasonings, lusts, and they would throw me into their sucking whirlpool, and they would have me.

Fear, the pee spurts and burns on your thigh, tighten, tighten, yet your legs—O tight so tight to the withers!—will not cross. Your eye will not move, your hand unclench from your books. Your breath will not come, the silent scream splitting the dark, splinters ripping the pudgy flesh, sour stinks and poisons.

"Come now, Miss Tocca, have you no smile for your professor, Lily, may I call you Lily? We have your research examination we must work out together. Next week, I believe, yes, just so, just so."

oil

Tap, tap, tapping on the desk.

and

"We must be friends, Lily. We have so much in common. Our Europe, our perhaps being not completely understood in this country, our deeper awareness of the life processes. Emotional affinities, Lily. How important they are for fullest understanding! Come, we shall review the specimens together."

bitter bile

The tapping stops. Yes, it is you, Lily, little Lily. Cold and the smell of wet wool, standing, moving, steps, quite away from the screaming and the trembling rage. Forward into the dark where he would point out life processes, bottled, graphed, pressed, dissected, stuffed, tapping again with his . . . O God, O God, O God! And turning to you again in the murk and dust, the stale air, the scream starting again from the far end of the room, crushed under the blue light.

black

"You see, you see, Lily, how our affinities work, confronted with these, this nature? Do you smile?"

contains

Wool, wet in the dark under the trees whispering to you. Blinking into the stars, whimpering perhaps from the cold place. Until he comes and you wiggle out and stand and reach above your fuzzy head to his great hard hand that leads you beyond the campfire and fumbles your pajamas. I kiss you, I kiss you, Papa, kiss kiss kiss like all the stars.

white

"Yes, yes, we shall be friends. We are so much alike. Look how your head comes to my shoulder. What pretty hair. Let me show you, here, your hand, how unbelievably strong and . . . "

The tightening, it snaps through every cell—the flank behind the blue worsted, the greasy hand, the foul breath—the scream splits between you. Flesh scraped under your fingernails, the poison drips from his face, from his closed and naked eyelids, from his flaccid fingers.

pity

laughter

skipping

Slowly, Lily, turn slowly or every muscle will snap like rods of glass. Turn slowly, with your books pressed tight to your breast, carefully, your thighs together, walking from your knees. Cold grease, the slippery doorknob, shocks you shivers to your heart. Ahead, another door, the blonde, how can she matter? Wool, and are there drops glistening on your stocking, and does the bulging glass, Seth Thomas clock behind

in the dust

72

your bloated head, fracture with the echo of the scream?

You will not pass, Miss Tocca.

From the black behind you, the black before you.

Ladies. Ladies go there with their fish smells and their perfumes and their bitter piss. Lily, with her tears bleeding down her cheeks, vomit searing, dripping, a curled black hair on the white porcelain. Sobbing, her knees sharp pain on the sticky floor, her head raised, bowed again in the dry convulsion under the graffiti of men's enormous things.

Will you ever know, Lily, will it someday come to you in a dream or a revelation or a stranger's word, how you left there, how you found your way in the stifling smog and the dingy streetlight glow where no one walks? Where the music pulses from open doors and tires slap and wince on the streetcar rails. Where newsboys are orange metal racks with smeared windows and ten-cent slots. Where rats peer from the drain grills in the gutters, and mankind is motionless behind the glass, tweeds and two-pronged sweaters in the glued-up autumn leaves and shellacked cornucopias.

How did you get there, Lily, where you looked across the room, strange to you, loathsome with its clinging smoke and its humidity of beer, as if you'd known he'd be there? Eyes that greeted you, that told you it was all right that you hadn't found your room at all, that made the wool all right and the scream fade some, that knew how you'd scrubbed and scrubbed your fingernails in the slimy liquid soap, that could see with no shame where the tears ran astringent on

sun's

path

across

the sky

73

your so cold cheeks. Eyes that came toward you, bright blue, help where nothing nothing else could . . . *Eyes wide to the burning sun, eyes filling with desert sand, eyes drawn closed to their hateful chapel music — so few months, Perry distant at my side.*

He took you to your rooming house, he left, asking nothing.

So you sit here alone, Lily, at your table piled with open books, digging in the pine wood with your ball-point. Blind with tears and anger. You will not pass. Again you will go up there, up those same steps and down the same corridors and past the Ladies. The blonde, the greasy doorknob, the murk. The Project Committee, three, he's one of them. He will trap you among the specimens and the explanations. You will not pass.

"We're sorry, Miss Tocca. You are rather weak here. You must prepare another project for next term. You know the Department's rule, no degree without a satisfactory project."

my

rainbow's

gold

So you will choke on the smog. You will take your last few dollars that Pa sent you and will buy a bus ticket out onto the Mohave, Quail Springs beyond the mountains. Somewhere the sun must still be burning, the air be pure, and people touch the ground.

He will come again, Perry, with his steady blue eyes, just as you are leaving. He will take you.

Flowers from the ruins, Lily. Perry a tree of a flower, you a little lily. His long blond hair, his huge eyes, his cowboy walk with all but his thumbs shoved into his back jeans pockets so his elbows idle, tall in the Joshua trees. You, to wander off in the yellow flowers of the cholla, to crouch in the sand, and feel

74

the breathing about you, the sun flowing, the birds singing for themselves. The calming.

But this desert keeps its secrets, withheld, not yet for you, my Lily . . . *Come with me, Liliana, come with your Colin, to old Will's, the high desert. You'll learn the secrets. The sun will flow into you, the birds will sing for you, the flowers will bloom in your heart.*

Return to where he's sitting, staring out across the hostile sand.

Let him tell you of his country, of his Canada, high against the northern Rockies, the wilderness. Where his horses range free through the winter, to paw grass in the deep drifts, coats grown long against the sixty below and the mountain winds. Where bears and wolves and cougars pull down the old and the sick. Where the elk and moose and the caribou lick salt at his doorstep. Where the glaciers rumble through the summer and the avalanches can uproot trees a half a mile away with their blast of wind. Of rodeos, of packtripping for weeks at timberline, of canoeing the wilderness rivers with the beaver swimming under your bow, the trout as thick as the mosquitoes, a coyote pup playing on the sandy bank.

Forest

bride of

the Sun

Of another life, his life in San Francisco. Burlingame, the Pacific Club, the parties at the Mark. Yachts with the Golden Gate vast against the sky. Europe. This car of his. College, his fraternity, his basketball. The floating blondes, the Jewesses, his sisters in their snobby school, the black girl who taught him how to dance. Debutantes and champagne and five-dollar cigars.

my

pauper

And now, animal husbandry, keep the foreman from gouging: Recreational ranching, but how does it touch your world? A plaything of a livelihood. Pa, the black fatigue on his face from a foaling or a colt lost on the back pasture or taking off honey from eight hundred hives when the nectar runs heavy. Perry, so tall and at ease, who outfitted a pack train—ten five-hundred-dollar riding saddles, the pack saddles, the tents, the grub, the horses he was short—just for the fun.

Good, good, good that when one has it one can enjoy it. Not wrong, not resentful, not even for Pa. Each his own. The dried-up puritans, the reformers; not you, Lily.

wrong

wrong

Perry, who talks so evenly, who accepts you, who makes no fuss about anything. Who is interested in your hell, and even, as the weeks pass, somehow seems to want it for himself. Your life, so bitter and empty and endless now, so remote from the smogged reality around you, he would call it the reality, he would learn from it. He would learn to suffer, he says, he would learn to be unprotected, exposed, the violent reality, primitive forces. His words, not yours, Lily, and you'll never learn them for yourself. Nor did he.

and the

evil

even

line

O Perry, Perry! Was there no way? What did it mean, where did you learn that lofty smile? Should I have hidden me from you? But I cannot hide, nothing.

"One day, you'll see, Perry. I'll be waltzing in silks at the cotillion, right before your eyes, and I might or I might not let you cut in. I'll be blackballing with the best at Burlingame. And I'll live on the top of one of your hills, higher than anyone else."

The smile, the deriding laugh. Turn from him, blindly. A cab, the meter clicking till the last dime is gone. Blindly down the empty streets, to the in-

Tocca Italian

queens

fernal trembling room, trembling from my sobs, from my breath that rushes in at the last moment of agony, from my heart that hardly stirs.

Calmly, Lily, calmly. You will see him again, more than once. That day riding high in the piney hills, and you could see his dude seat for all his talk, and his stumbling for the pain when he dismounts. When he'd come for your tagliatelle you'd do on your electric plate, but only once to Ciro's and with such sarcasm for aristocracy.

A last time, you know it will be, even before you start that early morning. Vacation in the spring, you the weeks between quarters, he the whole summer. And he will take you home, on his way to Canada.

Seven hundred miles. Dawn from the mountains, the sun rising out across the desert. Cajon Pass. And north, the dry salt-lake playas and the salinas, the yucca and the sage, the thundering double trucks and the house trailers and the campers, the filling stations signaling for miles and miles ahead. Granite Pilot Knob at the end of Cuddleback Arch. Bonanza country, Kern County, red mountains bored and scooped and streaked with the tailings, blacks and grays and yellows and greens, calico. Across the borax road.

And mostly, except the moments — scene or mood, colors in the hills, desert flowerings, a word spoken straight, a grin from a truck driver — mostly the sense of ending, doom. Suffering, the sweet imminence.

Coyote Holes, the Sierra Nevada climbing up behind the deerhorn cactus, signs to the petroglyphs. Lava cones and congealed black falls, half down the face of a precipice, never to arrive. The Cosos and

north, up

through the

hole in the

sky

77

the Panamints above Death Valley and the Inyos and the White Mountains. Dry pine and snow patches to the right, hazy, foreshortened in the slanting light. The Sierra to the left, picked out in the morning sun, spruce valleys, rock faces, snow fields glistening. Gold country, ghost towns. Camps and motels and Best Trout Fishing, animal farms and Kiss the Kobra & Rattlesnakes, trailer parks, ski lifts. Oldest living, highest point, lowest point, largest state, tallest tree. And still the glory of the Owens Valley remains.

Mono Lake, the high passes, the walls of rotary-plowed snow, the heater on your toes and the ice on your ears. The catsupped hamburger which no Italian, however aristocratic, could abide. Discreet disappearings to the Rest Room where no one rests — you prudes, you puritans, repressed, all all all is form. Though your eyes could smile still, O Perry, Perry, Perry.

Devil's Gate Pass and the long valleys, the opening range, down to Carson City. Reno, the unbelievable town, will you ever understand? The Nevada deserts, mile upon mile, salt flats, dry hills, a glimpse of the Cascades far off in California. Asphalt turning to dust. Antelope, the ranging cattle.

Still you're in your separate cubes, you and Perry, sealed off. Do the hours that reel out into the roaring wind bring you nothing, Lily? Can you not break loose, break him loose, or chink through somehow so at least he can hear?

O listen, listen, listen, Perry! No blame, no forgivings, but accept me, wherever, or I can never see you again. Look, there, far off ahead and to the west, those are my mountains, black against the white

my

failing

flight

78

evening sky. And this is my valley, leading in from the desert, and this, Perry, is my town, my Valley Hope. Further on, further on a bit to our ranch. But what would you there? This is not your route, and you would have left days before. You say nothing, you ask nothing, you hear nothing.

They are waiting for us on the porch, against the yellow light of the open door. Fling out, almost falling, rush to them, rapture of embrace, joy filling and filling. Oh! but I shall never never leave again, nothing can make me.

parting

going

Yes, this is Perry. Ma, Pa, my sisters. You've been waiting for us all this time? You must be starved too. Supper, oh! supper, my supper, it is, it is! Polenta, I smell it from here.

the black

suffocation

Cornmeal mush spread hot on the marble table, the sauce and the cheese and the sausage in the center. Each his sector, seated round the table evenly, start together, the sausage the prize. Chattering, stuffing, shrieking, faces leaning into the disappearing circle.

Perry, can't you, can't you?

OK, you can't; but try, be funny, be embarrassed not at us, at you. Not like that, Perry, closed off, the motions, remote, studying. Look, it's us, it's me, me you rescued once. But it's you to be rescued. It's me, can't you hear me, won't you?

your

gentle eyes

So tall he'd be, high on our biggest horse, and I'll show him how to ride with his shoulders steady and his hands light and high, his heels down, back on the saddle, with his blue blue eyes and his long hair beneath the curling hat. And I'll teach him about polenta and how to laugh and what is family and what is love. And he'll teach me something, that other

across the

smoky room

world, where everything is possible and there is nothing you cannot have.

But: "Must leave this afternoon, must get on."

One night, a morning in the bee house, and exercising the stallion who must be kept in now. His eyes slide down and to the side. He has left you, Lily.

Your eyes will fill with tears, Lily, your heart and your breath will stop. Again, again. His eyes will only slide away. Otherwise might he suffer?

High on the mountain table, high where it tips into the sky, a horse is racing, all honey white, racing with a girl lying lightly on his back. All dressed in a silver robe shining like dew, her hair the yellow heart of a lily. Her face in his flying mane, her body resting so gently, like a moonbeam, on his withers and loins. Her toes stretch out bare on his croup. Her arms lie almost around his neck and her fingers are twined in his thick wild coat. They leap like one, high over the flowering blue sage and the wild grass, ever higher into the black sky. Beneath her she can feel his wings spread out and with great slow sweeps carry them on up into the sun.

blue

'tween

white

and

black

She does not look below, she does not think of the earth they have left. On and on they fly and the air is so clean and sweet and the light so cool. Their bodies seem one. The wings seem to spring from their very soul, rushing and rushing in the wind, the great feathers snapping, the muscles so pure.

His ears are turned ahead, pointing eagerly. His head is thrust forward, his eyes so black and true. From his nostrils, sucking sucking, blows warm foam.

From her heart she cries out to him so gladly,

"On and on and over the sun!" The words blow back to her heart and they are cold like flecks of ice.

The foam blows back, ever more. And it is red and burning hot.

She opens her fingers in his hair, rises to her knees, tears mixing with the foaming blood. She raises her arms in the glistening tunic, she catches the wind and is torn free.

Slowly she turns, resting on the air, her face to the sun, her back to the earth. Above, beyond, so white against the arch of the sky, is her horse, still with the great wings beating, the hoofs prancing on. Even from the widening distance she can see him, as she hadn't need to see him before, in every detail, and she can see that his ears are wildly back and his eyes turn white in fear. There is heaviness in his muscles, but on and on and on he races.

Ever higher, smaller, a shining point, a star fixed in the black sky, following, following the sun.

She, slowly she turns, slowly she falls away. And now the air that presses on her is in her face, drying her tears which have washed clean the blood. She is facing downward, her features in the shadow. Her robe, now brown and coarse, it cups the air. Toward the earth. Turning turning beneath her, coming to her, she to it.

The desert, stretching pink and red and yellow on and on, spinning past. Then pale greens, black volcanoes, the far wrinkled sea. The great outer ring, warm desert colors, cool plains and mountains, the warms again. And an inner ring, the dazzling white of the salt playas with balloons of heat rising from them, and tight beside it the narrow green strip of

finish, Lily

don't let

the birds

sing yet

81

wheat fields and corn and fruit trees. Changing to blue lakes and dark green forests and there the miles and miles of spring hay fields.

Just beneath her, slowly turning too, the mountain-tops, shortened and softened, bare in the velvet of the fir. And the high plateau, the Landing Place, ever bigger. Quite gradually she settles down, the earth comes to her, circles. The center, the flowering blue sage and the wild grass. Her wings enfold them, they reach up and receive her. Her flowers, her snow-brush, the wild peppermint, the tiny blues bending under the weight of a bee.

that
complaining
kitchen
pump

Holding; the ancient home, the earth

Wild flowers leaning in a jelly glass, Welch's, flowers that came in the evening. Some close, some wilt; others survive, proud sun, spring rains. Leaning out over the oilcloth, over his twisted hands that lie on the black pages of the album; sympathy, tears drop on his wrists.

Dry desert; twists, blacks, the pine planks, suffering.

Dry sobbing; faint in the still between harsh breathing and the rush of the night wind.

I the home — my voice.

I, collecting you, protecting you, holding you, weeping with you. Lily, new tears, new presence, clear heart in the dark beyond the lamplight. Old Will, tears of time, the silent shaking of his shoulders, trembling the floor, renewal of courage.

I am here: to contain, to store life, to give it its place. To be there, within the reach of habit, the familiar. Familiar to the recesses of the heart, to the search of the memory; light to the eye of the soul. To receive.

Who else to comfort you, to embrace your pain, to answer? Me that you reconstructed, warm around you. I reach back, old Will, far back, and you are the inheritor. Your secret valley of the high desert, secrets reaching deep into the earth at our feet. Crumbling adobe, mud and sticks, hide tents rotting in the sand, barricaded caves in the ringing rocks.

83

Place, that is what you found. And do we sob for that, for those distant pains that led us here, for the sufferings of the search? Or is it that we can see no farther? Are the cyclings ending, are we the last, Will? No inheritor?

Willy; Spider Woman, give Earth's Treasure

Who'd shake me so, who'd make old eyes blink so, who'd want to tell me of the end? Lot to remember, lot still to do, and they'll be taking it over when I leave, won't they? Their Park, their museum, they say. Old Will won't be forgot. Why's that an end, why do you tell me still that this place ends? Why do you shake me still?

impatient

blackness!

Have I cried, have I dripped tears here on my wrists? They're wet when I wipe at my eyes and cheeks. Here, this little brown photo, now that I can see good. The soft dark hair, the eyes, the lips that seemed always half ready. What moves behind the lamplight, what eyes are wet with tears?

Did you weep for me Jenny, as my hoofbeats died, did you play your waltz some sadder that desert afternoon? Did you mean for me to hear it?

Jogging off after the sun; young feller, sad at the mouth. Best look ahead, young Willy, plenty to see up ahead. On where there'll be the Walapai tribe, high in the wild country, the red country, the pine country. They'll take you, Willy, they'll make you a brother and give you a name and you'll ride bareback

85

and whoop after the antelope for a second shot. Speare, you wrote it, 'cause the Court Clerk said so. Thieving, judge said, damn half-breed, till your brothers came whooping on their horses, hundred'r more, and said you'd with them, no thief, and plenty of trouble if you'd be kept a piss-time more. Ride off with them, hair all tied behind, maybe a feather too.

Chloride, Arizona. Ride in, running, on the Fourth, you and your Walapai friends, fat from the summer hunting. You'll loosen the dust at the Half Moon Saloon. You'll pay down your fee from the hides you'd sold. They'll cheer and whoop you when the announcer shouts out "The Indian!" Your riata'll whistle, steer-tying, and maybe and maybe not you'll get a piece of the prize.

That's them, the Walapais and me, foreman took the picture when I went down there—over from Needles—to get turquoise for the tombstones. Still keep going, they do. I knew them well, back in the 'nineties. Good people, good friends, loyal, honest. Savages! Who'd be calling who? It was a Garden of Eden, America—who knows the debt we're in? Colonel Chivington, at Sand Creek in Colorado; the Cheyennes, just remnants of them, camped, treaty with the United States, he orders "Shoot them at daybreak. The only good Indian is a dead Indian. Women and children too, nits breed lice." And he was a preacher once. Shot'm down, every last one. The women pulled their dresses right up, over their heads, to show they were females, but he shot'm all.

Scalping. Y'know who did the first scalping? Back in Virginia two ladies were kidnapped by the Indians. Some good reason too, probably. Lived high, on

barbarian

hordes

we,

crushed

against

the Baltic

86

maple sugar and all the meat they wanted, said so later. Stole some knives, slit the throats of their guards, sliced off their scalps, escaped. And they were paid for the scalps. First time anybody'd ever thought of scalping.

Yuh, good people. Sober, protected their women, sort of instinct toward the female. Kept the family small, like the quail won't lay eggs in the bad years. Have some sort of herb medicine to take when they don't want children, squaw told me of it, don't know just what it was. Just one wife.

We were all gentle once, in this Garden of Eden. Cave man was naked and he wasn't ashamed. Fruits and nuts and maybe eggs, but never thought of eating meat. Then the ice moved down from the north and he didn't want to leave home for the south, so he took the warm skins from some animals he'd trapped. Threw the meat away, but his dogs ate it, and he got the idea too, though his teeth aren't made for it.

We'd never hunt but what we needed. Here too. Leave the bighorns and the wild burros and the deer and the cats, leave them for the Indians if they wanted'm. We had beef cattle; why take another life? Hills here, up in the high desert, were full of those wild burros. Then they came along, rounded them up, slaughtered them to feed the foxes, fox farms down in the valley, still going I'd reckon.

That's how it is, Lily girl. Here, let's have some grub, corn heating. Mind it in a cup? All I got. Spoon's over there. Saltines? And there's a good bit of your watermelon left still.

Were your eyes like that, Jenny? Did you look at me straight like that?

Whitsuntide

slay

the Wild Man

of straw

night

snarls

down

by

the

river

bank

87

"I'll pick up and take right out'a here, Willy boy, if'n I hear another word about that Jenny. Snotty from the East with her ways."

How'd you know then, Bucky O'Neill, what'd you know of Jenny? And what'd you know of Willy? Whatever, it'd not be long, you with a rope around your neck. Partners, you and Willy, but how much did you know him, could you even give his last name? Dan? you'd never heard it Jenny? just another college girl come out to get educated, high-class music at the Fashion Saloon.

But Willy'd knowed you some, Bucky, kind of looked up to you, when the Indian doings wore like a girth sore, last name leastways. And best damn cowboy in Arizona Territory, working sometimes alone, sometimes with young Will, sometimes with your brother.

How does it go, how does it fit together? The Parker brothers, Frank Parker and his brother Jim. Switched their names for the Rough Riders, 'ninety-eight, you all did. Willy Dan, on the roster you're William Franklin Speare — Buffalo Bill, William F. Cody, what better name to take? Buffalo Bill the old gray hero. Neighbor of your uncle's back at North Platte. Remember, Willy? El Centro where you went to see him with his show — the women had cut your hair and your beard by then, Will my boy — and he took you round to show you how he'd always get them glass balls that no one else could but once in a while. A bullet made of wood, looked like any other if you weren't too careful, that sprayed out like a shotgun, couldn't help but hit.

Willy Dan, Jerry Dan, wasn't that the last time? Eighteen and ninety-seven. You'd see them again —

Old Tales

close out

Volga mist

Hero

who

escapes the

88

train from somewhere, Denver and on up to Nebraska — dusted as ever with the flour, cold silent about your hair.

But Denver'll wash it off and their holy crossings and mutterings and the brothers doing so good in school. Denver, all hazed in the whiskey smoke, tickling, such ticklings with the prostitutes. Shows and plays and the opera.

Give in to it, Willy, the prostitutes, the liquor and tobacco too. Trespass against nature. Temptations, all around, for cowboys. Perhaps they'd jack off too, out on the range. Wrong, but there weren't the females there and there was the need. Fool youngsters now, with their pushing the liquor and the cigarets on the girls, their automobiles with the corruptions, the raising hell; life's wrong today.

The last time, eighteen and ninety-seven. Send them money ever' so often, a letter, a Christmas card from San Quentin — no, must of been dead by then. They'd get you all tied up, like a steer, and you'd not be castrated and you'd not be branded, least not Dan or Danziger. Speare, William F. 'd do fine.

All signed up. And then you bust your ankle, Willy boy, and they'd off without you. Jim Parker, he made it, off to Cuba and they'll hero him, you'll bet. Frank (though, "Bucky Boy" you'd like better), they got you. Smart fellow, the sheriff, George Ruffner, and he got you. Everyone'd knowed, Ruffner too, and to switch your brand wasn't quite enough. Held up the Santa Fe, you and Jim and the others, just this side of Ash Forks, before Peach Springs. Some gets killed in the shooting.

And now they'll hang you for it. Your friend Willy's

Great
Mother

to the

multiple

womb

escapes the

Phallic

Orgy

and the

Rites of

Castration

89

here, your partner, whooping you on where you got to go, with the tears running like the spring thaw. Did he put you to it, fool hold-up? They stand you there before the crowd, up on the trap, with the bandana over your eyes and the green hemp loop around your neck. George Ruffner's there, in charge, and you tell him, loud so's we all can hear for sure, "Pull the string." You're twisting, Bucky, twitching, but you could hear the snap, loud like you'd yelled it out yourself.

A good cowboy, the best. And Jim, never did see him again.

> Wipe off the tears, young Willy;
> Tie back your hair and leave.
> Limp to your mare, the pinto;
> Not much a use to grieve.

(hang down

your head

Tom Doola)

> Back to the Walapais, boy;
> You'll have your troubles too.
> Give her her head, she'll know where;
> There's nothing here for you.

But troubles. Their law, reaching out for you; grabs you sometimes, how often? With the sheriffs and the deputies and the D.A.'s and the wardens and judges.

D.A., the one without hands, how'd he lose them? Dixon. How'd he know, how'd he found you? How can you help the killings if they get in the way of the shooting? And how can you keep'm off your range if there isn't shooting? And they couldn't but agree, so's they let you off, but only after a pile of words and legalizings.

You'll be on now, young Will, on till they hear your whoops in Boston and L.A. and they're eating like burros out of your hand. The Walapais, but they're kind of retreating now, and you've got an idea you'd kind of like to move on, get over the Colorado, on into the desert, the real desert they call Mohave.

A few dollars, Will, and you'll be freer. And that's what George Briggs offers you, at his saloon in Needles after you've swum the Colorado on your mare — save ferry money. Herding cattle. Suits fine. End to the Rough Riders, and to the Indians, though their pine mountains are still black to the east'ard. Cowboyin'. And come the Fourth you'll be up at Chloride again, steer-tying, and maybe then you'll be yelled out as "The Half-Breed!"

That'll be the last one, Willy, the last time before all them hooting chittering spectators. The rush out from the chute, lariat onto him, the mare skidding to hold him tight, you're in the dust and follow down the rope, throw him with the trick you learned in Nebraska, whip your piggin' string around his legs, your heart stopped to leave room to breathe, your thigh throbbing like a one-stamp mill for the kick he gave you.

The last time you'll be cowboyin' for another. The gold and the big time, they'll find you, and you'll be strutting like Gardner's peacock on Boston Common and learning how to do hypnos' from a Harvard professor feller. Cows sure, plenty more, twelve hundred head, but they'll be your own, here on the high desert where the Joshua trees do for tie posts. You'll be the one who'll be hiring for the herding.

You'll be glad to be getting on, to show 'em back

Hero

who

escapes

to

the

Treasure

91

in Boston, and perhaps in Nebraska too. But you'll keep a hankering too. For the soft swing of the saddle when you lope through the sage. For the wild fool look in a steer's eye, the feel that your rope is as sure as your forearm let loose to loop round a hind leg. For often as not a night up on the rise under the circling stars that they don't have back in Boston, with the coyotes to sing to you when they've done feeding on mice and rabbits and are feeling harmonious, with your horse tethered and your saddle to keep you 'wake enough under the back of your neck, stretched on your Angora goat chaps, and a serape, for your cougar's long since worn to nothing, to keep off the dew. For knowing the Walapais are racing *O Indian* bareback for the wild horses off across the Colorado, and for maybe seeing their smoke from the top of Pine *friends* Peak where the old ones'd be telling the Spider Woman tale. There's the greasewood smoke and the *of earth* bacon and the being 'round with the others for the company now and then. And there's the desert range sliding off into the horizon, its pockets to learn where the cattle can hide for a year, the washes with the mesquite and the cat's claw and the white flowers in the early morning like bottles on the Elbe.

The hankerings, got'm still, old Will, always, one way or other.

But Willy boy, you're a kid no more, and maybe *the* you don't know where you want to get to, but cowboying ain't likely to get you there. So's you've met *Hero's* this Ike Crabapple fellow and he wants you along, *voyage* for there's gold up in Death Valley he says. Better pick up, what there is to pick up, and go. Crabapple, *begins* that's him with the white goat's beard, fifty years later

92

it'd be, dolled up with the dude buckle and choker and professor spectacles. Serrano Palms, and who took the photo couldn't say. The Missis between us with her bonnet tied on with that scarf, looking like she'd got a roast 'bout ready to please old Will. Weren't like that back in Manvel where he'd tired of swamping on the borax mule teams and he and Scotty wanted you with them to get yourselves some mines. Swamper, who got all the work and none of the glory — but you're not so bad grubstaked now, Ike, down there with the fancy folk in Serrano Palms, some photo, and the Missis passed on not long after. Swamper, who rode the rear wagon brake, and got in the firewood every night, and the rocks for the skinner — lording with his whip which you could work better — to throw at the mules, and squirted castor oil from the long-spout cans into the hubs and corked them up. Swamper's life a short one 'cause the skinner carried the gun and wouldn't take much to get heated up.

Scotty. Was he rascaling even then? Still, Willy, you got yourselves some mines all right, you and he, Crabapple just kind of disappeared. The Golden Girl, the Red Cliff and the Two Leg and the Old Whistler, others. Scotty mostly drunk, parlaying himself into this and that till you kind of parted company, least for the time. He and his Mystery Mine, his railroad race from L.A. to Chicago on the Coyote Special, his big thing in L.A. which he had you talk up all over Rhyolite, his castle, and his Wingate Pass, and his riding in Buffalo Bill's Wild West Show. (Most he ever saw of that show was a wintering with them on Long Island, so Tate, the show's gunner, told you, whatever for his cigars from the King of Spain and

search for

Sun Father

Hero

with

his

Hero Twin

Buffalo Bill turning jealous and ordering him to keep his place.)

Gold kind of got you, Willy, in those first years, you'll say it now. So did Scotty. Locating there on Silver Lake and Soda, couple of days south of Death Valley. Horning for gold in secret, though wasn't really horning — the old fellers who'd, for lack of better, use a sliced cow horn as a sort of spoon for washing a bit of ore. But then there was that bonanza in Goldfield in Nevada, so you just gave your claims to Adam Crow, and Abel. And wished you hadn't after when Goldfield you'd found all used up.

That's when you took up with Panamint Tom, Indian Tom, who knew every spring in Death Valley, though not so much about minerals — comfortable feeling in that country for a young feller who didn't know his way about much.

Prospecting.

Quiet too at the first. The borax boys had gone off to Calico and Daggett. A few hopefuls passing by, heading for Tonopah still and Goldfield. Just that caretaker up at Furnace Creek Ranch, Greenland the old-timers called it — say you can buy your nuggets air-conditioned, read up on the great Scotty at the swim pool.

Then the discoveries, Skidoo, The Bullfrog, Harrisburg, Furnace, Greenwater. And they swarm up the hills and the canyons. Most of 'm prospecting the outcroppings, but then there's the claim jumpers. Not too healthy, out alone. Tom, and later Indian Bob Black, they keep you more than company and refreshed.

Bob Black, with for a brother-in-law Jack Long-

Spider
Woman

smoke

rising

from your

cave in the

ground

O Spider

of Gold!

give

to your sons

94

street who had a ranch beyond Ash Meadows at the mouth of Forty Mile Canyon. Kind of helped each other out. Jack, who'd had the law after him about always for his fast draw and his good eye and the few folk that got in the way. Kept guns strapped on even when haying and would disappear up Forty Mile Canyon when called for and no one would be just about to head in after him with the ambushing so good. Bob, a bit wild too, but he'd come in handy. Time comes when you've been out for supplies and you're packing back in to the One-Man camp. Five fellers sitting there, taken over, armed and nervous with their right hands. Kind of suggest you just move along, and there's not much to argue on. Get set to move off, slow-like though. And they'd like to know if there's anything in particular, any special reason for not getting started right quick. So you let on that you'd thought to wait for Jack Longstreet and Indian Bob who'd be along in a piece. Such magic. Just kind of faded away.

Bob, the same though, who's drunk at Wingate, year or two later, who shoots up Scotty's brother and a mess of trouble.

Maybe he'd find a few mines, that Scotty, but it was not finding them that makes him his name. Never got further up One-Man Canyon than the spring at the foot where he might have pitched camp once or so, the canyon where you've your Golden Girl, Willy, best mine thereabouts. Yet they'll call it Scotty's Canyon, and how long'll Willy last?

Still, you were never much for competing, 'specially with one like Scotty, his shenanigans. And maybe you'll have yourself a museum, kind of a national

Protecting
Charm

feather of

alien gods

and

Magic

eagle's wing

monument, yet, old Will, if you'll wait it out. Not so bad, even though Scotty got himself that castle in Death Valley and the rest of it.

Nineteen oh two it was, Willy, when you rode down from Nevada, town called Bonnie Claire it was with the saloon closed, up over the Grapevines, and down the narrow valley which leads out to the north end of Death Valley below Ubehebe Crater. Coming down to prospect, you'll be picking up Panamint Tom in a piece. Camp high up at Jake Stenigan's ranch with the water bubbling and the willows all green and the vegetables fresh and the grapevines tended nice. Would you dream of a castle going to be there and Scotty as fat as his burro telling stories to the tourists?

Always moving, Willy, moving on. Sometimes grubstaked, sometimes not; Cranton from Worcester, Massachusetts. Good claims and you'll give'm away, or just let'm sit. Got yourself a name too, several names, what with the Cave Man, and the Cherokee, and the Choctaw, and the Wild Man of Death Valley. A burro and a blanket and you'll be knowing every spring in the six hundred square miles, maybe better than Tom. With your brown hair down your shoulder blades and your beard over your breast and your Levis and your ten-galloner. And like as not you'll be moving with Scotty, least till the Under the Box Car contract is ended at Lone Willow. Fifty fifty it is at first, you and him. Though there isn't much to fifty. Johnson's his real mine, Johnson from Chicago who came out for his health. Going to die, they said, for all his millions, and took to staking Scotty as a hobby, never finished till he really did die. Staked him to the Coyote Special train race, and maybe even that's how he's

to face

the Dangers

of the Way:

Boiling
Sands

that

overwhelm

96

salting his Mystery Mine, buying high grade to mix in with the gravel and show to the dudes. And he'll stake him to the castle.

Still, you whoop around more than a little, and you're young fellows and you don't do much harm, least not at first.

Like how, to keep the mystery good and stirred up, Scotty would kind of keep out of sight for long periods, sitting easy up on Tin Mountain, or over by Ballarat, or up in the Bullfrogs, and he'd send you in to Rhyolite with a big roll or some salted high grade for assaying.

Yuh, Scotty's digging hard now, up on the east slope, and when he digs he's got to have plenty of whiskey — be packing it in soon now — get some assays made too — buy from you folks cause you're honester than over at Montana Station — big thing will probably be pulled off next spring, should be L.A. — and the women's juicier here.   .

And riding back you'd hurry, though the booze beat hard inside your head, to catch up with a couple of riders up ahead; company's better than being alone and there isn't much choice. And stop to tighten your cinch and a bullet'd cut into your saddle — would they have thought you were going for the saddleboot? — and your horse takes off and you for cover behind some rocks. And with dark you hear a prospector banging by on his tin-pot one-blanket mule and you take up with him. But there's no sign of them two or your horse. Till you find back at Scotty's camp the next day that Chief Jecopa of the Paiutes in his stovepipe hat had taken in the horse and they'd been getting ready to go out for your remains.

Waters

that

poison

Reeds

that

cut

97

Like Tully Canyon, George Ratford's saloon. Sees you and Scotty after a long drought, extra long 'cause your mule fell off a cliff, earthquake perhaps, and every last bottle was broke. Raw whiskey on empty stomachs, no time to eat, and treating all the women to champagne. And Scotty rides off with your rifle and whiskey's the only way to trap him and you'd like to be getting on after him. So you're back into the bar on your horse, twelve hundred pounds, just a couple of bottles but they give you four to get you on your way, and all twenty of them Swedes took off already for fear the bullets'd start buzzing.

Rocks

that

crush

Or Janice. Miss Acton when she got off her little horse and was asking for Mister Scott. With pink lace flowers in her big black hat. Straight by train from New York society, with her eyes so green and gold — would the clear waters in the sunrise off Ellis Island be like that? And by stage and by pack train from Rhyolite, over the Grapevines, down across Death Valley, and up into the Panamints to find Scotty's Mysterious Mine just to show him he can't skalawag a woman, whatever the men'll think.

Pits

that

trap

"Scotty's away, M'am, gone to New York on mine business, but I'd be more than happy to have the honor to show you around and you're welcome to stay."

"For a Choctaw you speak English very well, Mister Speare. I know of you, you are Mister Scott's head scout."

Careful, Willy, careful does it.

So she stays on at your camp. How many days has it been? It all seems one. Riding up the black willow canyons, up onto the skylines, over to Gopher Mine, abandoned now, to show what a mine looks like. (It's not hard to hide a Mystery Mine which ain't. Keep a close eye on her pack crew, Panamint, wouldn't want them finding us out, one way or other.) Up to Tin Mountain top where the snow still lies and you can see Whitney and Telescope and Furnace Creek down in the Valley and south to the Mohave. And you'll tell her tales of the emigrants' bones in the Valley and of cowboying and cougar-hunting in the Rockies and of the Walapais, and maybe of rodeoing at Chloride — not easy to show off much on a burro or one of your mules, and her little horse is all skin and bones and she's sorry she's brought him for she sees now how the burros who were scrawny on camp garbage back at Rhyolite are thriving on the grease-wood and the cactus that her horse won't touch. Maybe you'll get her a rabbit up there in the scrub oak and you'll roast it to liven up the sourdough bread and the fancy canned grub she's brought. Spring water, almost taste the gold, can you?

Cane Cactuses

that

tear

Careful, Willy. So you're a Choctaw, and like as not it's better that way. More exciting, and with the long hair and beard, and easier than the talk of Russia and Boston balls . . . *Jenny, Jenny* . . . And the girls at Chloride, or maybe Rhyolite, whooping up with the whiskey and the petticoats and the frilly drawers and the soft sweet things and the giggles and the kind of fainting and the shame. Miss Acton, Miss Janice, and then she doesn't seem to mind if it's Janice, from the distance of a real live Choctaw. Janice, who can snuggle a bit, who can laugh in your eyes, twist a braid into your hair, call you quaint so saucily.

Where the pine needles lie soft in the dry grass, the lizards snip up crumbs. Would she? One last day, to show her the Paiute campsite where they'd come to work their Lost Mine and bury their treasure. The wine she'd brought singing in the brain, the sun so warm and the air so still. Would she?

Her fingers fumbling to find her hat pin, "It's stifling under this silly hat, help me Willy."

The pink wispy sticks to your rough fingers like to briars. How her hair tickles on your wrists, can she feel the heat of your breath on her downy neck? Would she, would she lean back now against you? Oh how strong you are! Close her eyes with that light far smile on her red red lips, the pulse beating on her throat. Lying against you, sleeping in Eden, and you trembling to keep off the swelling and the thrusting that she would feel. Would she?

Her hand stirring in her sleep, finding yours, lifting it gently to her breast, sliding your fingers in the buttons. Her legs, the brown skirt so wide she'd ride astraddle and still it'd reach to her little ankles on either side. One leg draws up, the knee to the side, the foot in against the other thigh under the skirt. Opening, and maybe ever so little a lifting. Her other hand, would it? Searching for yours, finding, carrying you to her, pressing. If you move, though, if you move.

"You forget your station, your place, Willy Speare. You will take me to camp now."

Jenny, Jenny, down by the river bank.
Pity, Willy, pity for them.

You'll be all right, you'll always be all right. Like the mountain quail that'll wait for the good years, like the desert flowers that'll come back with a good rain however foreign soles may have crushed them.

O Spider Woman

give him

Strength

to find the

Sun Father

in his

Turquoise

House

100

*The foreign ones with their hidden curse, the outsiders,
the city ones, the East, who would suck off the honey
without touching the seed. They who dream of differences, superiorities, because they're afraid, won't
hear man whooping with the buzzards and the sand
devils, would put him in little boxes, all buttoned up.*

*Wait, Willy, you'll see, like you know you will. You'll
unbutton a few of those boxes, and you'll show them
what's station, and you'll not care nothing left for
their differences. And you'll be back in the desert and
you'll bloom with the rains while they'll shrivel sterile
in the smoke.*

So she'll sleep a last night in the dugout Scotty and
you made for special guests and maybe she'll learn
in her dreams why the snake with its tail in its mouth
is for an Indian the night and the day of life. Roger,
who lives under the dugout's adobe wall; no need to
rattle and flick your tongue and show your fangs,
unworthy of your poison. Gently, Roger boy, up on
your plank and Willy'll take you out into the afternoon
sun. And you'll be sidling up, rubbing on a boot, at
sundown for your plate of whiskey, and faithful you'll
be slipping back under the warm adobe for the night.
Circle in her dreams, Roger boy, couldn't but do her
a piece of good.

And you'll be off Willy in the morning black, and
she can come too if she cares with her burros and her
saloon boys who wouldn't know pyrites from the Tsar's
crown, or borrasca from jewelry rock. They'll be
burying Old Man Finley down at Manse, and you'd
be there, women or no. So she'll sing over the remains
with her high-class voice, and be stuck up that it's the

under

the

Tree

past

the

Poison

first female voice singing in the Valley—which wouldn't be at all true, but let the history fellows straighten that.

She goes east, you go west, back to the Panamints, where the mountain wind'll blow clear the perfumes, where velvet is mine-profits gravy and lousy rich is ore. Windy Gate Pass.

They'll near get you there, Scotty boy, at your Battle at Wingate Pass, you still nearer Willy, though you be forty mile off. It'll be Janice Acton to get you off, in a way, and maybe that's to be her parting shot, who controls things even out in San Bernardino, or maybe it's her best regret. Janice who'd touched you to her in the mountain sun.

It's steady, see; it may claw a bit at the album, with its calluses and its twisted joints, but it's steady as the oil flame, see?

The Battle of Wingate Pass. You're in your luck still, Willy my boy, forty miles off, at your camp, for you'll not be seeing much more of Scotty after Lone Willow. Lone Willow at the entrance to Wingate Pass, where you'd finally split with Scotty, ended the Under the Box Car agreement. Down in Daggett, that agreement. Scotty and you at that hotel where you'd agreed that when the deal went through with Johnson you'd be getting the two thirds and Scotty the one third. And Scotty with his fool ideas: though it was getting dark he'd for going outside and down to the train yard where he'd crawl in under a box car with you after him and scratch his hieroglyphs to make our contract, couldn't hardly write, but Willy, you'd taught yourself.

So now he'd be wanting the two thirds and you'd be telling him to go to hell. And that'd be the end of

his

Charm

against

the

Thieves

it, right there at Lone Willow. And you'll be forty miles off from Windy Gap.

First you'll know'll be Sheriff Ralphs trying to serve some sort of warrant on you at Ballarat and you'll have nothing of it. But he'll get you later. Twenty-seven days in the San Bernardino jail. While Scotty's off scot-free on his Mysterious Mule, or some such.

Scotty there, harder pressed still, now that you'd pulled out. They'd be wondering the more without Cherokee Speare who'd show more'n a few claims of his own without no mystery. And they'd come out to see for themselves this Mystery Mine they'd bought. Hard pressed plenty. Easterners with the financing and the experting and the engineering. Sinclair, Delisle Sinclair, and that Owen fellow from Australia, and A. Y. Pearl from New Hampshire, and Johnson of course who'd kept Scotty out of jail before, and there was Scotty and his brother Warner, and Bob Black, all whiskeyed up. Quite a pack train, heading up Windy Gate. Not more'n a few hours, it was, after Jack Hartigan, the deputy sheriff under your friend Ralphs, had been pot-shot at. You'd never thought they'd gone cahoots, though.

Come afternoon and Scotty sends Bob Black up ahead to locate the water hole and get fixing camp, plan to head up the next day to the Mystery Mine. Not long before the lead begins to fly and there's whoops and Warner gets one bad; the whiskey's paid. So they'd had enough, with his piles of high grade he'd showed'm and the tailings in the distance on the mountainside he'd pointed out. And Warner bleeding heavy. Call it a day, head back. Bob shows up and his rifle's hot and he claims he'd shot it out from behind with

his

Magic

against

the

Arrows

103

couple or three masked fellows, drove'm off before worse could happen, who hadn't probably never seen such fancy gents in the Panamints.

Wasn't on the program, Warner shot like that, nor for Sinclair to get so suspicious and get Ralphs to swear out warrants. Back to Daggett, scared but kind of angry. And Warner bleeding bad. But Scotty's not so drunk that he can't try to turn that to his favor, with his headlines in the *L.A. Examiner:* "Aids Brother in Rain of Lead—Stands Before Ambuscade and Defies Four Hidden Assassins." And his thousand dollars to the doctor of the California Hospital who'll pull Warner through.

So they'll pull you in too, for who'd heard of Scotty without Speare for more than a few years now? And there'll be Scotty too for the night. But Johnson has him out quick and he skips off fast to Washington and Oregon and San Francisco and Saint Louis. With his Mysterious Mine Show and he'd go right on the stage with his burro and his tin pan and his campfire; fat, though, so'd be hard to take full serious. Saint Louis, that's where he'd be with the show, drunk so's he fell and bust his gun and yelled shit at the audience and said they could have their money back 'cause he'd not go on.

And was it from Oregon, while you was cooling in the San B'doo jail, that he sends a telegram asking for you to come join the Taylor show?

So'd be Janice Acton, who'd heard tell of your plight, who'd turn up Judge Bledsoe, R. E. Bledsoe, or was he a Judge only later when you'd be fixing to sell out to Boston? With all his golden talking, had Judge Oster convinced. Forty miles away. And then

Hero Twin

that

fails

him

104

they'd find the shooting was in Inyo County instead who'd refuse to try the case at all . . . *Janice, your best regret, your hand or Willy's? . . . O Jenny, Jenny!*

It'll be today they'll let you out. Twenty-seven days is cool enough. There's a room or two above at the back of the saloon. Temptation's tempting and her thigh's big round as a pig's belly. Twenty-seven days and there's no Cherokee as white as you and maybe just it's time to trim up a bit, with your hair dragging so's you trip on it and your beard getting splashed when you piss. And after the barber's done with you, so chilly 'round the neck and your chin all naked like the saloon girl's rump. All giggles she'll be, husky with the black hairs on her chin, and all the petticoats to corral. There'll be a bitter taste about your heart, though, and you'll wonder who this is so sweating beneath you.

You'll be thinking of her, heading back for Death Valley, stopping over at Coso Hot Springs, and with help from whiskey and the boys you'll mold her in mud and salt with her great breasts staring at you through their cherry nipples. You'll sit at her feet and they'll photo you, with your hair all slicked and your mustache all curled and your eye looking out on the world secret proud.

They'd tell you how Owen, fellow from Australia, died not long after Windgap. Scotty'd camped down at Lone Willow, give Warner a rest, get some blood back. Drinking heavy all round, Owen like every day for weeks. And he with the heavy fat he's carried before. How he'd bedded by a bale of hay and the next morning they'd worried him to jitters saying he'd slept on the

Charm

that

forgets

its

power

Magic

that

105

bad-luck side of the bale, dangerous. They had him in the wagon, layed out, all deflated from the workings of the whiskey, moaning in his sleep. Hot like a griddle, twenty-five miles up toward Granite Wells. And he woke up and yelled out murderous to Pearl that he was bleeding to death, all warm and wet underneath. But it wasn't blood but his gut all emptied from the shits; the sun and whiskey and the fear when the lead was flying the day before can do it. Got him a nurse when pulled in to town, shipped him to L.A., to the Hollenbeck Hotel. He told the police he had a story, a big story to tell, but they shipped him under escort to New York. Couldn't even recognize his wife and children and he just up and died, up in New Hampshire. Story with him. Scotty's luck again.

Is it then you'll meet Arthur Jakewell again? Another one you and Scotty'd four-flushed. To show him where the Mystery Mine's at. Packed out from the Nevada camps, through Death Valley. His grubstake to his last penny. Showed him the hidden grade, salted good as ever, but kind of steered clear of the Mine, "Being followed, can't afford to show the way, government land so's no claim, secret even from such a fine fellow as you, Arthur Jakewell. Virgin gold, almost, for the picking."

And on across the Panamints, down into Inyo Valley, back into Death Valley, and through Windy Gap again, and Black Pass to Barstow. He none the wiser, you two fed and traveled free. And not to leave enough alone Scotty'd pawned Jakewell's horses to landlord Parks for board and drinks. Poor Arthur boy'd not believe it in the morning, a writ of attachment served by friend Constable Stuchberry, when

could

die

eternal

Spider Woman

give

Strength

to your

Hero Son

106

he came to take his horses, and landed in jail for two days for resisting an officer while Scotty swore he'd keep him in for six months, Easterner, looking for adventures, eh, well here's one.

against

himself

So, help him, Willy, nice sort of fellow, you know your way about a bit with the San B'doo law enforcers where they'd shipped him by train. D.A. Hugh Dickson, and that Waters'll get him out. Poorer and the wiser, after you'd talked Scotty from leaving him out on the desert with only a few pounds of grub.

Money'd be coming from Chicago. Back to dear old State Street.

Sitting for your photo. Willy with your shiny shirt and dark wool jacket and big white ten-galloner with the fancy black band—looks same as ever, always kind of self-contained in the eye. Arthur with his black hat cocked like only a dude from the East would think you should, bandana not at home, and the black mustache slowly growing up to be like yours. He'd show you his girl, tucked in leather by his heart, framed in oval cardboard with her twin sister. This one, she'll be for you Willy, I'll bring them both. The Wellington girls.

here

painted

in the

sand

the

Ending

But she'll never come, O Willy. Just Arthur and Frances, Christmas Greetings. Most years. Sixty gone by now, and still somehow his arm's on your shoulders. A first-rate fellow. You'd be done with Scotty, though, once too often. And it's time to be back in the Valley. Roger to feed, pencil assessments to make on your claims, bit of developing till it's ripe for experting with the Boston fellows.

Maybe too just getting good and out of civilization'll be good. All these people and their dirt and their noise and their shenanigans. Willy Speare, that's who you be and there ain't nobody who's going to make you over. Choctaw or a fancy-pants cowboy or Jerry Dan the miller boy.

Up there at the Golden Girl, not much to it, just keeping your claim up, scarin' off the jumpers, you and Panamint, waiting for to sell when it gets too much botheration not to.

But there's a lot of just settin' to do, and getting up to the skyline to see what your neighbors are at, and all them one-blanket fellows nosing about — maybe see one somewheres two three times a month — see what the weather's going to be and how the sun's getting on, and the purple shadows stretch down the canyons and the flowers come out after a cloudburst.

Cleaner out there, and you'd like to be clean, what with the miller's flour and the soap perfumes and the jail stench and the tobacco and the cunt fish that you'd not wanted much anyhow — just kind of got in your way — and all their powders and paints.

The desert wind and the dew under the moon and the sun so's you know every shade in the Valley and the rains and snows and kind of the wash of the great sea that threw surf on the red cliffs, cutting into the bone of the earth.

Fossil bones, fossil shells, geological specimens, stretched out on planks and tables and the old troughs, like from Russia clear across Europe and the Atlantic and America to all this monzonite and the pinto gneiss. I'd not bother you with all that and their fancy names. Learned them since a little fellow: where the rivers cut through the Russian plains; where they dig,

ponies all blind, out under the Irish Sea; where the
Rockies kick up through the plains; where the seas and
the great ice and the craters and lava flows and the
gnawing wind and rain made these valleys and deserts
and mountains and left minerals enough to buy off
Armageddon, if you but know where to look.

its Bone

The Missis planted that bamboo, must have been
when she first came out here, nineteen eighteen or
nineteen, and never could get rid of it; just kept sucking away at the other things we'd put in — all weed
and thistles now — never could get rid of it, kind of
fond of the well.

its Flesh

Walter lying on the arrowheads. Can he smell the
rabbits' blood?

its Blood

This way, Lily girl, where the stone's finished for
putting out where I shot Crabble. Still snow in the
shade from last night. Not enough to settle the dust
or open an aster.

Over there, now, over that fence of Joshua trunks,
that's where maybe I'll find more than a bit of gold.
Stamp mill'd set there first. Pretty crude, lot of gold
got through I'd never recovered. Sometimes, you
know, in the mornings, hot sun coming in, and still,
like now, sitting at my table maybe writing me some
poetry, I'll get a feeling like a sort of magnet, pulling
at me, real strong, right from over there. Had it before
and it's proved out. Must be a good pile there. Get to
it soon. When I get done pulling in all that fence wire.

its Treasure

109

The earth holds this lightly, waiting

Collecting, gathering in, the infinite evidences. Sixty years, mining, ranching, farming in the high desert; sixty years draining back into the sand. The means — wagons, trucks, rails, rakes, picks, the stamp mill, bed springs, Hercules Powder, horseshoes, an acre of nuts and bolts, shackles, hooks, buckles, pulleys, wedges, tires, a saddle frame, pipe, hose, axe heads, saws, shovels, hoes, scythe blades, steel traps, a coffee grinder, post holer, curry comb, buckets, pots, ore pans, cultivator, branding irons, chains, stirrups, pitch forks, the grindstone, mine cars, barrels, funnels, gears, bee houses, a baby buggy, a scooter, the fence wire, rolls and rolls and rolls — laid out in a sort of neatness over the valley floor, bleeding, dying the bones back into the sand. Tombs under the Joshua tree.

The earth holds this lightly, waiting. Always the scars have healed, always the taking away is the giving back. Always the dying is the returning is the giving life.

Lily of the Valley, so slowly turning from you

Home, little Lily, returned to Valley Hope. The sun shines in from the clearest blue, through the yellow poplar leaves, through the morning voices of a million birds, through the mist of muslin breathing gently in the air, the floating fairy dust, the secret princess perfumes, warming the tear on your cheeks. Thin, so pale and drawn, with the green eyes looking up at the gabled ceiling, looking inward, homeward.

Somewhere back behind your eyes, back and far far down, the black oily roar, the long corridor, the tap tap in the wet palm, and the reasoning and formulae and books and ritual symbols. A shuddering back of your shoulders, swallow to clear the smell and the sting.

And somewhere in your head, maybe at the roots of your warm soft hair, hair slept on against the lie leaving a crease of pain, somewhere an ache of hurt, of his going, so blond and tall and handsome, so silent, so afraid.

The ceiling, rippling from the leaves, white shelter, reflections of home. Pots and pans and hot honey for the flapjacks, up through the rattly register. That complaining kitchen pump. Hands and her humming voice.

I,

a Lily in

the earth,

a Lily in

a vase

111

Hoofs on the barn floor, a creaky gate. Long thin legs, high-heeled boots, a great floppy hat slapping at the rumps, his sweating face shining with love for you. A calf bawling in the west pasture, a tractor starting up at the Pini place for the plowing.

Bathrobe spread, green like the peacock Mario keeps for shrieking at intruders, with an ache of will, slowly rising, up from the grass, up through the poplars, a little more effort, up into the sky to sail so easily. Pa's here, take his hand, he in his bathrobe too. The sun is so splendid and the tops of the poplars are feathery plumes, and the doves fly about encouraging, giving tiny downy shoves. Cedar-shakes roofs among the swaying branches, white clapboard with the two-pane windows, brown bare-wood barns, white front fences, cedar poles and barbed wire in the pastures. Greens and the black plowed fields and the dusty white road, purple mountains and the blue blue sky. Stores with their false square fronts to make two stories of a peaked roof, lining Elm Street. The church all clapboard white with the open bell tower, the bell swinging soundlessly under its pyramid roof, ginger-bread on the eaves and the pointed windows. The pioneer log cabin with its tippy roof, but the tourists never come to Valley Hope. Flower beds through the oak trees, hollyhocks and pansies and geraniums. The mothers in their bonnets, the fathers in their black suits, the children swarming 'round, clusters moving down the lanes and out to Elm Street and on to the church.

can

I

ever

land?

Fly on and on and on, hold tight to his hand. The others don't know how, earthbound, but you and he, you'll fly forever, up where the poplars point so stiff, reaching for the sun.

ever?

ever?

The screen door slams, his heavy footsteps in the kitchen, the clanking of the pump. Sudsing on his strong fine hands, strong to hold you and keep you and protect you and never never let you go, fine to love you and be so tender and give you such beautiful gifts . . . *Why does he tremble so?* . . . Throw off the covers, race in your bare feet down the stairs, your long robe streaming out, fly into his arms. Tears and screams of laughter and the tarantella thumping on the linoleum and suds and the pump still splashing as the handle sinks down.

Never never never will I leave you, and never will you ask me to, and I don't care at all if I ever see him again, no, I shan't see him again. I want nothing nothing nothing but to stay here and go riding with you for the bees and be in my own own town.

The amused look, the quiet look, the wink to the others as the flapjacks are forked out and the honey pours golden with the bacon from last Christmas's pig so crisp along the side. You love each other so, Lily, you and your best best father.

Every moment, Lily, every single instant bursting with fullness, shouting to be heard forever and to admit none other.

Bareback, though Ma would have you clean off of horses: stretches who knows what, and isn't fitting for a young lady, college and all. Bareback with just a hackamore on your little mare Stella, down Elm Street and Orchard and Bari, "Hi!" here and there, maybe Bella, "Gosh, college hasn't changed you much!" And then maybe, "It's awful, they flunk one out of three, hardest field there is, I'm doing fine."

Out into the meadow land beyond town, along the valley edge. On to the creek, willow banks cut down

my Prince

so

strong

beneath

me

in the sandy soil from the freshets. Follow it east toward the desert, bubbling, lesser lesser, until it simply disappears in the sand. Our water has a way of doing that.   •

carry me

on

You see him there, a stranger; still, loose in the saddle, leaning with his elbow on the horn. He must have been watching you as you lay out on Stella's neck and kissed her and told her you'd never leave her again. But you don't care a fig, and you swing over to him and ask, "You're a stranger, lost?"

"Not likely, I own this."

Turns out he's the nephew from Alturas, got this ranch when old man Rocca died in the winter. Taken it well in hand, Pa said just this morning. And he rides so easy and he talks so soft, and it won't be more than a mile before you'll be going with him to the barn dance Saturday in the Servadio hayloft.

Spring, with the winter hay gone and the new hay not yet in. Dances in the church from now on. That hangs a weight on you, though, a kind of dusty deep organ note on a fiddle and an accordion and a tambourine, a kind of upraised vestmented hand which slows the pulse of pagan whirl. So who'd miss the last hayloft dance? Who'd miss the rites of spring?

In the late twilight his shiny pickup comes dusty up your line of poplars, and he's at the garden gate, his boots, all shiny with their stitchings and their inlays, reach long up the pebble path. His tight twills, his heavy belt that a man'll work a winter on with its buckle maybe an Indian did, his sleek white gabardine shirt so tight to his body with its pointed buttoned pockets and its obsidian arrowhead at the throat — so tight, so strong. The Sunday-go-to-meeting hat all

my Prince

114

stiff and sitting straight, so proud he is, so steady he moves, like in the saddle, under that Stetson hat.

It's the only hayloft with a stairway instead of a ladder up to it, and at that it's narrow and you yell at the bottom for right of way and your skirt all standing out brushes along the walls and picks up some dust of the hay but it doesn't matter at all or if it did you wouldn't be there. It smells of last year's hay and the milk cows and the girls' perfume that hasn't worn off yet. At the far end the table with the punch, at the near is the fiddle and the accordion and the little fellow from up the valley who does the calling when they do the reels and the squares. Light bulbs strung along the rafters, all swept up clean, and the folding chairs from the primary school. Wax in little lumps still on the floor.

The tarantella, whirling whirling in your heart, the tambourine shivering hot under your skin, and you're out there, your hair flying in your eyes. He's there at first, you see his face so serious and proud and detached with his black hair loose over the sunburn line. Everything rushes past behind him. Then there's nothing but the rush inside you and the breath burning on your lips and your skirt swings out on its own and you're stripped bare to the sweat on your throat and thigh. You feel the swelling of your breasts and the shine in your eyes and the dancing of your feet high over your head where the music spins.

The music stops and the room swings about you like atop a haywagon all piled high across a rocky field. His hand is strong on your elbow, the punch is sweet lemon and honey on the tongue. You stopped 'em all, Lily, and they clapped but you'd not have

my father

soft

opening

for

my

Colin

115

heard. And the air outside is cool with the desert dew, the light from the hay door above, roped so's not to fall by mistake, makes the shadows so black, and the fiddle makes the owl's call silent.

I think he'd kiss you if you'd help him just a little, but you'll not have thought of kissing at all, you'll not know what it is but for the movies and Pa's cheek with the after-shave lotion. If he touches you it is to help you, if you were to touch him it is the better to talk and maybe the better to know how strong and true he is. And somehow he knows that and somehow he doesn't.

slim

the hard ribs

under

my breasts

What is it, Lily, that makes them tremble so, that makes their voices go hollow and high and lose the song? Or the others that reach out, tap tap tap tap, with their eyes on you? Or the others who hate and hate? What did he mean and who was it told you, innocence corrupts?

Power, Lily, you'll not learn until, no, not even then, until it turns full on you and drives you to the edge.

Almost every day Stella to take you to the north range land, or the haying or the shearing or the branding, and he'll be there, somewhere. And he'll come over when he's able and he'll touch your elbow when he says hello, and he'll talk soft to Stella and ask after Pa and once he'll have a lead rope that he braided for you, white and black and roan, and joke, "But you won't take offence, will you, Lily?"

day

night

wrap

the

He'll come when Pa invites him to supper, late, when the sun's gone behind the mountains. Straight in from the haying he'll come and he'll not touch you on the elbow and he'll talk about the bees with Pa

116

straight through. And about how Ma's risotto is so good. And he'll say "Goodnight Lily," so correct, so formal, and you'll not help but smile and laugh at him a little and Ma will look so black.

Your room, your sheets, so icy with the window wide from the sunny day, with the cold midnight air flowing down the mountain in streams. Remember, on the back of your neck, Lily, when you've come down the canyons evenings with Pa, packing out the hives when the honeydew in the white fir has stopped, late August? Felt it sliding in under the hot breath of the black rocks?

Ice sheets, and there'll be your cotton flannel gown, but even not and your ooo's! would be so happy. For that's a part of being home, you see, Lily? Exiled, alone, and the chill touch tightens around your heart. Home, and it drives in the warmth to bubble in your heart. (Fannie Farmer who would have you plunge the baked potatoes into cold water to drive the heat to the center, and Pa would laugh so at it. But that's what happens, you prove it every night.) And the warmth creeps out and out and out, and so slowly you relax and sneak your toes down, opening, an inward opening.

You'll not think, not for the tiniest moment, and anyway it couldn't possibly be, that anyone or anything could make you go away, leave where your heart's so happy, where men are tall and can sit to the saddle, where everything reaches up joyfully into the air, where you can fly.

Tomorrow, tomorrow is dumped on you, a black suffocation. Your breath stops, you will not breath

red Earth

skin

of the

Earth

117

again, ever ever ever. The tears are ice, the cold turns on you, you close, you hate, you curse your father who would so kill you. And he, who had said that he's loved you, who'd asked you to come up with Stella some fine day and hand him the braided lead rope and stay for the rest of your life, he too, even he, would talk so, the reasons, the opportunities, the honor, the getting ahead, the never regrets, the being so proud, the new horizons, the duties and the oughts and the musts. Reasons reasons reasons, and the unreasons which stream from your eyes and your heart are weaknesses, to be noticed only by not noticing, by putting you on the bus, behind its black glass, in its stinking shuddering inferno, and driving off fast up the line of poplars where the mountains shade off the moon. Weaknesses, which must succumb to reasons.

shudder

the

Earth

Here the moon shines in, tinted black.

Let them be so sure, all rightful and satisfied. With the heavy boots that swing along unseeing and crush the little flowers. They'll never know nor understand nor want to. But someday they'll be sorry and they'll want you back and they'll want you as you were and they'll ask for forgiveness — and never never will they have it.

Sun

is

reason

They'll want you back, but you'll not return. To Valley Hope? Why? With their prejudices, their country hick ways, their poverty, and they'll never understand you, Lily. Let them go, like they want you to. One-horse backwater where nothing ever happens, ever. Never go back.

Changing buses, waiting in the candy wrappers and

the gum spots and the piss smells and gassy fat bodies
about you, waiting and you're already there. San
Valentino. You'll get another room, an apartment
with a kitchen and its own bath and Pa'll just have to
pay. You'll put blond streaks in your hair, like Zena,
and you'll learn to smoke, and you'll wear falsies.
They'll have to pay.

    Tight against the window, watching the freeway
unwind, tight so as not to touch or feel the body
warmth or even the existence of the arm in the aisle
seat. The arm in the dirty rolled-up sleeve, inching
toward you on every swerve. The arm with its freckle
blotches and the little red hairs, with the fingernails
all chewed down so the flesh swells over the ends. The
rotten breath, leaning across you to look out at nothing.
The wet stain soaking out from the armpit. The foulness that is man, and the weighing down on you and
always the pressing of their ugly minds and bodies.
But they'll have to pay.

    All night the tobacco smoke seeps around you,
settles on you in a film which you'd scratch off screaming with your fingernails if you could. All night in the
slimy air-conditioned air. The morning breakfast stop,
the women lining up, elbowing in ahead of you, for
the stinking toilet. The grease and the rotten hamburger and the catsup dried blood on the counter.
Fly specks thick on the fluorescent tubes. Outside,
Lily, quick before the vomit. Stand in the valley wind,
so cold before the dull sun gets in. Stand, Lily, look
back at the mountains, and let the cold in, deep to the
very center. That is what they want. And maybe you'll
freeze and you'll never have to move again, to move

antlers

stag

so strong

against

the Sky

mountains

peaks

so pure

against

the Sun

119

on, pressing pressing pressing on you. Is that what they want?

But Lily, Lily, it's no use. I can see you clear from here, through the embracing sun drinking up the last few shining crystals of the night's snow flurries, liquid in the desert air, far out across the sage. And you're ugly, Lily, and you're lying, you're holding off the truth. Can't you see, can't you feel, isn't there something wrong, letting first the brilliance and then the shadow overwhelm you? Or will you never learn this, not even now? Will you be torn apart?

Move on, Lily, move on, the bus will carry you on, and somehow you'll survive. Or maybe it's not survival but death and birth. Is that what they wanted?

On. The Valentine city, waiting for you, waiting to devour you, swallow you down without a hiccough.

Nothing will be waiting for you, Lily, no one, and your tears are your own and they'll run dry, tears of powder salt. And just then, just when you've stopped saying you want nothing nothing nothing and the breath comes into you strong and bitter and you look out along the low gray corridors of the bus station, just then he's there. Still tall, slim to his boots that have never touched manure, neat to his long blond hair.

You see, Lily, the meaning of the bitter breath? But no, you wouldn't see, not now. Later later later. Now you stand there, simply stand there, you let him come to you. Nothing stirs about you, your hair is still, your heart is the ticking of a clock, your breast is made of bone. Perry, who's somehow found out your bus, and it doesn't matter how, Perry, above the rest, aloof, conserving.

120

"Hello, thought I'd give you a lift."

"Hello, Perry, I expected you, my suitcase is over there."

The corridors are hollow to the click of your heels. The air-conditioning sucks at the heat.

"Nice trip down?"

"Thank you, Perry."

That was when it was, just at those words: thank you, Perry. A concidence, a moment of resolution when all the jiggling stops, frozen, all motion stops, it drops in place? Or hadn't you, Lily, already done it, already stopped the motion, already engaged yourself to Perry and known that he had too?

Lily and Perry, engaged. Short, pretty, the great green eyes, glimmering still. Tall and strong, elite, the quiet easy way. Engaged, and you'd never touched, never met, never communicated. Together, for refuge.

A keeper, to hold you in escrow; your empty body plays out its role. Perhaps a man intensely self-alive, charged with the supremacy of each moment and each thought, could not have held so much. And perhaps he never knew what it was he held. And now it's too late. Had he to die that you might live? You'll not know, it will not come to you at all until now, out here riding over the hot sand and into the hidden valleys. Only now do you know what happened there in San Valentino, in the bus station, in the roar of the sports car, in the dusk under the dull orange city sky, in the rock band beat that bangs your solar plexus, in the hot smoke bitter in your throat, in the sheets that wad and turn slowly brown.

Get on with it, Lily, as it will be done. The feather bleach, the bouffant, the nets and sprays and tinsels.

Emptiness

created

by loss

of substance

required

for building

Heaven

121

And the shopping shopping shopping, through the acres, the miles, the unending searches, with him always there accepting, dazed but accepting. And on and on.

It's all jumbled together, like through the porthole of the laundromat. Nothing is apart.

Bribes to get the course papers written, but it's only right because you're a girl, and anyhow who doesn't?

oh!

let

The hi-fi turning turning in the dark rooms where shapes move alone untouching or in clutching weary pairs. Where liquor, bring your own, sloshes from glass to glass and you'll stop caring which is yours, the community of embalmed germs. Where shapes slouch to the furniture pushed against the walls, the never-ending walls, or to floors, so tired, in ones and twos, to murmur and fumble, or to the bedrooms where the rhythms change in the dark and you'll feel nothing at all as you pass by.

me

sleep

The crib sheets for the exams, so finely done at such a price. He doesn't seem to mind, and maybe you'll still need help when you go out to Ladies; there'd be any number. The honor system.

The letters you never write home, for there's nothing left to say except, somehow, don't come and thank you for the money, send more. But you don't really need it; he doesn't seem to mind and you've forgotten how.

The tobacco smoke indelible in your hair. Light another so's not to notice—and it trembles in your yellow fingers and it tingles sick in streaks along your arm and catches at your heart.

It's all so gay, and you'd love to, you'd love to,

and if only they wouldn't touch you at all. Call him, if they start again. Perry, that's your role. Such a very good party, so different, just graduate students, mature; the new records, and she ye-ye's like a dream. And someone will ask you to do the tarantella, and, "No, but not tonight."

They clear the floor and they have your record and your feet move heavily on the floor and your head absorbs the cheering and they catch you just in time.

Your fingertips that prickle and the sun that's too bright and coffee coffee that's all you want. Your head all emptied, pressed by the vacuum.

Racing off in his little red sports car, he so solemnly gay, with the top back and the wind blowing your hair forward, just the right effect. Off to the city, somebody's brother, and it will be such a good party. Pink eyes soft about you in the marijuana smoke, the quiet slow motions, the sweetish smell, the gentle conversations, the melting of the sexes.

Entrance fee: your pill box properly punched SMTWThFS, one, two, three, four. The lunar box, Perry has it all poked out to get you in. "Abort (Shithouse) Abortions!" pinned on the bathroom door. You hardly shiver.

The passion-cooking types, the special delights. Rehydrated dips on the Ritz, casseroles where everything becomes nothing, the gallon jug of red wine, the rebaked half-baked bread sponging up squirts of garlic juice and margarine painted on, salad just swimming in Six Selections Mix, frozen goodies, the cooky jag, ice cream made last year from the back of the freezer, real honest percolated coffee with the powdered uncream and who wants Sweeta?, real

teeth

my

teeth

falling

like

tears

brownies from the aluminum foil tray you can get at the Klassy Katch.

The elevators, down and down and down.

And always men, to your green eyes like bugs to the headlights, stuck glued or glancing off, to some promise you never thought you gave. The young ones, stumbling or sly. The PhD's and assistants, maneuvering for position, the sophisticated remark, the intricate gamesmanship, even already the stupid envy of those younger. The older ones who somehow always would slip in, temporarily attached (some wide-eyed girl), unununderstood, the superior slant of the head, ready to pounce on any immaturity, their thirst for a second life, deeply ashamed.

Everywhere you take your knitting, click clicking away, in the psychedelic shoulder bag, the gossamer cashmere yarn. Perry and your knitting, always with you, your safe-conduct across the Styx, past the reaching reaching figures, the obscenities and the drugs and the intense melancholy of youth. Detached, cold; sought.

Everywhere the knitting, the scarf. Your favor for Lancelot. Yard upon yard, and you see it wrapped about him and streaming far out behind his MG. With your lettering, almost finished now, between gay white flowers at each end it'll be LILY OF THE VALLEY. Sometimes you whirl it around you when you dance your tarantella, and you hear their admirations and you hear their "Where is your valley, Lily, when may we visit it?" And you understand?

Night upon night: you have no home.

It was all a shadow dance; why could you not see

Spider

weaving

life

weaving

the web

of

death

124

it, Perry, why could you not save her and yourself?
Who were you, that would never say no, that would
stay there every night, hour upon hour, you who never
danced or drank or smoked or talked but in answers?
You who never saw the sun now but through the smog,
who never were touched by your Lily and only watched
and watched as her green eyes faded, as her feet were
ever heavier, as the glimmers died. How you must
have suffered! But you too, though, surely you were
seeking the shadow dance also for yourself. What
were you unable to release, even back as far as that
awful day at Valley Hope? Best not to ask, you'd say,
enjoy yourself, Lily, that is all I want. Was that your
way to love her, or did you know it was all but shadow?
You, her keeper, she might have loved you one day,
when she was ready to receive her soul. And you
yours.

It is his birthday today, the Santa Ana's blowing, the sky is almost clear. Round and round him you wrap the finished scarf. The day has finally come. Finally, do you feel freed, is there a moment when perhaps you've touched? But still his eyes are so soon turned aside, and yours, so faint with the lack of hunger, can they look at all?

To fly up and over the mountains, free of the choking air. Free and on to the desert, where you had first talked. Shining in the pure sun, on and spinning on. Does something stir inside you, is there still the faintest flicker to start the pulse again? Is your laughter opening, can your feet dance again high over your head where the music spins?

Streaming behind him is his banner, snapping in

white

horse

wing

the

sky

fly

the

sun

125

the wind. And somehow, for perhaps an instant, is not there a light in his face, radiant at the end of that gaily colored scarf?

A sharp cry, his hands to his throat, he is gone.

blood

Forever you look at that empty seat, the black leather holding his shape, the wheel slowly turning, the silence rushing past. Forever the cry hangs there where his hands had clutched for his life, where the shadow had swept across him. In the instant you know, and there's no unknowing, Lily. You know the absoluteness, death the plucking of a flower, by you, as clear as the voice of the lark in the desert racing past. Past belief, past understanding, only the knowing. You know that you love him.

foam

There, where his hands were, slowly the wheel turns, ever so slightly. The car is lurching, throwing dust, crashing through the cholla. Stopped. There, in his racing-tread tracks, the torn end of the scarf, torn, THE VALLEY, the flowers all crumpled, the long end wrapped on the racing hub. Back, at the foot of a barrel cactus, torn, OF, LILY, the crumpled flowers. His blond hair in the sand, the blue eyes wide at the sky, his lips parted to the sun straight overhead. His body lies so straight and tall. You cry his name, and you love him so, and you throw yourself to him, and you kneel above his head, and you hold his pale cheeks between your hands. How easily his beautiful head moves to your touch . . . *No touching, please . . .* how warm is his skin, how the light shines in his eyes.

the

whirling

earth

Lean to his lips, how strange, all upside down, you would kiss him and he will wake to take you finally in his arms. Yet you would not know how to kiss, and

126

he would wake to laugh at the shame of your innocence.

Look up, Lily, you must. Can't you see? It is not enough that somewhere behind you know already, you've seen already. Those gentle shoulders, that long slender back, the narrow thighs, the heels in the boots that would never wear spurs, stretched so carefully, his heart to the earth, stretched out under the sun. His patient hands resting by his sides, breast down, face straight up to the sky—twisted around. Oh God! unwind it, release him, oh Perry Perry! The gay flowers unfold, one by one, and, quite as if he would have it so, his head turns slowly away, do his eyes close?, his face so slowly from you, down, a hollow to receive him, down into the sand.

the

dust

the

flowers

Look up and see, oh Lily,
Look up and see and cry.
Loose him, his neck so tortured,
Let him turn from the sky.

(hang down
your head
and cry)

Face to the sand, he'll rest there,
Heart to the sand he'll lie.
So strong, so true, so noble,
He's oh so young to die.

Cry his name, shriek his name, as even now the buzzards wing over.

Your face is in your vomit in the sand.

They'll come, with shrieking tires, and they'll say "Jesus, two," and they'll go with shrieking tires.

Sirens winding winding, dying as the feet crunch in the little flowers. Silence, the idling motor, and "This one's had it, look." The rough grasping of your

127

shoulder, the thumb in your eye, the ear to your breast. No, no, no, no! Shudder the breath back, bitter, bitter gasps.

The face, so slowly turning from you, down into the sand. Never to breathe again, nor ever you. Silence in the roaring of your heart, in the dying of your heart.

"OK, start it. For Christ's sake start it!"

You never asked how you got home, back to your room where you'd hardly been for weeks and weeks. Was there a hospital? Were there reporters? Pictures, the long columns neatly clipped, they're lying there on your table. How? It does no good to remember, it's all there, ready when you need it. And if that is not enough, there are the embarrassed calls, the embarrassed absences, the silences wherever you go. Solicitous, or as if it had never happened, or just one of those things. But usually nothing nothing nothing.

For was he not your keeper, did he not hold you, cupped in his beautiful hands? Safe-keeping, what there was left after the bus stop, the freezing wind. And now his hands are clutched in the sand, the lilies lie crumpled beside him. You are nothing.

Can I remember, and honestly? Is there such a thing as memory, for is it not always of the present moment? Can I, sitting here, now, this moment, the warm granite, Will with a cane pointing to the shadow paintings back in the shallow cave, can I cancel everything that followed, can I forget? Remembering is forgetting, forgetting the future of the past. How can I, when each moment vibrates so, is so complete that there can be nothing else? How can I forget?

You'll be there, Lily, somehow, and you'll be

lilies

pure

burial

controlled, oh so very calm. No tears, no fevers of regret. How well you take it all, Lily! Letters from his family, from yours, writing them all so correctly. And the inquest, and the coroner, and the police, and the reporters again and again — he'd have been amused in his anonymous way. He's dead, that's all, head twisted right around and of course he's dead. No use turning inside out, these things happen. They just happen.

It's the only way to do it now, the modern way. He's there in the coffin, his head's on quite straight. Flowers all gay, hardly crushed, though someone mutters over the champagne, "Pay for quality and get supermarket seconds, guess who rakes in the difference."

Waterman's, the Funeral Home of Distinction. Even the Burlingame high-class uses it. Such a sad occasion, but so nicely done, so pleasant and efficient, really quite painless. Who'd wear black these days? So funereal, and I can tell you, I'd like to know, when I'm lying up there, that everyone's having a real good time. Real French stuff, lovely music. Such a nice young fellow, lucky the girl didn't get killed too. Rock of Ages, the Chippendale Room, bereavement, the purring limousines, so well arranged. A fine man, Bob Waterman. Oh, are you the girl? Such a sad occasion, and my how lovely you look, a picture!

Not far either, you can hear the diesel working, like a little bulldozer or something, the gravedigger, and he has an umbrella over his perch to keep off the California sun, and he'd never know if he dug up some poor fellow's skull. Electric lowerers, the gray gloves. Leave as soon as decent.

black women

shrieking

to their

emptiness

sand sifting

through

cold fingers

129

Lily, standing up so well.

The helping hungry hands. Yes, of course, you'd love to, seven-thirty? Nick's, well why not? A new band, the dance floor's bigger, the bar is very very chic, so very dark. Of course, of course, and why don't we dance again? Yes, I'll have one, and cigarets please, gold-tipped. I never eat. No, do not touch me, never touch me. Please don't, please don't, damn it! don't!

Old friends of his, they'll comfort you, take your mind off it. His roommate. At least he's learned to keep his hands to himself, or to others. No, no, there's no reason, you just find it so disgusting. And he doesn't talk about it, thank God, you'll scream if you hear it more, or do you remember how to scream? So heavy with smoke where he takes you, you wouldn't know this place. Grass smoke, but he'll not bother you with it; he's learned.

Faces in the dark, passing, passing, floating with their smiles and postures and vague or clear desires. Desiring, it has nothing to do with you. Sex, like a taste for olives, or beer which you can't abide, except that it's bad and wrong too until it's for keeps, and then, well, you just do, even if it is olives.

Sex, this hunger on the floating faces, it's evil too, this way, it's evil like the grass because they make it so, they would have it so. It washes and breaks on you like the ocean on a ledge, without effect. All so strange. And sometimes, for an instant, Pa flashes before you, and then it hurts and you turn quickly away.

Back to the floating faces, the game, the reaching for you, the dodging, the simulated laughter. And

sweet

dewdrops

on the

petals

Colin

Colin

always the twisting feet and the gesturing hands and the swinging hips and the shoulders always beckoning — the rock-hard driving music. The game, but you must be different. The other girls — and how much they hate you, hate you, hate you! — the other game, the prize so plain for all to see, so easy, so bad. You, it's the brilliance, the noise, the dance, the floating pieces of people, the tight tight closing out. Men the accompaniment, but always hovering, never alighting.

His roommate, so docile tonight, yet an extra way of sliding his eyes away, of giggling, of sweating on his narrow forehead. And a sort of shiver. And the hard voices with his friends and the silence when they see you coming back from Ladies. Always the pressure, hard as bone.

"Here Lily, here's your stinger, your day's ration. Wish I could get high as easy as you."

"It's because you start so low, you see."

Drink down the stinger, Lily, straight down before the burn and the awful taste catches up with you. Don't grimace, it wouldn't be the game. High, how could they know? Every nerve hollow, the endless echoing, the blood so thin and dry. But what does it matter what they know?

Drink it down. It will be your last one, ever.

The glass, why won't it set down straight? Eyes of lead, so very very tired. The music retreats, tinkly, yet is it not really right inside my head? How overbearing it was, blasting from the speakers, what relief. Except this bang banging on my temples, the last blood I have, all pumped there. Why must it, banging, banging, banging? Floating faces, hovering,

moths over my flame, feeble flame, to burn their
wings if they alight. Nicer this way, nothing matters,
rest a little, lie here a moment, just a little. Banging,
banging, banging.

Yes, yes, take me home, that would be nice, very
nice.

"I've got'r OK here. Take her feet, Pecker; won't
be long before you take the rest too, man, or what's
left from Perry. Man, you really doped her! That's one
way. You bastard."

bull-roarers

Where is the sound? Help, oh help, oh help! But
where is the sound? Help is an idea, help is a sound.
Where, where? Clawing, but my fingernails are empty.
Strike, but my hand drags on the dirty floor, dirty,
dirty, dirty. Banging, banging, banging, upside down,
the hurting hands. So dark.

Is that light, fire in my blood, the color of pain?
I don't know that ceiling. Why won't you take me
home? Aren't my eyes crying, though you've killed
my tongue, can't you have pity for me, pity, pity, pity?

Through the numbness, what is there, this numbness, black and rotten back of my eyes? Why are
there no answers? Crumpling. The thinnest thread
of fiery heat. Draw it tight, is there nothing, no
will? Draw it tighter, burn, sear; hovering, never to
alight.

Unconnected, foreign masses, hollow numbnesses,
unconnected to the hot thin thread, lying dead, pressed
under the strange ceiling. Pressed, under glass, the
stiffening moth, fluttered so in the bottle, chloroform.
No connection, no meaning, only the thread.

The color of pain in the black rottenness.

Draw in, there's no heat left. But the heaviness, a

132

mountain of seaside sand, and so far away, unconnected. Widening, widening, no, no, no, but the will
is dead.

Pressing. But this is me, there's no room, there's
no room, there's no room. Closed the numbness,
closed against oh God! Where can there be pain?
It's something else, it's birth, I'm being born of me,
bearing myself. How can there be room for pain? Oh
God to cut the hot thin thread!

The wrenching, pressing, the convulsion tearing,
tearing to the soul. Hot stink roaring. Sear. The
thread of my soul drawn from me. Oh God that I may
scream! The hurting, hurting, hurting.

The light, it hurts so. Why do you slap me, again,
my cheek? You're saying "Get up, Chrissake, got
to get you home, taxi, Jesus what a mess, how'd I
know? expect me to believe Perry that he'd never
touched you, what else for? all that time, all that
hard-to-get and the flirting, Chrissake stop crying."

You're saying? You're talking to me? Words, but
they can't get in, nothing can get in, nothing can
alight, I'm Lily and my father's Joe Tocca who won't
let anything happen to me, never.

Let me sleep, and the light, why must you carry me,
can't I just sleep? Hold me, Pa, I'm hurting so, press
me tighter, tight, no! no! it's hurting hurting, why do
you go on hurting little Lily? Let me sleep, please let
me sleep, please, please.

So you'll sleep, little Lily, and you'll never know
how long. Waking sleeping waking. Sometimes the
roaring traffic and the blotched familiar ceiling, turning
slowly. Sometimes the dark and the smog stench.
The bed so hot and narrow and where are the cool

bee's

Honey

133

edges? and the sheets are bitter wrinkles and you have no strength to move. The bed trembling to your chill that shudders in your skull, clutches, closed so tight between your legs, so private and yours but why spasms, the hurting? The bed so heavy, pressing. The bed, floating, hovering, turning slowly, dipping slowly, your feet whirling and whirling over your head. The sheets, crumpled, smelling sweat, and the slime if you move however little.

sail

the Winds

keel

the Seas

Sleep and the throbbing throbbing pain, when do you separate it, where is it? When finally is it a knife pressed to your bladder till you would burst? The ache, the floor of ice and are you naked?, and you'll not have time, and the seat's so cold and you flinch on the ache and nothing and little spurts and your breasts tighten to nubs of pain spurts and spurts till the ache is taste. And the other pain and you'd open your eyes and you'd see oh God! Black, caked and cracked, smearing your thighs, knotting your hair that you'd never never seen . . . *Black ringlets, hidden.*

Vomit, the gluey mucus. You must not remember, you must not remember. Anything else. To piss again, it hurts, it aches so still. Bloated full, if only it weren't cold, if only you were not shaking so, if only you could find some warmth and put it down there to relax, relax.

It's no use, you remember. "Doped her, doped her," the pressing, the ceiling, the searing thin thread, oh pity, pity, pity!

Shaking retching. Crawl, the slime, and even crawling fall from the convulsive cold. The rug, the smell of dust, a corner pulled onto your bed, that's all you can do, the blankets, half doubled, the gasp of the wet ice sheets.

134

Let no one ever come, let you never be seen again. Shame, shame that must end everything, and you wouldn't die because then they'd know. No one left, no one, nothing but to hate with all the last strength you have, you want nothing nothing nothing. Each face hovers and you hate it away, hate it for ever away, to never never come back. Tap tap tap, flexing in the fat palm. The long corridor. The black glass dimming to nothing the headlights along the line of poplars. LILY OF THE VALLEY. Slowly turning, turning down into the sand. So well arranged, so comforting, so smoothly lowering, lowering. Here, the braided lead rope, whirling in the hay dust, in the puddles of lemonade. Snap snapping in the wind, clutching, slowly the wheel turning, turning. Cunt stinks, you can say it now, you can say it now, you can say it, and you'd never even heard it had you? stinks in the Ladies, the cold wind from the black desert daybreak. Yes of course, of course, of course. And who'd be able to eat polenta? And who'd be able to stop screaming with the sand of the Santa Ana grinding in your teeth?

There, Lily, it's over, it's finished. You have come to your end. It is good to know this, that there's nothing left. Peace comes from that, the hollows fill with peace. A kind of warmth that slowly makes its way out from the bitter sting of the center. Shame becomes a passive thing, the soul can loosen, ready finally to move on and away. You must let it, you must help it. Poor sweet soul that has cried so many tears that no one has seen, that has always wanted only the sun and the buzzing of the honey bees down in the yard, the rattling and the bacon through the register, the blue sage tipping up into the sky. You will let it go.

"out

of the

lowest,

the

highest

reaches

its peak"

135

Desert voices

Let us receive this soul, this gentle sad soul, we the desert, the olive hills and black peaks, distances down the curve of the valleys, the pure sun slanting up the canyons.

Yes, we receive, we accept, those that would come to us. There were so many, there are now so few. But now is nothing, time is nothing but the cycling. Forever is moments linked to this circling sun. We are not indifferent: each is all because there is no all, so we totally accept. Come to us, let the leaves fall as they will, lie down with us, join us, be the eternal rebirth, received and receiving.

We bear your scars: the asphalt and the concrete lined over us; tracks deep in the sand, uprooting, the clutch of rigid hands, the scream of the sirens; the borings and strippings; the rippings and the pluckings and the cutting, cutting, cutting; the burnings; the debris, the stinks, the creeping pollutions. We must heal; O let us!

Hear us, for we speak to you too, as we do to all. Let our voices be. You who walk in our valleys, who have known our summits, who have drawn your food and drink from us and have given us back of yourselves, you do not deny our voices as the others are wont to now. You listen, you accept, and you reply. And in us are your ancestors, the line of life from the far past, and through us they speak to you and you to them.

How many centuries of summers, up from wintering in the plains, up for the hunting and the gathering of the pinenuts and acorns and

136

berries and bulbs, grinding grinding on the granite? Metates of the Chemehuevi to grind their foods, worn into the ledge convenient to the cave entrance, the pestle still hidden in a crack of the stone face. The fruit of the earth against the bone of the earth, feeding its children. We speak to them.

Mysteries accepted, the magic from the rehearsal of the hunt, the harvest, the healing. Magic on the cave walls: palm trees, children, the cross and the bow and the deer, the snake to bring him calm, the flying arrow, the fish and rams' heads and flying double geese. Others voiceless. While she, how many many is she?, crouches naked on her haunches, or rabbit skins on her shoulders for the evening cooling, grinding grinding.

Acorn meal. You learned that too, old Will, from your friends who'd wait nearby the stamp stamp of your milling, ready to drive an arrow from their stiff bows — strange wood, not from these parts at all — into the gathering curious bighorns.

Yucca fiber sandals, baskets, pots, the seed-beaters. Yours are different, yours do not always nor even often spring from your own hands. Yet somehow they speak.

They speak to you. But there's the fear and the loneliness in your heart, thinking sometimes that there will be no one after you to listen and reply. Silence is you, shutting off your reply, for you would not tell them that the end is near, that their magic and maybe the very voice of the earth itself will perish. You who came so far to hear our voices and to speak, from the banks of that weeping river, from the flying manes and the streaming tails over the steppes. To join them. The last.

This girl, this Lily girl, can she, O can she too hear our voices and reply?

137

Stem of grass: Willy's shaman rope

Down in the canyon bottom. Arrow-weed with its rose-purple blossoms: arrowshafts, prayer sticks O God of the Giant Lily, animal traps, baskets, eyewash brewed from the little new leaves. Inkweed for the basket designs. Peach-brush to give its sweet fruit, jointfir brewed for squaw tea. Cattle spinach where the Indians tethered their horses for the browsing — in Death Valley we'd be calling it saltbush; that's where it grew best, mostly.

Desert holly or sheep-fat you'll call it down in Kern County, but here it's just saltbush. The Cahuillas, you've seen them grinding the seed in their metates, cooking the meal in salted water, and the ground roots pasted with spit onto ant bites.

In the saltbush, beyond the Tule springs, going after his burro in the morning half-light, he said, that's where Michael Carroll come up on it. South of Furnace Creek, you'll remember, Willy boy, maybe twenty miles. Some time January, come into your Golden Girl camp all excited. Wouldn't go back but told you just where and you hadn't much else on your mind so's before long you packed up and went for to see for yourself.

Earth's

fruit

for

its

children.

Wm. S.

138

Back in the saltbush, poke around. Sun's gone and the light's a sort of blue and it doesn't help to know what you're looking for. White is going to be awful white. Half dug up, it's over there, coyotes and Carroll who said he was pressing or he'd done it himself. Not above looking over your shoulder yourself and wondering how long the light'd last: might not do in the dark and camp wasn't quite hard by.

Not much to dig, never was more'n a foot or so deep. Bones, white where the sand had blown off, browner when you dig down. Lying there, all doubled up like a jackknife, dumped in, feet higher'n head. Long brown hair, goes on growing when they die, sheriff said — you'd hadn't the experience — stuck to the skull here and there. And the hole knocked through, shape of the head of a prospector's hammer. Striped trousers plenty oversize by now and the number-seven prospector's boots. Under the saltbush, towels — one-blanketers'd take the damndest things — and a pick and a shovel, chewed piece of a valise. Over there by the greasewood a little pile of sticks, rats'd never do. Poke and there's a bit of canvas. Blood stains and F.H.

shearings

pinned in

the album

strength

to the

Missis

Berryman or Dusty Rhodes Titus, the Desert Post, or one of the others or some fellow nobody ever'd missed? Mule-wagon tracks near, in from the Bennett Well road.

Kind of creeps on the shoulder blades. No harm in looking behind you, more'n once, never can tell. While you're wrapping the skull — just fell loose — and the bit of hair in the towel. Take it right in to Los Angeles, be going on mine business.

Nothing to dig for here, that's clear enough. Not

139

like Old Man Lee, Lee brothers' dad, them fellows who located the Lee district. He'd dug and dug round Salt Creek, for years, looking for the emigrants' treasure they'd buried forty years back when they'd knowed they was done in for water and grub. All of'm dead, down by Salt Creek, fifty-two, bones strewn by the coyotes. Found three miles of logging chains near Keane Springs they'd left when the weight bogged them in the sand. Back in 'sixty, figures. Used the chains to lower their wagons and horses down the cliffs into the sink. Be you, Willy, to find the treasure, lying right there in that leather sack Indian Mary showed you. Up at Ash Meadows, the daughter of the Paiute some said'd massacred the lot. And for two horses, a good hundred and fifty dollars in those parts, she'd traded you that gold watch, Howard, full-jeweled, in the hunting case, which they'd got so excited about in Rhyolite when you'd showed it. Lot of other jewelry, diamonds, too she'd not give up, and she'd said how the old brave had sworn her never to show none of it to a white man and how now she'd be cursed.

labor

to

dust

treasure

to

dust

That's what it's like in the saltbush, or when you run clean out of that too and it's just sand and devil's salt. You'd know, Willy my boy, you'd know all right. Ghosts aplenty, even when the sun's straight up and the wind don't hardly whisper. Ghosts of the fools and the heroes who got themselves burned and thirsted and hungered to death, or maybe an arrow through their ribs or lead or a hammer in their skull.

Distance just don't stop out there, keeps on stretching ahead. Thin boots and you'll dance on the burning black cakes of mud, no blanket and the shivering can kill you with the night wind roaring down on you from

140

the Panamints. It's the thirst though, mostly, most part of the ghosts are dead of the swollen tongue and the lips all blistered black and the skin cracked dry and the desert whirling and whirling till your legs cave under and there's no getting up and crawling'll get you a few yards to die, if you're lucky, under a greasewood before the coyotes start tearing at you. You'll know, Willy, and it's many you've saved from just that. Two down in the Mohave, remember them?, and two more up in Wingate, the fellow at Hidden Springs who'd never have found water, how many in the Valley?

There's ghosts aplenty, but not of Willy Speare. Know the springs and the coyote wells and where to drop a rabbit or a kit fox or a coyote, old Tom had taught you well, know where to find a bit of shade when the sun's getting heavier than you like, know the eye's a liar for distance in the Valley and the shimmering can move a mountain twenty miles. Then it'll be mostly all right. More'n that. It'll be home, for a good stretch of years, though maybe not much longer. Under a tarp tent, or often as not the sky, or a dugout and a bit of corrugated and the powder boxes.

There's the ghosts of Dan Mullan's friends. Tells the story while you're sitting helpless and remorseful under the Bullfrog barber's razor. Yup, take'r clean off; not touch nothing else, though, be needing the mustache and the long hair still. Slicked up for going East . . . *Jenny, Jenny, will you be at the ball?* . . . Naked and pale like a baby, you've lost your old friend, Willy boy.

Dan Mullan he'd knowed the Valley some. Must've been other routes, though. Headed out with two

soft rain

deep well

Robin

Robin

lakes

to ice

to snow

windmills

frogs

the

Volga

reeds

141

greenhorn fellows after gold. From Bullfrog, in the summer, for the Panamints, pack train of burros. Got himself lost in the Valley sand. Hot so's they could hardly drink the water in their canteens. You'll know how that can be. Lost, and they pull into a canyon for some degree of shade, five o'clock maybe on the second afternoon. One fellow left about dusk on foot to search out water, never did come back. Next morning the other left, looking for his friend. Never showed up, neither of them, till prospectors found them few days later mostly eaten up, not far apart either, from the tracks you could see they'd never known it. Dan Mullan he fired his revolver now and then and built himself bonfires as signals. Two days more, a swallow or two left, maybe half a pint, canteen in the shade of a rock, provisions piled some protected from the sun. The burros had already wandered off looking for water, never turned up again . . . *Plenty wild ones still, Willy, or have they shot them all too for fox food?* . . . Must of gone delirious, but he wakes one morning and sees things clear and takes a raisin or two and another swallow of water. Dozes, wakes again to noises and sees shaggy-tails, rats, and he's too weak to move now or even yell. Busy taking off every last bit of grub, piece by piece, bringing pebbles and twigs in trade. And they knock over his canteen. Next he knows he's slung on a Mexican's burro, howling like a coyote. Months before he got his right mind back.

First time you'd known of trading rats, where was it? back in Arizona Territory? when your boots were gone and some fellow's thrown-away hat in their place, your apples gone and onions instead. And you'd got pistol mad and there'd of been some, more'n some,

skunks

a case of

White House milk

142

shooting if they hadn't showed you the tracks.

Arizona. Jerome, alone in the desert, though they'd no lions that you ever saw, nor any Bibles either for that. You'd told her that and she'd laughed so pretty. Down by the river bank, where you'd told her and you took her hand and her laughter changed and your heart turned all to ice. Will she be there, Willy boy? Oh Jenny, Jenny, will you be at the ball?

All slicked up for going East, outfitted, grubstaked to look for greenbacks in the East. Riderson, powder people, got you mostly talked into it, C. P. Riderson, whatever that fellow Hatch telegrammed them. Hatch, engineer fellow, down from Lead, South Dakota, to expert the Golden Girl, with grub and equipment piled about. Came in to Ludlow on the Santa Fe, transferred to the Tonopah and Tidewater being built. Up to Salt Spring, still constructing in the Amargosa Canyon. Came up in a borax wagon and twelve mules, men and supplies, up through Saratoga on the south road into the Valley. Kind of sketchy, your trail up One-Man Canyon, hadn't figured on the likes of them. Bit of jolting didn't much relish, and Speare's Camp conveniences weren't famous, least not to your hearing.

So Hatch he takes one look up the hillside, next morning, where you point out the mouth of the Golden Girl, says, "It's too far away, we're not interested."

Doesn't even trouble to go into the mine. Just takes up and gets set to take off. Gets the borax wagon filled with grub and hay. Seems like a poor way not to sell, nor would you want your reputation suffering from wrong impressions he might be going to send East. Thirty-thirty, that'll hold him adequate, hold

wind

in the

mane

away

him while you get out ahead, unload that grub too, hardly seems right to haul it all the way out again. One bag of oatmeal, hundred pounds, that's a lot of oatmeal, keep the camp and the Indians in the neighborhood going for a good piece.

So's you're out to the Silver Lake telegraph office and Riderson replies you'd done right by Hatch and he wants the mine, Hatch or no Hatch. Which makes you wonder why in the first place . . . but no matter.

So they'll have you go East, fix the deal, and that's what you'd have too. Twenty-eight years you've got, gold and greenbacks in your jeans, and you'd not been East—except for Ellis Island and the heifers and Ma still smelling of lye soap made from the drippings. Best get slicked up.

Wine, T. J. Wine, you'll be going with him, company. Finest fellow you'll be likely to know. Yankee fellow, real Yankee, Sommersworth in New Hampshire.

Gnädiges Fräulein Lily. You'll come with me, won't you? Help me with my German, Hamburg, till I get it straight again. And we'll go to the Volga where the cream's so thick. And we'll go to Siberia where the radio rays'll melt the arthritis. And to India, they know, they know about the human soul when no one here would. You'll come, won't you, Lily?

Wine, been Weinberg and he'd changed it. Promoter, rich, but he must've wanted to be richer. Poked around plenty in Death Valley. Come up on him when he's staying with Scotty down at his camp at the mouth of One-Man Canyon. But he'd figured Scotty pretty well by then and it didn't need Wingate the next year to be convinced. Inventor too, he'd got an auger that'd make a square hole; that's some trick.

lunchpails

in the

orchard

away

144

Good times, that trip, a fine fellow, human, you couldn't imagine, from the East. All slicked up, but your hair's still down to your shoulders and you've got a fancy cowboy shirt and a tailored buckskin and your boots and a stiff new hat and your pistols and your rifle, and you'll show them a thing or two back East.

Shooting practice, every stop along the line, Santa Fe, for the leg-stretching and the grub at the station restaurant. Get a bit of a crowd and some bets, and Wine to stand behind you so's nobody'd notice. Practice for Boston where Wine had got them already primed. Wasn't exactly cheating, not like Buffalo Bill and the wooden bullets, just a kind of trick. You'll be showing them. First thing when you get there, almost. The Boston Gun Club, Wine and his long-haired fellow from California. Bets. Watts the Chief of Police and some fellow Glidden and the whole Club turned out. Beat'm, cleaned them pretty good, with that trick of yours to make sure. Wine right close behind you so's they couldn't see you'd had your knee wedged and propped in under the shooting-gallery bench; cuts the weaving so you'll get a good bead.

And that's just the beginning. The ball, it'll be later, so you'll not be thinking too much of Jenny at first. Jenny at the piano smiling to you over her pretty shoulder. There's your historic tour, with Longfellow's house, and Harvard where Ed Lemmon's a professor who's to be president of your Speare Gold Mining Company and who's done a bit of prospecting himself; but no, guess it must be Technology where he's at. And there's Bunker Hill right next to the rooming

hurdy-gurdy

monkey

on a

string

gypsies

their

performing

bear

house where they've put you up, and the Massachusetts State House which isn't much. And at Harvard they take you to see Tom Lawson, big promoter, and you go through three outside doors and offices before you reach him and he'll be asking all about Death Valley gold.

Ed Lemmon, who's something to do with a paint company too and you'll never get it quite figured. He's the boss at first. And he and the group, that fellow with the textile mill, they put up fifty thousand dollars and they want to get in and out quick at the Golden Girl and you're sour and plenty sore because that's no way to develop a mine. So Riderson, they kind of take over.

the hand

to cuff you

lye

flour

law

Speare Gold Mining Co., Office, No. 80 State Street, Mines in the Funeral Mountains, Death Valley, California, 65 Claims, William Speare, Field Expert, Boston, Massachusetts. Card and all.

And Wine, he'll be taking you up to New Hampshire, there on Lake Winnipesaukee, where he'll take you over to the party at the Colonel's. Horse buggies and automobiles, brass all shined up good, by the dozen. Little girls opening the gates, and the band and the fireworks and the duckpins down by the lake and the fancy guest houses and all the servants and the swimming which is something you'll not be bet to do and they get you to put on some shooting and you talk it up good and they heave up bottles and you bring them down without any wooden bullets. The yacht the Colonel has, steaming and tooting among the islands and the dance out by a lighthouse he'd built. And they play Jenny's music, waltzing and whirling and so sad it's lucky it's dark. And on the way back in

146

the dark they see a swimming deer and you wouldn't shoot a deer like that and they pull on the steam whistle and careen around and run him down to his screaming fear and you're plenty mad.

Is it the next day? Wine, he takes you someplace and there's the professor, Lopliss, and he and Wine talk about the hypnos' and before you hardly know you're in it too and they've taught you a bit of it too. Still don't use it much, seems kind of unnatural, though Wine he says he only does it for knowledge and for benefit. Kind of thing they'd do in the East, though. Don't like it much, hypnos'.

Woodes, he's the one, editor of that Boston newspaper, he's the one who'll be doing the ball for you, at the Young's Hotel. They'll not tell you much but you give them Jenny's name and her address and they say they'll be sure she'll be there and she couldn't help but know you're in Boston what with all the newspapers writing about you and the photographs and Wine talking things up more than a little.

Your wavy hair and your mustache waxed and your pistols shined up — so's your boots — and a black suit that's just a little less city swell than Woodes's own. The champagne, and the long table covered with little bites that don't seem much, the orchestra playing very dignified and they get to that same waltz again and again. Jenny's waltz.

But Jenny, she'll never come, and the best you knew of Jenny was down by the river bank.

Boston. It hurts, Willy, it hurts you deep and you're going to be back and it's going to hurt some more. And never will you see Jenny again, though you heard for certain she got the invitation.

corruptions

desert

antelope

bones

147

It hurts, and it seems like they want it to. When they whisper behind they make sure to whisper loud, "Outlandish," and "What will they think of next?"

Wine, he gets it too, with the talk about Jews, though a finer man there never was, Yankee, real Yankee.

Like they've got something you haven't now nor ever will have. Like you're a part of something naughty they don't tell their wives about. Like the effort's not really worth it and it will be a considerable relief when they've seen the last of you. Protecting and protecting, all fixed up in their big houses and their big families, preserved.

Boston, with all that racket and the stinks and the buggies and automobiles coming at you from every side and the crowds hustling you where you'd not be going. Policemen whistling like marmots, the fire engines clanging and stampeding about. Electric lights like they'll no more need the sun, or the gas that hisses and rattles at you. And no one picking up, though all those crowds and they'd know what a mess they can make. You'd have to scratch under the sand to find the ashes before you'd know most any campsite in Death Valley, and not just so's you'd not know perhaps where they'd been prospecting.

Be best out of it, Willy boy, best well away. They've had enough of you. They've got your mine and they've had a good look at you and a good laugh at you, and . . . Jenny, she never came. So you've had enough of them, and you'll be getting on.

Boston to Death Valley. Shake it off, shake free, like a dog coming out of the river. Breathe, Willy, let the air clear you out, the stinks and the shadows and

corruptions

city

citizen

bones

148

the highfalutin ignorances. And if Death Valley isn't enough, now that they've your mine, and there's a telephone line across the Valley to keep the claims speculators informed, and almost a hotel at Furnace Creek, and the borax boys cluttering around, Scotty turned to showmanship and hoaxing: guess there's nothing to keep you, plenty of territory empty.

Field Expert. Little printed card. All right, then that's what you'll be getting to. They'll be needing you for a bit, and you'll see, you'll see.

Jack Canterbury, they'll be putting him in charge, out at the Golden Girl. Good mining man from Tonopah. But nothing for Willy Speare. Maybe disappeared too much, not the show and the shooting like the others.

Spear's Outlook: lie still, Jamie Pope, when the north wind comes cold across the sage, Spear's Outlook and now it's Smoke Tree View to put the twist on old Will, and he wouldn't twist and so it stuck and it's on all the signs and they're all beginning to forget, and the last there'll be of Willy Spear is here in the Joshua trees where the bighorns peer over the granite rims into your secret valley—or the Volga, and oh come! little Lily, come with me to paradise on earth.

Good fellow, though, knew his mining well. Good mine you sold them, Willy. Five hundred dollars the ton and she producing for ten years. Till Jack goes over on his own at his Carbonate on the other side of the Valley.

And all them other mines, kind of pressing on you, Willy, kind of scratching away, and you wonder. The Ibex in the hills back of Saratoga Springs, with the talc mines coming in. The Confidence between Sara-

but the

crowdeder

the

emptier

Old Will

moving on

the accepting

hold

it

off

149

toga and One-Man Canyon (Scotty's Canyon) by the Mormons in from Salt Lake, first mine in the area, the Confidence Mill well the oldest in the Valley, maybe, though there's Surveyor's well north of the Stovepipe Sand Dunes . . . *Ruins, they say, dying in the sand.*

And Scotty's Mystery Mine, keep it up, Willy, and who'd not story the emigrants and the greenhorns? Augustus Enfield, he'd grubstaked Scotty at the beginning and he'd got hoaxed at Windy Pass, and he'd sent his man, his explorer, out who gets to the camp down at the mouth of the canyon and, like usual, there's no Scotty but there is Willy and you take him up and up the canyon and to that red-yellow hilltop where you could look down and across and up to the black cliff, two hundred fifty feet up, to where the hole is and you, "Think that's Mister Scott's mine."

stolen

There's no getting to it, so he can get home happy about how he'd seen the Mystery Mine and the thousand dollar a ton and the nuggets like cows' teeth. Better than Windy Gate, where things kind of went wrong and they got shot up more'n they'd figured and a thousand dollars if you'll save my dear brother's life and a bullet through Pearl's hat with only an eighth inch to spare 'cause his mule bucked just then. And still there's them that swallows it whole like J. Levin Meld from New York who tells in L.A. about the fellow who, he won't tell who, said he'd ambushed Scotty, though he'd not meant a bit to shoot up nobody, he'd just wanted to capture Scotty and find out where at's the Mystery Mine.

Volga

apples

her

cuffing

hand

Scotty, he'll drop dead of a stroke, and long before old Will who even him he'd tried to hoax. Scotty and

150

his goldmine, that fellow Johnson. And the Castle, right there where you'd camped with the grapes and the vegetables and the willows and the creek flowing to vanish in the desert, first time when you'd come in from Bullfrog. Towers and battlements, his automatic orchestra, the imported masons and wrought-iron artists and the carpenters, marble and carvings and skins and the prospector weathervane frying bacon to the north wind. Go up to see it, Will, before they'll be sending you off to San Quentin. Scotty and his mules and his mottoes and his emigrants pouring through the turnstile. And Alla, his wife, she's left him.

Johnson, he seems to make a better partner, or a better mine. Got himself crippled on his own railroad and his doctor tells him he needs hot climates and that's where he finds Scotty who's looking for just that sort of mine. A. M. Johnson of the National Life Insurance Company, Chicago. They'd slept together there in that little shack, the Original Castle, and they'd let Alla go. And when there'd be tax trouble, Johnson, he'd get himself two million dollars on the Missis' life: shove her from their car, some said, and off a cliff. Alla when she's left off with Scotty, she'll be suing Johnson for half the Castle and Johnson'll pay her off handsome for he'd rather not they'd hear about that mishap on the cliff, some said.

corn-holing

black

range

nights

Easy, old Will, old Will of the Joshua tree.

Look out, Willy, out from your rock, the soft one, is it worn by the seat of your jeans? On the ridge above your camp. Home a camp, and for more than a few years, whenever you're around. Not much time you've got, for lazying, not much use for doing nothing when something's always to be done. Still, though, last looks. You'll be going, Willy, moving on, for there's nothing here for you, not much. Kind of say good-by.

Here where the burros are browsing in the sage and switching at the flies and braying like the heaves, cursing the water trough so far below, and the echoes come back in herds from the cliffs of the Golden Girl. Where the bees come poking in the beaver-tail blossoms and you've found wild honey in the crevices and the piñon stumps. Here where the early sun comes in first while you're chewing maybe on your jerky with a can of coffee. Comes in to cut the winter frost and stop your shaking and you're all clenched up tight, to shine on the snow of the Panamints across the Valley and reach down into the desert and the sand and the salt flats and the Badwater and the tracks in the saltbush where the antelope step lightly on the graves. Running up to the north, into the haze where the desert'll rise gradual into Ubehebe and the craters of the Indians' evil.

O Mana

sweet

juices

Or where noon'd burn you off quick and you'd only go to see who's coming, knowing they're coming from the cicadas and the marmots stop their racket and then the echoes, freak, a whisper in the canyon throat. Coming and you could spit on his hat, or just not be there, or make him turn quick with a rifle and its echoing sentinels.

And where sun turns the reds to blood, when it lowers by Telescope, so the Indians call it Bleeding Brave. Lights straight up the canyons on both sides for a few moments, this time of year. Turns cold by the coyotes' cry and the hooping of the owl. Camp

152

smoke rising straight up to find the last sun, white, high above Jubilee. And the stars are ice for the last time, through the dugout door.

Not much. You'll be getting on.

An old Indian, it was, told you how life is the rising sap. Up the stem of the grass, up from the earth and the dark moist and the roots, up into the light, leafing one way, then another, together in the strengths. Moving up, up with the others, but always also apart. Stages of life, he'd say, if you don't get cropped or droughted out, or rise too fast or slow or miss the desert rain. Toward the sun, leaves of grass, till you're rooted in the sky.

Shamans and their ropes you've read of here under the oil lamp when the Missis has gone up hers and looks down on you. Her window in the sky. Keep climbing, though there's few who can, few who are given ropes to climb. Hanging down from the sky, reaching up from the earth, tying, for a few. You'd known it, too, way back, maybe where the bottles sparkled on the Elbe and Ma said you'd never fear. Maybe where the warning came to you, the cougar's tail switching, the high hissing of the snake's rattle, or the bawling of the heifers on the heaving sea. Maybe where the Omaha Indian girl, back in the hills, took you to her and caressed you so gently and asked you for nothing.

Climb up the rope that's offered, and if you don't you'll die.

tying

Earth

to

Sky

climb down
the
Rope

Willy–the weaving threads–Lily

The web and the weaver, threads in the design. Threads, if you'll see them, tied to the wind, sails for the spider who would climb to heaven. Threads of gold sailing in the sun over the black water, black under the rock walls, white under the sky.

O Spider

Hoist up, me, old Will, steady with the two canes, two extra roots into the earth, steady with the buzzing behind the eyes. Up the old steps, I'd know them in the night, up the shoulder of my dam, Third Lake. Here where I'd fell fifteen feet, young fellow of sixty-three, onto the pink granite and could walk off, not even a hand from daughter June and Mana. Crazy old man, June'd said—hush up! Hauling on the cable car: lugs concrete to pour at the top of the dam.

Finished now, long finished. June in the Vegas corruptions, Mana her window in the sky, the cattle stole, this land and its water lie black and useless, acres, thousands of tons. I'd done it, Will, dammed it up, one old man and the womenfolk, for the cattle I'll never have again and the hay and the grain and the fruit I'll never grow. Dammed it to leak away, trickle there where the moss and the poppies grow in the cement face, thousands of tons and the humming-bird hangs on his invisible wings drinking the drops, and the bees skim the puddle below, thirsty, where it disappears into the desert.

Out on the far side, Lily girl, that's where the big-horns come to water, and before there was this they'd go twenty miles summer nights and back. That track is the cat, you'd know it from up your way, and the coyote and the kit fox, in the mud edge — wider every time, bleeding away, bleeding away.

Easy, down on the hot rock where I'd stretched a tarp once for shade — need the sun full now — and'd eat a pail of food the Missis'd fixed.

Over by the edge, there, you can look straight down into the water, see the fish sleeping. Stocked them in the first year, after the rains.

Know

the passing

the tearing

the re-
weaving

Know

the thirst-
ing

the hunger-
ing

the replen-
ishing

155

"Sit here, girl, I brought these cookies. Closer, I'd
see you. Cataracts, yuh."

> Clouding over, old soul needs the sun. This Jenny?
> Touch lightly, Willy pains here inside. The others,
> crowding, silent. Where? *shark's teeth scattered on
> the sand*

"Pa loves cookies too, eat a boxful; half and half,
splits, if I'm there."

> Halving: two wholes. Pa in Valley Hope, honey,
> currents of time. Lily in the desert, Valley Hope
> childhood past—love Pa steady with the half smile.
> *stone Hero: storms, the rounding, worn to flowering
> sand*

"Pretty hair, Lily. I'd not have liked it short. Colin,
he told me. Kov women too, cut their hair off for the
grieving."

> Hair tips tickling on my lips when Janice she'd turned
> away. No no, my Mana, they combed it nice, a ribbon,
> like you'd do; Will sniffling by the casket. *womb*

156

"Pa wanted it long, but it's really growing back for
Colin."

> His hair caresses, my cheek sleeps on his heart.
> Touching when I never would before. My Colino
> only, like the sun: the moon on Valley Hope, thin
> shadows, past. *solar phallus*

"Yuh, yuh, your pa, he'd like to see it. Like he sent
the honey."

> To June from his Loving Dad. Why'd you have to,
> Juney, Dad here, looking on'ard, free like the air in
> the Joshua; you there, all fouled and your sharp
> tongue? *breathe, Willy; Boston, shake it free*

"I know. I'll go, with Colin, when he comes."

> Here too, though, Will, I'll be here, you and the
> Joshua, you'll know, you'll see. Now I touch you, like
> I didn't that first night—so you'll know. *high desert
> graves, the joy*

"Be getting on, girl, just I'll rest a little spell."

157

Look, straight down, down into the useless dead water. Dark shapes, waiting, slowly sliding through, through long honey hair falling forward.

Almost a bighorn would peer over my shoulder down into this dark mirror, almost. Will sitting behind, his knees in the sun, dozing. Dreaming. Trickling, leaking away. Swallows picking bugs from the lake's surface. A lizard flicking at an ant. Water world, propped up here over the desert by this flimsy curve of cement, seeking to die, to abandon these lives. Holding the buzzards high in the white sky, two hawks, the granite rim, the long hair swinging.

I turn to me, I must.

A leaf falls free from my hair, up into the image, ripples distorting.

So too shorn hair . . . *Comb it out with your fingers, lift it, wide with the scissors, slicing, slicing. Sudden cool weightless, the locks fall softly, lightly on the glistening sand . . .* Here it would hardly stir the surface, floating gently, drifting, threads settling slowly through the shining surface into the black water.

So too salt tears.

final

dissolution

my
Upper Ocean

to
Lower Ocean

158

Sad flowers, Lily; the passion dance

No mirror saw you then, Lily, and the mice carried off your hair during the night for their nests, and the sand drank your tears. Sand which still held the tracks, criss-crossing confused, would hold them forever. Flashbulbs scattered (your bottles shining on the Elbe, old Will?) where his body lay.

Sit there, cross-legged in the sand, your hair strewn about, the cold evening air on your cruel new neck. A lone car's rising rush and the falling! . . . *Doppler dwindling — yes, Pa, I know now, your Doppler effect* . . . Teach your little Lily, your Liliana; it's too late, much too late, and you'll never know for I would not hurt you still more. Enough this. Oh, if there were but another way!

The hollow where his face turned so slowly from the sun. Had you never loved him, not now or ever? But his eyes would shelter, and he followed you uncomplaining to the end.

How had you come back here to the desert, back where the buzzards circle forever? Maybe some bus driver would know or a motorist lost by now in the vultureland of Las Vegas. It doesn't matter. There's

Head's Hair

let

it

fall

the

end

159

no one to see. Maybe later, when they find you, stretched in the sand. Will it matter? Will it matter, will they have to notice, that even now, after how many days or weeks, you still couldn't wear panties, they hurt so, remind you?

He'll know from the hair anyway, Pa will know, or will he think it was for Perry? But it does not matter, dear Pa, there is nothing left.

And maybe, Pa, you will know now what you did to your little Lily, driven from her home where her heart could sing. You who could talk of loving her: you who could put her on that bus. For a better life, a future, opportunity, for this where the mouse even now steals off with the beautiful shorn locks. Vanity and pride, Joe Tocca, that killed your heart and your Lily.

I hate you, Pa, I hate you, I hate you, I shall die hating you.

Cold and clear like your heart under the fading moon, under the coyote cry, cold, Lily, till the last trembling has left you still. Ready, it's so very easy, you just breathe no more. There's no one here to crush the breath back into your empty heart. That's it, so easy, no longer to disturb the silence and the rest with the futile suckings in your breast. The tap-tappings in your head, but they are fainter now. The shooting star over Vega, even it has stopped its flight.

each

breath

a

death

Yes, it was so easy, Lily, everything ended forever. And maybe even then you smiled as the dark closed in, for even then, at that very end, each moment was absolute, the only absolute which you could ever conceive.

160

The next moment was of the cold driven down and down into your core and then slowly melting out to disappear in the sand. The warmth shivering on your thighs, the sun rich red to your inner eye. The sweet desert air flowing through you. A motionless stretching of every fiber of your body.

Now, now, now! Hold on to it, Lily, let it be in you, let it grow in you till the last instant when it must burst and create a new moment. The world to be seen and so to accept you. Open your eyes, but there's no choice. A stone world living. A stone that holds all history. Lichens, reds and yellow-greens and blue-grays, whorled and convoluted, mites laboring through the towering jungle (the north side, Lily, that's what Pa would say).

Built into a crevice to catch the morning sun, the honeycomb of the lonely desert bee, of sand and resin. Ants pull at her dead body, twisting and shoving. A punctured hole in the cover of a cell, a crack, gnawing, the new bee emerges, rubs her nose, stretches her limp wings in the sun till they glow iridescent and are strong.

eternal plan

A world of tiny flowers, towering flowers, swaying in the early wind. The blue butterfly, tired from the morning honey hunt, ready to rest now that the wind has come. He lights on a round pebble, folds his wings upward, gray-green now of the saltbush or the desert floor, across the wind, hooking his three feet on one side to his pebble, tugging, rolling down flat, anchored and no longer bothered by the wind.

Nothing to remember, nothing to forget. What is there? As for the butterfly, the moment, indivisible and unending. It's best that way.

Standing by the roadside, the wind feeling you all over, the sun lifting you in its embrace, the lark golden honey in your heart. The distances drawing you back to nothing and filling you with all.

The familiar jerking bounding of the pickup . . . *familiar; is that memory, of what? nothing, nothing, nothing* . . . upholstery shows the cotton matting, wounded, tool kits at your feet rattling, shiny with use, sun-tans, heavy greasy hands. White hair all standing straight like cholla spines, the deep creases and the blackheads at the back of his neck. San Francisco, yes, that's where you're going too. Maintenance tour, some kind of special machinery, his beat. No need for meaning, reasons. Accepted, going on from there, from the sun.

All is detail, for him and for you. Like coffee at the Shoshone Cafe where everything's in the silver bubbles that rise in the glass globe, globs of steam in the greasy air. Like swerving from a rabbit without thought for your neck 'cause that's just your nature and there's nothing for it. Like piss time and no fuss . . . *Perry, the American malaise, camouflaging, posturing, snickers* . . . Like the universe turning on the North Star over the Funeral Mountains, the heavy black Death Valley air, salt-stale, the steel and dust smells of your blankets bed in the back of the pickup under the looping cries of the owl. Like no difference from taking and giving.

Oil drums: the truck-driver stops; the farmer's yard for the bimonthly overnight with venison sausage for breakfast; hitchhiker if he'll ride in back.

"Take it, get some duds, Penney's, I can spare it, you'll be showing through soon, someone will need

Body's Hair

the

moment

transcends

all

162

it from you sometime and you know's well's I what you'll do."

One

Over Tioga, Tuolumne, Yosemite Valley. Where the thousands and the thousands busy on their cracking nerves to be "unnaturally natural in unnature," as Henry says. Henry and Lily, your oily rusty-blue pickup so proud among the campers and fly-proof tents and bar-be-qued Smokey Bear misery. They stare and stare.

is

"Maintenance man, Stevie, not everyone can have fun."

All

Mother Lode. Pan Your Own—$2.50 An Hour. Mark Twain Slept Here. Real Facsimiles.

Henry and Lily for Salisbury steak and a plate of pie shared and black coffee.

Yellow poppies for a hundred miles. The Central Valley. Thunderclouds and the cows bawling to be milked and the lark tumbling in the thick air.

No thinking back, no distance, all distance.

"'Bye, Henry." Like kissing a sunny tree trunk. Good. Rattling into the distance, the clean oily smell.

Saint Francis

Lily with her Penney's paper shopping bag, her head all chopped so her ears stick out, and her neck too flat in back. Sandals and a denim skirt and twenty mules climbing over her sweat-shirted breasts. Not much.

That's you, Lily, this is you. And everything around you is you, wherever you may be. Which is here. The Panhandle, trodden grass; eucalyptus trees lonely between the lines of one-way traffic. Drift with the other few, west, to the Golden Gate Park. Gathering and gathering.

These strange ones with their sad soft faces. This

163

silent world. Feel it, let it slip around you slowly, time, Lily, time. Later you'll see, now you'll simply be, a thing at a time. Try, let there be nothing wrong.

Figures, sitting on the grass, sit among them for you must be of them. Jungle drums, skirls of a clarinet, pink palms under the black hands throbbing, pulsing against the genteel park greenery. A trumpet on a complicated lonely trip, winding in the interior convolutions of closed eyes. To the side, a monotonous tambourine shivering by a blue-white face, jaw slacked, tongue bloated growth, uncontrollable, eyes the vacant pink.

Take it, Lily, sit there, your paper bag between your knees.

Black goatee on the black face, licorice-black clarinet, red felt squaw hat, beads and bangles, a mail-armor triangular chastity belt hanging low around his waist, curled-toe Persian slippers. Black jacket, black leotards, and a burning red codpiece, huge, with yellow LOVE.

Can you look, Lily, past the music — oddly 'thirties "Honey Won't You Hold Me?" — past the gagging tongue and the grinding codpiece? Past, through the musky-sweet smoke? Can you get beyond it? The ravaged beggar showing something to whoever will look into his secret trembling palm, leering spit. The honey-blond boy with the sinking mustache, naked to the waist, pale pale and ragged blue jeans, bare feet caked with dirt, the pink pink eyes looking only inward — LSD, man, can't you see? tripped out, man so high — wandering in an eternal dance, muscleless, head sagging far back. Squat fat stump-legged girl with a black baby in a stroller sucking wine from a

Time

that

ends

unhoneyed

164

Coke bottle. Beautiful miniature Black, the hearing aid, the waxed black mustache, beret, beads, buttons, keys, bells, flowers, purses, slogans, doves of peace, slung around him like seaweed. Woven belts, sombreros, serapes, net body-stocking with great orange beads, beards and tangled manes.

Gentle, so peaceful; why your terror?

Banging beer cans, the endless rapping of disconnected words, Indian elephant bells, hollow cheeks under the Digger hats, temple bells from their elbows, feather boas, furs, antlers, headbands. And everywhere the flowers.

He was a voice behind you, just a voice, so soft it was part of the baby's laughter at first.

"You'd be a lily if you'd want, so I'll call you Lily. Now you'd not want, though. Tight, Jesus so tight. Let it out, Lily, you can, everyone can, even without the dope. Think of how you feel after a long shit that keeps coming and coming — don't be offended, no one should be offended here — think of that, of how you sink down, shivering, loose. Look around at me, your fear is like a porcupine."

Great dark eyes that would swallow you, the neat half-beard, tight black curls on his bony white forehead. Look away. Look deeper, maybe you'll know.

"I'm high now, you can see it in my eyes except you look like you've never been here before. Don't be afraid. Kiss me if you will, you will see. Let the trees come to life, let them hear you. Think how it is to have leaves all over your hands and to be in the wind and to hear the cloud laughing with the Giant Purple. Let the others, straights, hate, be tight, be distinguished, play the game, cruelties, irreverent

End

that

is

nothing

165

thoughts. Smile, Lily, there's no reason not to smile. A stranger God, not the Devil. You are not alone and never have been. Listen and it's you that you'll hear. Listen and you'll hear the wind in your leaves. Cool it, all that tightness, let it drain out right here on the grass. Can you believe that you could dance like those over there? They're in the universal pulse, you're out of it and that's why you're suffering."

liturgy

the sign

of the

cross

Focus, here's a person, a man, quiet, his voice doesn't press on you. Focus. Let the scene settle, it's too much, yes, that must be it, too much to take in. So sad, his eyes, so kind. His lips are outlined by his beard, full, pleading maybe, trembling a little to be sure he's right, trembling because the rest is too still, stretched on the dirty grass, propped on his elbows, swaying is he, ever so slightly?

Come in, Lily, come up, come back into yourself.

He can smile, and you too can smile. And even you can laugh a little, at yourself, because you've dropped from your tension, just as he had said, and everything's purer and much more yours.

And it must have been almost funny to see that dropping down.

Still, it's much too much and you'd like so to go. And he must have sensed it too for he's taken your hand and you're walking off. Where the rhododendrons give shade from the oppressive sun and the distance helps. To lie on the bare earth, to say nothing, to think nothing, to feel the motion of the universe, unscheduled, unconcerned.

Rose Tree

mandala

Feel the multitudes who have been before you, supported by this same soil under these same broad leaves, each with his love and his soul, whatever

166

else might be his suffering. You, Lily, who know the earth and the leaves as uniquely yours, yours together with the creatures of nature, yours where no human has trod nor maybe ever will. Can you accept this difference? For you this is the human multitude, for others it is solitude. Join, accept and join.

Do your thing, they say, whatever it is and whatever the others think. But don't they also say do it like we do and pretty much with us or it'll not be right? So what the others think matters after all.

Join, but only when joining is freeing. Accept, but only when accepting is being no one but you.

It isn't going to work, can you see that? You'll go along for a time—so empty, so unprepared to judge, oh let there be no more pain: is that remembering, is that removing from the moment?

Go along. Take his hand, and your paper bag. The strange streets and faces, the painted windows, wavering designs, clusters in the gutter, music that beats in your stomach, your womb, fuzz prowling in their cars with their red lights civil-rights silent. The pad, decayed gentility, the cellar grass-matted for Linda's acid hip ballet, porches and turrets and gingerbread, grand stairs with the treads worn splintery, up and up into the gable rooms where the sun is heavy in the musk-sweet smoke, clean, empty, full of the few bits and pieces each one has, the mattresses blotched and blanket rolls, the john all painted in psychedelic fish and rusty and really overused and no one knows much about plumbing. The girl who pulls her dress over her head and "Don't you wear underwear?"

"Just at first." Turn quickly, Lily, find something

one

fruit

another

tree

167

to see. Nakedness you'll not have seen, not even your own.

Aimless little children, the pink eyes, the bare bottoms. Shaggy hair, plaited hair, tangled hair, glossy, dirty, bushman or savage-shaved naked. Sworls painted in primary colors on the window glass, the melted letters of their love.

What holds you, Lily? You would say you have no debts, that your promises are canceled. Then what is it that holds you? Why would you not smoke their grass, try their pills, open yourself to their love where it lies so quiet, gently stirring on the mattresses?

Because . . . you hardly know. Because joy is internal. The rest is substitute. You are waiting.

They'll let you stay, they'll be kind to you, though sad too and maybe pitying—yet sadness is their way. And in the morning they'll show you the dance workshop, where maybe, because you used to dance so much you said, you could get a job: "We're pretty broke and our Diggers are losing heart so we're looking for jobs."

With the morning the fog has blown in on San Francisco: clouds pouring over your mountaintop, shredded by the sage. You walk between the feeble frame houses, all flaking and gaping with their single-pane windows, and the endless stream of monstrous spewing cars. Black faces and Pizzas and Cocktails with the neon martini glass and it's you, Lily, that makes the street so hostile.

The address, just another row house. Up the steep stairs, white with the black dance posters: witch postures and a mouth stretched open in ecstasy and naked figures back to, reaching up from the dead. No

sad

for those

O Lily

your

love

that can

split

the earth

168

one. Clothes strewn in one room, sandwiches, paper cups, the musky smell. A throbbing back behind the walls. Push open a door. Huge man sitting on a platform, a tom-tom between his thighs. People walking in a circle to the beat.

"There are two ways to walk. Either you walk on the floor or you walk in the floor. Good, very good."

O run

O leap

A hairy man in nothing but a jockstrap walking like a giant, a girl slinking in her leotards, the mincing one in a turtleneck, little children skipping and who'd expect them to walk? And she like a genial circus master, in the center of the ring, scrawny, ageless, a bangle and modest Indian beads. She talks to you like anyone else, "Let's try for a while and see how it goes."

in the

sun

Is it weeks? Time is so unsteady. Still an outsider, but accepted. Will it always be that way? Tonight you are a part of the workshop troupe. It's all so strange at first, even for you who've done it before, the unrehearsedness, the audience joining in, mixed in with the troupe and then you're all divided in two. One group into the other big room while your half prepares Disorder.

Cartons, ladders, ropes, sheets of plastic, rolls of paper, old wardrobes, kitchen chairs, hand spotlights on their snarling extension cords, hula hoops. Arranging and rearranging, peaks and valleys of disorder. Gradually the audience members of the group joining in, tentatively often, skeptically, cynically, and some committed. Begin your Dance of Disorder, Yang-yin to orgiastics to indifference to violence. The lights, yellows and reds and oranges, spotting, flashing, unrelieving. Cruel altars, love dances with

magic union

space

169

closed eyes, epileptic seizures, harmony in the disarray.

The other half let in, watching, not understanding; understanding, joining in disorder. Sweat and dust, groans, high discordant hums, crackling paper, shuffling, the tom-tom beating, fire engines sirening through the ghetto, grime and other people's smells.

Watch him, on with your mime of rejection, watch him with his beard and his eyes shining through as he stands to the side under a web of ropes, studying the strangeness that he paid two fifty to be in, unknowing, withheld for now. His eyes and his hands beginning to move. His mouth for a moment twisted wryly, derision, then settling on its course. Slowly his hands rise, stretch out. Do they appeal to, do they draw from, this great room of disarray? But for his eyes, drawn in on himself, he seemed to seek to disappear.

He opens, he fills. Slowly he unbuttons his shirt, takes it off. His body grows, takes on strength and life, his mouth opens in a silent shout. Is it triumph?

Strength from disorder.

Watch him, Lily, how brave he is, how he challenges his bonds! Does he turn toward you, does he see you, can he understand your rejection of order?

The groups change place. They are to make Order. Your group to the other room. There to divide into pairs of strangers, interview each other for five minutes, and then one by one to describe to the group what you have learned about the other.

Little Lily, sitting apart, on the platform. Watch the others pair, talk quietly. Two homosexuals, so pleased. The stringy blonde with the brown teeth, you hardly know her, finds an awkward sweating out-

to

time

170

sider, takes him by the hand. Adonis, his eyes so
pink, and a fiftyish love-eager woman; he draws her
down to sit facing him straddling on his lap and their
interview is a wordless rocking embrace. He will
say, "This is a beautiful person." He always does,
and she, whoever she be, the same.

Is he coming toward me, the beard, the strength,
the perceiving eyes?

I am Colin.

I am Lily.

Will we ever learn all the rest?

But wait, Lily, wait. You're not me yet.

Lily. He'll ask to see you again, even before you
rejoin Order and wrap yourselves in sheets of brown
paper and look so internally ordered. He'll ask and
he'll lose strength and be all drawn in and self-
denying and resigned to external walls and angles
and blocks. But you saw him before and his eyes still
look in on a different world. And his hands, you'd
seen them from the first moment, containing something
unexpressed, power, will to be reborn.

How many times he'd say, later, how he believed
he'd saved your life then. So drawn, to a fine blue
nerve, jittery like chalk on a blackboard, transpar-
ent. Hating your father, loving him, smothered still
by San Valentino. Living in the empty love of the
flower children, yet reserving, withholding, resisting
with instinct. Giving away whatever you have, forgetting to eat for days and then an apple or some
nuts, or honey. Unnourished by the dance that asks
the spirit to be free but doesn't know what freedom
means.

Every moment, every word, every gesture. You

contain them, they are at your source. There; true, reliable, constant.

The restraint of your first meetings, the central flame of I'm sure I'm sure I'm sure spreading out and out through your whole being. (Square, you'd suppose: tradition of the unfolding, the prolonged discovery of love.) Resonance in another, the inner conversation, the inner touching. Two passions, two longings, two to one, reaching out, so unprepared, so hidden from the conscious, so without control.

He? Colin, dear Colin. Has not your Lily saved you too? What was it you would tell her? Of the crush of the world, of the pollutions and saturations and destructions and killings. And of your escape, your retreat into the last wilderness, walking the mountains and the valleys. You, writing and lecturing of this bitter despairing escape, thus destroying the escape itself. You could see the irony, yes, remember, as you would talk so of it? But what recourse, the final frontier found and destroyed? No further task but death itself. And you were ready.

Your passion, the blade of grass, the drop of dew, the tremble and the stillness. The doom closes in. Neither touch nor be touched, man was all menace.

Your infinite inner solitude. Your despair.

Your fate their progress, your end their goal.

You knew it, all this, yet you were helpless. Memory, nature, but relation cut. Inward, to yourself, but in absolute isolation.

You knew it, these are all your words. Your Lily, though, she could not have put it so. How could she have understood an onanistic attitude, a life so closed and silent and drawn in, an embryo seeking

surpassing

space

and

time

reason

death

172

the womb in the self, in death? She, who had so often made laughter from dust. She who held men's inner images, the keeper of the projected dream. Eternal daughter, eternal mother, eternal lover.

anima

woman

in

man

Yes, you, Lily. You, that skipping step of joy in the midst of tragedy, that love from hate, that paradise regained.

But you'd not have thought like this either, Lily, not have known yourself then in such terms. Life, an intuitive process, not to be understood. So gay at times, perhaps when he is somber, dancing ahead of him, turning, laughing in the sun. Or hurled down into the shadow, the dark side, sobbing under the gray moon, irreconcilable whatever his gentleness. Until the inner light changes.

Go! Go with him where he will. Whatever the burden of his past, he has withstood it, you saw that strength in him that first night, there is the source of your trust in him, in events which seem uncontrollable. Sometimes a wondering and almost a fear: how could this be, how am I here? But still you go with him.

animus

man

in

woman

Tests: dragons to be slain, the elemental attacks, the clouds racing through the sky, the fateful cycling. But still you will go on and on and there will be no end.

The stolen time, stolen from his desperate rush to satisfy a publisher, from his past, from your sad soulless dance on the fringe of the flower children, from reticence.

The paddleboats in the lake, bicycling down the midday park lanes, the Basque restaurant where your Italian mixed so prettily with the Spanish 'round the long family tables, the Fairmont tower to see how long you could stay before they'd catch you and want you to gulp petits fours on their merry-go-round when you'd so like just to stretch your arms to the Bay and the Bridge and the Pacific and watch the sun drop into the distant fog. Dragon Go Go rock blasting their electronic sadness into tinkly Chinatown, topless breasts swaying in the dark over lonesome men and seventy-five-cent beer. Fish where the violent becomes the poetic, where love is an image of the self, where art is sometimes born of disconnection. Cross-legged on the wall-to-wall carpeting where the black glass trembles to the bellowing foghorn, hoping to avoid the empty disagreements of public issues, hoping lives can be given words.

The miraculous time, time the ancient fateful pulse, beyond limit and understanding. Time no longer a flat distance in continuum from the horizon behind to the horizon ahead; time turned, tilted up onto its edge, reaching from the center of the earth to the heart of the sky, with you complete in that dimension, containing it all so that it is no longer that continuum but an infinite moment holding all experience, all moments.

Landing Place

How can I remember, then, with time tipped up so? How can I sort out events when there was no progression, when everything happened at once? San Francisco, so many images, so many moments, the stitching together of time. Our trip, our Calabrian trip to the back of time, to ancestral mountains. Can I ever remember the way other people remember, step by step, building like a plot even if it never was that way? O my Colin, my companion, my liberation, my life! You could take me where you would, you could bring me such discovery—and I you. How dare I

174

remember, how dare I touch the miracle we found?

Let me wait, hold off the elements that swept us up and bore us into existence. And savor the waiting. I'll try, but later, please, please. Now let me be here.

With Will. In his old jeep held together with fence wire. The cat claws ripping at us as we spin in the sand and sage. The buzzards still circling over the pink peaks which hide his little lake now, over the thin concrete dam sliding out of view. Along the wash bed, the going's best, least brush. "Indians' summer campground over there, water here them days, good location for the hunting." Olla bits, charred bones, a metate stone.

A tumbleweed still rolls, restless in the dying wind, but old and silvery, its seed spread long ago. "That's Russian thistle, Lily, that tumbleweed, came to America recent, brought here from the Volga, rolled here maybe, like young Willy."

Stretches of the evening primrose, opening now in the fading afternoon, yellow which will soon turn orange. Rattling along and up onto the old desert road leading to the ranch. Black willows, yucca, Joshua trunks pushed aside, wild pear.   time

Up into the opening in the hot granite pinnacles that leads into the hidden valley. Here he would stop. To show me the graves. Stop the jeep in the middle of the track, no one coming or going now but Will himself.   tipped   up

Graves, they busy Will these days.

175

They'd roll no more

Desert's edge, to the boulders and cliffs where the bighorns had stood against the sky, curious at man thunder, where the Joshua tree throws thin shadow, where the tumbleweed rolls to a stop.

Four stones standing, reaching up still into the low sun, holding their place there for yet a time. Guarding, at the head of each plot. Where the sand drifts in and the wild grass grows again and the bobcat's track is blurred by the lizard's tail.

The tallest, rounded at the top, decorated with a border, an arch, a whirling sun in turquoise . . . *Walapais, over across the Colorado. He'll jeep out there soon, one of these days, when the foreman writes they've mined some more, they'll give him some and he'll bring it back and cement in other designs, pretty on her stone, pretty on theirs, green blue* . . . The others with the stars and the sickle moons: the two sides of life, the Indians knew.

HELEN JANE

MOORTON SPEAR

BORN SEPT. 8

1886. DIED

JAN. 19 1963

ROCK OF AGES

176

ROBIN		
JERRY SPEAR	SPEAR	SPEAR
BORN JULY 21	BORN SEPT.	BORN SEPT.
1927 LIVED 13 YEARS	1923. LIVED	1920. LIVED
3 MON 4 DAYS	3 DAYS AND	3 DAYS AND
DIED OCT. 25 1940	DIED	DIED
OUR JOY	OUR TEARS	HEART'S CHILD

Half hidden in the wild grass and the dust splashed up by the last rain.

Who will there be to chip out Will's stone, cut him into the rock, lay him lovingly under the Joshua tree? Will, why do you cry? Younger, you'd have been ashamed, you'd have turned away from another, from this Lily. Now there are tears on your cheeks.

Me, Willy, I'd roll on, more

To lay me out under the Joshua tree. This button of a girl. She stands there by the Missis. June, she's gone; and she'd called me a weak-headed old crank and would say it's uncivilized to want to stay here, a pauper under the sand.

These that stayed at the gateway to my valley. Their stones, they blur in the tears and the time. They'll last, though, and there's no coyote that'll dig them up.

Lily, Lily, why do you kiss this stumbling dirty old man? You, so fresh, I wouldn't want to disgust you. I know old men, knobbly and sucking, with their dirty necks where they can't reach or remember to wash, the fetid smell, the bits of clothes that have become a part of them, the old eyes and the twisted hands. How can you kiss this old man? Don't, please don't, I'd not have you so close, the white stubble on my cheek, the dirt and the blackheads in my ear, the tremble.

This warmth, and sweet like a flower . . . *O Jenny, Jenny by the river bank!* . . . I'll leave it all, how can I hope, little Lily? On where paradise stretches out

Jerry Dan

Ancient

of

Days

178

to Siberia and no one hurts for want. Leave here where it closes in, where there'll be no one to stretch me out under the Joshua—not you, Lily, not you! Where they nibble at you and blast in the Indian blue sky and in the red earth under your feet. Where their black pollution pours out onto the desert: antelope ran thick there as Nebraska buffalo.

Four of my heart, three of my loins. Look close, old Will, draw to them, down, on your knees—patched and padded with the trembling stitches, don't look too close, Lily—to the boy, Robin. Your shoulders are shaking some.

You can hear her calling, strong and firm like always, but scared, and the bell you'd hung up ringing in the rocks. Scared, you too, Will. Wouldn't be ringing this time a day and calling out without something wrong. Your Robin, lying on his cot, his eyes open, so quiet.

Gone to help his Mana, always helping, always the laugh and the skip and, "I'll do it." Plenty of tank water there was already, but he'd knowed she'd liked it cool and fresh right from the bottom of the well. The crank windlass, a lot for a little feller to manage and the heavy bucket halfway up when the handle must of slipped and spun with the weight and got him on the forehead.

He'd be all right, he'd be all right. Scurrying in the rocks again, bringing us his bits of this and that, never but gentle with his sister. Quieter though, failing, will he be all right? Never, never, never! They'd send him to the hospital, L.A., operate, tumor they said, but all you know's he never come back but for you to lay him here under the sand.

Beside his brothers, babies, and now their Ma.

I feel your hand, Lily, light like the sun, on my shoulder.

Yet how'd you be here, Willy: this cove in the high desert rocks, down across the Mohave from your ridge above the Golden Girl, from Death Valley; this burying, knees in the sand; this desert flowering, this desert dying?

homeward

Gold in red rock, Willy, your Desert Lady

Death Valley drops below, climbing over the pass. Wave your hat, all stiff and new, to the men who lie down there, the ones you've found, buried them with a sermon you'd penciled in poetry. To Indian Tom, even Scotty with his rascal ways, the prospectors. Single blankets. Seldom-Seen-Slim Ferge, Ballarat with Jim Sherlock, and Shorty Harris. Shorty who struck it good over near Skidoo with Anglebury; called it Harrisbury Mine; asked to be buried next to Jimmy Dayton near Eagle Borax.

ghosts

Looking around some you'll be. The Mother Lode. Nevada City, gables and the balconies of the National Hotel. The high-country camp at Alleghany. Comstock, Virginia City, most dead. Kern County for a spell, the Yellow Aster at Randsburg with five- and ten-stamp mills, open pit. The Dale District — east, beyond Lady Mountain from here, on into the Pintos, more'n a day by horse — the Virginia Dale Mine, Dale the Second . . . *June, will you take old Will there again one day? No, no, you've gone, Will knows that: Las Vegas, lost in their corruptions, turned forever from your Dad your desert your little brothers waiting*

busying

about

in the sand. They'd read me your last will and testament like as why they'd buried you there and how you'd not be moved home by the Joshua. Old Will, he'll go alone. Dale Mine, just the headframe and some rubble the tourists haven't got, they say.

And the Desert Lady, your Desert Lady mine, here, just on beyond the ridge where the sun hits golden, she who brought you here, her red rock with the gold.

Mana

Mana

"So flashy," Helen'd say.

Bowman, it was he'd found you, Wm. F. Speare mining man, Death Valley Golden Girl. Good pay, stock in the company. Pocket mine you'd bet, and you were always one to smell out pockets and you took the job, with Bill McQuillen.

by the

well

Bill, partner, like a dad, in the albums, was it just last night? Beard white as the snow around your cabin, still there back of the adobe, and you'd come to eat the Missis' cooking that last winter, and you'd old Will to chip your stone down at Serrano Palms.

Bill McQuillen with brother Jim who'd run a pocket dry, the Desert Lady, she'd brought others up short too. Feller found her in eighteen ninety, then got bushwhacked dead by encroachers, two cowpunchers. They were tried in County Court and it was Hale Minton who saw they wouldn't be working that claim for more'n a bit and he jumped it and worked it, Bill said, five years till the pocket thinned and sold to Jim and Bill. Till theirs thinned too and the San Bernardino bank took over, cattlemen then. They'd got a stamp mill in and were rich till it petered out. And the bank sold to Bowman. Bowman, he couldn't pay Will Speare like he'd contracted, so he'd give him stock instead until the Desert Lady was yours, Willy boy, 'fifteen.

182

Still golden shining on the ridge, and red on Lady. Up on Lady, where Tucker'd been—never'd had time for strolling yourself, especially straight up when there weren't a reason—and seen the Indians' tripod of sticks across the cave's mouth, all covered with grass. Gold in the quartz, all sparkling red, they'd seen it and knowed the white man's passion; the tripod to protect the treasure from that evil. Filled with desert-rat nests when Tucker'd got there. And under the cap rock on the top, Indian hier'glyphs.

For a pail of cool water, Robin, he's left. Full of life, helping his Ma and his Dad. Built that big cage over by the arrastra for the little eagle he'd found up in the rocks. Fed it with mice he'd trap. It's yours, Robin. Got to understand he'll owe his life to you and you to him, for he's wild nature and without that we'd be nothing. Water too. And a rattlesnake in a box, and a coyote pup. Knew a feller, over Coachella way, smashed his wrist on a well windlass, slipped, started whirling, tried to catch it, busted all the bones. Standing right there'd been Robin, in the gap in the bamboo the Missis planted and could never get rid of. Took the windlass off, dangerous.

Same well Minton dug when he homesteaded here in 'seventy. Built the adobe barns, built well too, in good shape when you came, Will, forty years later, though you got to coat the outside every so often, even the best adobe, or she'll wash away. Pretty gone now.

Sixty years back it was you come here, Will. Some cash in your jeans still from the Golden Girl, and the Desert Lady yours. Been prospecting some on the side, poking about here and there. Worked a bit in the Two Skull area with Jamie Pope. High on the back side of the mountain; black up there, yuh, always think of it as black.

Jamie Pope, ⅃, drew it in the sand for you, damn little to brand by then, few mules, all his time on gold, though he'd run cattle once with that brand, back before turn of the century. And you'd showed him what your brand would be when you'd found a ranch, and you'd use it proper too, W↗, scratched in the sand and Jamie had laughed about how you'd not be needing a bull looked like, and you'd got kind of mad.

Twelve hundred head carried that, registered in 'seventeen. And Jamie crawling up your road. And Jamie, his mustache half off, rotting in the desert, buried down the other side in Two Skull Valley more'n forty years back for his loneliness and his gold.

Black up there, with only your hobnails screeching on the rock to break the howl of the wind, walking up Toole's road and on beyond his Two Skull Mine. Big operation, that. Headframe, elevator, mountains of tailings. Up to your black hole picked out in the rock.

Clem Toole, 'ninety-four he started there, patented in 'ninety-seven. Big operation, stamp mill, cyanide to dissolve the gold. Over the zinc filings, puddles of the black mud, volatizing, leaving gold.

Jamie Pope, gold you short-measured on the night shifts, gold you hid, gold you went for in the winter wind when you'd best be home with a fire and a family to look after you, gold that maybe's buried with you now. Beyond, to the back side where nobody goes, where you look out through the white flower stalks of the 'olina, out over Pleasant Valley and Malapai Hill all black over the purple desert and Squaw Tank, and beyond to the Hexie Mountains. Yucca and buck-

lie alone

die alone

for your

fevering

passion

184

wheat scratching in the wind. Your shaft, yours and Jamie's, almost hidden there in the juniper, black down into the hillside, into the rock, half plugged with the tailings you'd not time, for gold hungry, to haul out proper. Hope the melting snow of the last days has run off like it should, not backed up into the shaft. Mean, mining in the winter wet. Silent, he was a good worker when it's gold. Propping in the timbers, picking, picking, picking, with the gray light far back behind and the head lamp making things blacker. And when you think it's warm in there you know it's winter. Good, though, good feeling, get warmed up in there, feel the rock at your back, feel the pick . . . *How many are there, pickheads, worn to nubs, lying out there by Robin's scooter? Tires gone, wheels all twisted and the board's splitting, but I'll fix her up when I get to it, I'll fix her up, keep things going here, maybe one of Juney's kids—but they'll not be coming, their mother said so, and they'd whispered "crazy convict" and "Ma, he smells so bad"—or some little fellow out by the Volga, playing on the river bank . . .* Picks, picks, picks, shining points like silver in the black rock. Gentle in the high grade, kind of taste the difference. Reluctant, mostly, to give up her gold, a kind of game.

roll

on

more

Packing out the high grade on your burros, packing to the stamp mill at Lady. Weigh it careful, you and Jamie.

Back down Clem's road. Clapboard and shingle cabins, one'll be yours for a time, Jamie. Heaps of their tin cans, rusted and new, bottles, stoneware whiskey jugs—lose the instinct, Indians, prospectors, to clean camp when they leave. Around the shoulder and you'll see the sun's light coming up white behind the Little San Bernardinos to the southwest — where one day you'll be pulling a fresno scraper up to the ridge, finishing Spear's Outlook few days after you'd put Jamie to his rest, in 'twenty-five it was. Black the mountains against that light. And off to the north the jumbled skyline, where the red-tailed hawk is circling. The rockpiles to the west of Lady Mountain, rockpiles of granite, quartz monzonite, you'd know that or you'd not be a mining man, intruded from beneath into the pinto gneiss and left when the gneiss eroded off. Wonderland, where you got your ranch, where you'll settle now, up in the hidden valleys, your garden of the gods, rich and fertile pockets in the rock jumble, some encouragement — dams, Will, dams in the right places and the desert will be flowering for you — pockets where the wild hay grows up to your waist, where cattle will stay with just a gate between the rocks, almost, behind the ranch, walled in natural, thousands of acres, clear over almost to Willow Hole, though you might be losing some up in there for years. Hidden valleys full up with flowers in the early spring after the rains, thick like ripening rye — the sand verbena, primroses, harebells, globemallows, desert sage — scoop the wild honey on your hot cakes, in your tin of coffee.

Water, old Minton's well, put up a tank and windmill pump, dam right back in the rockpiles behind where you've got your privy over the wash.

Water for the final washing of the stamped ore, for you'll be setting up a stamp mill on the edge of the pasture, dry mining, and when you'll be short you

geological

tying

tying

inner

the

pockets

of

love

can reuse it by settling out the mud with lime. Eldorado, they'd had to pipe their water nine miles from Piñon Wells.

Water, you'll see an orchard, fruit for the picking, vegetables, melons, even cutting flowers maybe; but what'd an old feller of forty be thinking of flowers for? And a big washtub with the water sluicing through, wash hanging out, great white sheets in the sun; but what'd a mining man, a ranching man, alone in the desert, be having with sheets?

A lake backed up, ice, a swim, alders and cottonwoods and willows finding their way there after a bit. Drink for the deer and the bighorns; for the doves when they come through in the spring bringing with them the thousands of buzzards; bees dipping down before going in for the night. Kind of makes life thicker.

Home, Will.

Slicked up, Will, wagon to Banning, train on to L.A. Mining equipment, material for the dam you'd build, fencing, saddles, a long list for the ranch. Prosperous, Willy, Jerry Dan, who watched a cougar's tail flick, his saddlebags half empty and that's all he had but a lot ahead, a lot ahead . . . *Prosperous, gold in the pockets. "Looking for gold in the heart," you'd write in San Quentin, and she'd know what you meant. Gold in the heart. Soft eyes, to touch, to be touched. O Jenny, Jenny, down by the river bank. Janice, petticoated in the Panamints, set Choctaw Will a-trembling. Could tell about Janice, to Diamond George MacMillan, and the Chuckawalla Fiend, and Minton, who worked the Desert Lady, and Bill*

rain

sap

milk

blood

graves

they

need

tidying

187

McQuillen. But not about Jenny, with her fingertips on the ivory keys.

Slicked up and you'd be thinking of the figure you'd cut with your black hat straight 'round with none of that curl they'll do today to be smart, and your black coat to your ankles, your beard trimmed shorter and your mustaches waxed up nice. The flashing eyes, the dark blue shirt with the white tie, black button boots. And you'd get your photo took, one of those places where they set you in front of a painted background, tidy things up. You'd a cane then, shiny, for the show . . . *Touch them, reassuring, lying beside your tormenting knees, lying on the grave.*

The Rothenstein Hotel, all done up nice, the clerk banging on his bell, plush and velvet, oysters. So gallant with the girl cashier. So pretty and smiling, her hair all up, her dress to the ground all billowing and bows. And she'd join you with her two sisters if her mother said she could, for Sunday.

The beach, the Pacific stretched out to the back side of Russia, gulls the hawks of the sea, the pier walking out on its wooden legs into the dirty waves. Bill, three sisters, but only Helen . . . *My Mana, my Mana . . .* all in white. Her black brimmed hat tied on so dainty with a lace scarf under her pretty chin . . . *So soft and smiling from her window in the sky.*

don't mind

the other

rutting

rutting

Three sisters on a photographer's burro, side-saddling; prospector Will, who struck it rich, standing by. Posing together by the beach houses, then one by one.

St. Louis, they'd come from, back East, and before that from England, with their mother. St. Louis kind of wrote the rules tight . . . *Jenny, Jenny, you'll not to mind too much . . .* Helen Jane, I'll be back soon.

business, the ranch and the mine, and there'll be
postcards to send.

Helen Jane, will you have me,
Will you be my desert queen?
Will you come with me, will you ride with me,
Will you see what a home can mean?

One knee, Willy, that's the style,
Your beard to brush her hand.
And the parlor scene, permission,
Would Mother understand?

nickelodeon

the

boardwalk

Would Helen Jane, Miss Moorton, your daughter,
M'am, be thinking you've got a castle out there, a
kind of mansion in Eden? You'd be not one for running
things down as they are, let off how they could become. Will Spear, cut a figure you did, and the stories,
they had their way of multiplying, the loaves and the
fishes, though you weren't much one for the Bible in
those days. Four men to his name, though best not to
say just which. No stranger to places of refreshment
and entertainment. Scotty, no mean entertainment.
Scotty, no mean myth to be a part of, and the Windy
Pass, and the Boston Gun Club, and the Young's
Hotel ball, and Buffalo Bill teaching you his draw.
  A wagon trip, two good days from Banning over the
pass and out onto the desert and up to Morongo Valley
and high into the Joshua trees and on and home,
however loaded with high-price furniture that might
show pretty good and all that equipment. A wagon
trip can shake up more than some, for a girl all dressed
in white, so soft, no end of high-blown stories.
  But she kept the dust to herself, kept so much to

herself, or maybe mostly it didn't hurt, and when it did there might be tears and then she'd look on up ahead — where her firstborn, hers for three days, lay. Drawn, the twilight shining in her tears, and then the sweet smile as she brought you your plate, her touch as she lay by your side.

Two days in the wagon. How many times would it be, how many years before the stage, and the trucks, the cars that all but one lie dying in the yard, the buses, trailers and campers crawling in? Maybe once a year, six months maybe. One day, it'd take, down to Wilder Well; his windmill brought you water, and the hay carried in the wagon, and grass still, though dwindling even then, camped there for the night or maybe a bed and a meal in his ranch and bottle of something of this or that to leave with him on the way back. On to Banning, the Spokane Hotel, a week. Take in the shows, a livelier town there wasn't in those days, railhead. Provisioning a hundred pounds of flour, if you'd not enough, clothing, furniture, fancy things. The heavy equipment for the ranch and the mine would come out special with the carter's team. Sometimes the children too, June and little Robin.

Your doctor's there now, right where you'd camped — the buzzing and the itching's bad behind the ears, under your hat (hair to your shoulders, half-breed), the little blue-and-white pills for the blood pressure — in his ranch-style house with his airplane in the garage and the nurse'd say when you get there, three hours after sunup, "Uncommon early, seven-thirty, can't you read? You'll have to wait; all right, all right, I'll tell him." And the windmill's gone.

Or later with the truck. And then the touring car with the truck body on back for to carry supplies, and

the others

ribbons

on their

garters

no one

to

lie

me

down

190

the children when they came, camp all night, make quite a thing of it, even if the road's in good shape and could have kept on, out there at the mouth of Dry Yucca Canyon.

Or Cotton's ranch, Finn Cotton, the son, stay there even if no one at home and leave the quart of brandy under the hay in the manger.

Or on by train to Los Angeles, provisioning's cheaper, send it back to Banning while you'd be seeing the girls and Mother, and maybe see the magic show again and have a glass with your friend the magician; Captain Claude his son, L.A. fire chief.

There'd not be another I'd let take me like that, by the arm, help me to my feet; even she's drying *washing* my cheeks with her sleeve, this Lily. No, no, we'll leave the jeep, I'd like to walk home, watch the moon *my feet* for a bit, see if it's back in orbit, should be no more'n two feet above or below Venus, kind of feel it will be, *my* been out since the atom bomb. I'm all right, I'm all right, no, no, I'll get the firewood in (or would she be *child* doing this to make me young, not old?).

Walter, sitting on the doorstep, waiting for old Will. Walter and Will, when there used to be such laughter and running about and visiting, school, McQuillen, Jamie Pope for a piece, the teacher, the crew, and pets of skunks and snakes and the eagle and the coyote, the horses and mules and burros, chickens, twelve hundred cows, pigs. What else?

Fiddling for the keys, keys for everything now, and we'd used to leave everything open, even when *close out* we were at Banning maybe for a good spell. The teams would come by, help themselves to grub and shelter *close in* and the fire, and they'd leave off something, maybe money or provisions, and a note on the table, and everybody knew Will Spear. Only postbox there down at the junction then, for all to see, Speare Ranch — drop the "e," that fellow down at Serrano Palms — Leev Mail Here Pleas Serrano Palms Stage. Now it's a town and filling stations and old folks come up to retire and die. Nineteen twenty-one, and the nearest post office Serrano Palms and then Dale where Abe Grant ran it with the saloon, and when Dale closed up Abe took off with the government money and they're still looking for him.

Fig Tree John at Salton Sea, how's he fit? Don't remember.

Figs and fruits and all the fresh vegetables. Honey, wild and you'd be off with the Missis, with Mana, sweet Mana the children would call you, the only time you'd be got on a horse, off to follow the bees, and later you'd get hives with J & M, Minton's hives, when the wild bees began to disappear with the drying up of the high desert, and you'd no longer find their honey in the old Joshua logs and the rock caves, honey of the piñon and the blue sage and the mesquite, best there is. Flowers, the armloads you'd bring back with Mana and the children from Rattlesnake Canyon in the spring.

Kov orchard

sister

with the

yoke

The children, June and Robin, they'd learn to swim, back in the lake, the first dam you'd built, they'd helped with the hauling. Robin shooting black-tailed deer in 'thirty-seven, dead shot learned from Dad . . . *That cougar tail is flicking, Willy boy, he'll be on you* . . . Drove off twenty-four bighorns once, and the cliff hawk circling above them, diving at them, shrieking angry at them where her nest was, all white-

immortal cycling

splashed from the droppings, and slice down through the sky at you too, whistle by your hat.

Manzanita and lupin, the rabbit brush black with its silver stems. Would you be dreaming, Will, of finding a soft rock, stretching out on it, just feeling your desert around you? But it'd not do, with the south fence line still to ride and the bags of high grade from last season still to mill and Mana to be got to the doctor soon, her fourth. You can think it, though, and that'll be enough, and you'll never stop working while there's daylight. Bed happy, not long after the gold has faded from the rockpiles, always happy, kind of knowing there's something done today, results, yours and no one can cut you from them. Safe and self-sufficient and doing what you're made to do and it's what man's destructing now with all his machines and his pleasure-seekings and his fornicating when the female's out of season. Mistakes you've made too, Willy, but now you know. Bed happy, Helen Jane beside you, all filled out and the bumping inside, warm and gentle and you'd not want more.

Golden years.

Breathe, old Will, breathe deep. Give life.

Lose life too, four standing back there. Home, and the gray fox'll be sniffing there already and the kangaroo rats racing out of his way. Soft and sure in the moonlight. Four without regret. Two little fellows, three days, hadn't a chance, hospital and all. Robin, we've taken off the windlass now, but we'd done our best and we didn't know and your laughter still comes across the wash, and Mana's there beside you. Too, her time had come, the hospital, San Gorgonio Pass by Banning. Our desert lady, home.

O mystic
 Child

riddles

your

wisdom

The schoolhouse, fading in the light, a tricycle still standing ready in the sand. Behind the giant mesquite, rich in the graveyard of their pets. Weathered frames and a tight roof, stuffed now with old schoolbooks and toys we'd bring up from Banning. Ghosts. Nine children, with the neighbors miles off by Ram Springs. Their private school till San Bernardino took it on for a time. The Swenson girl from Sweden to teach, TB and you cured her up and fattened her to two hundred pounds with the spooned cream and the steaks you could cut with a fork.

you'd leave

they'd leave

the

meaning?

Good life, good for children, right way to bring them up, it'll stick with them . . . *You're alone, old Will, and where've they got to?*

Children, and they'd know the meaning of work, they'd be racing through stubble field and swinging on the apple trees, helping Mana and Dad with the preserving and the jerky-drying. They'd be off adventuring, maybe bring back a big black turtle — you'd bring them up to the lake every time you'd find one other parts, for they'd not be indigenous to the high desert here — for a special supper. Turtle'd soften Dad however he'd been storming; good meal, the best, like a cow's stomach, full o' vegetation, three or four different kinds of meat in a turtle and sometimes they'd be full of eggs, like birds' eggs, and Johnny Chuckawalla Wilson used to live on them. Or they'd be climbing over Jack the burro like he was granite. Jack, who knew you as well as the Missis and'd cross you just that far, no further. Jack, your friend, raised him, castrated him when he'd be so horny he'd be on a jenny, her neck with his teeth, rape her out of season, only time you'd knowed of animal rape, so maybe a

cling

to the

earth

Ancient

Claws

194

woman could be raped though the female lawyer claimed she couldn't: "Come out, Judge, in the back room, and try if you can." Though a lot of animals'll jack off, horses and burros they'll reach right 'round and finish off with their tongue.

Or they'd found an Indian olla back in the rockpiles in a cave, taken you up there. Half full of quartz chips and sand from dropping off the ceiling of the cave, the rotting of the rock, to give an idea of how long it'd been waiting to be found. Watch a lizard move across the ceiling and flick his tail and knock down one more grain into the olla pot.

Or an Indian skeleton buried all doubled up in an olla under Sombrero Rock. Big one, wrapped in palm leaves, hands tied under his knees so's he'd fit in, and everything he'd owned buried with him, his bow of the strange wood you'd never seen these parts, and his beads and bowls.

And the visitors, "emigrants" Scotty would call them in Death Valley where he'd be a-building at his castle now and you'd hear of it. Visitors from all over, kind of getting a name for yourself. And you'd be putting up another cabin or two and maybe thinking of a swimming pool.

Mattresses, piled and heaped on the old iron beds lined up rusty in the yard, cabins kind of knocked in, no need now for the double-holer you'd put up second time out over the wash, and all them road signs put up by the auto club out in the desert.

The Palm Springs Riders, hundred and fifty of them, in the 'twenties. Flew in fresh trout from Montana. Knocked down Joshuas to build a corral. Mexican dancing girls. Trucked in the tents and the Ladies and

my

heavenly

Jerusalem

salvation

Gents. Set it all up in the flat below Third Lake. Real live cowboy Will for local color, they said, and it didn't sit so good.

Still you see the corral logs.

Still you find arrowheads, specially after a rain when they've been washed clean of the dust and the sand.

Still it's your land and no one will come without you let them.

Like that Milton Hitter fellow who claims your black steer's his, or rather Branton's, and he'd got you so mad when he'd come up to the ranch that they'd had to hold you down. New Year's Day, that makes it nineteen thirty now, another year and you'll wonder if Mana's been draining the chicken well for holiday dinner. Today would be the day that Hitter just might try something. Put a sign up

HITTER KEEP OFF

by the Desert Lady where he'd been running cattle and stole yours.

Be over that way, Will; Hitter like to be along. And there's repair work to be done at the mine. And up he drives in that touring car with a crowd of others, women too, and he pulls down that sign and comes on in. Black and red inside your head for the rage, crack like a rock split open. Rifle up and he moves like to draw and you shatter his arm and turns and runs and you can get him sixteen more times wanting to but one's enough and he won't be coming back and you're still the best shot in that country . . . *Tail is flicking, Willy, flicking* . . . Chicken roasted right and just to mention, with the applesauce, you got Hitter good and he'll not be back.

my

Treasure

to

be

saved

196

"Sheriff's here, Will, like I told you he'd be. I'll care for the children while you're away."

Judges and lawyers and surveyors because what county were you standing in? And somehow, like lacking evidence, the whole thing just kind of disappears after a piece . . . *Not the next time, old Will, not so easy.*

Yuh, yuh, yuh. Forgive old Will, Lily girl, can't let'm go or I'll be suffering so's I couldn't walk more. Corns, terrible. That big rasp file, there on the desk, in the cubby hole with all them poems. Poems, they kind of rub the corns off your heart. Basketball sneakers, comfortable, and these socks, plaid, Mana knit, sticky. File them a spell, and that little bottle there by the jelly.

Curads, to patch the bleeding cracks in these callused twisted fingers.

Itching terrible under the checked hat.

No, we'll leave the oven door open to heat us up some, the old Majestic. That there's the Alcazar— Alcazar Range and Heater Co., Milwaukee, Wis.— bottled gas, but haven't used it since the Missis left. Gas icebox too once, and electricity, but the generator's a trouble and a racket.

Alcatraz

San Quentin

holy

gas

The wind's back rattling in the roof. Seems to shake the house too, rattle the empty Cactus Cooler cans. Coffee, orange juice, Ovaltine. There by the door where three layers of linoleum are worn through. Simmering, simmering, whatever it is on the back of the stove. Wilson's Certified Pan-Size Bacon, a good box for the trash. There's no need being too fussy about the dishes as there's only old Will to use them. Newspapers and the knife to cut them and the paste

197

to paste them in the books: prehistoric man, geology, history, Armageddon. Flashlight batteries, good to have a few dozen, emergencies, and the oil wick she sometimes misses being trimmed. Cutty Sark Whiskey, square-rigger on the open-sea calendar of nineteen sixty-seven . . . *Bawling in the hold, sailing the sea to America* . . . Deer antlers, Robin's, and the rubber boots for the snow.

Wind's right, there's a black cloud front moving up, and it's cold enough to snow tonight.

Joshua fire

Elements, Lily; the slaying and the sowing

Calabria.

Black clouds, the lightning, the fire that consumes the forest, the wind and hail and storm, flooded in the yellow waters, the trembling of the earth. Why these four, these ancient four elements of existence? . . . *Old Will, my friend, this tiny yellow circle of peace under the oil lamp . . .* A testing, to the underground, to the archetypal roots.

fire
air
water
earth

Of course, Colin, yes of course.

Words to things that were better left alone. Of course, though, best agree.

How broad his chest, with its thick hair, how lofty his words, and sure his step, and strong his hand! To feel him stirring when your thigh is thrown across him in the dark. "Bom, bom!" you'd say to each other, with your nose tucked under his chin.

rebounding

Chthonian demons, thanatic forces, the Erinyes, the furies.

rock

The multiplicity, the fracturing: the unity; the joining.

walls

His tests. Whatever.

Lily, little Lily, where light means dark, where dark

means light. Lily, carried on by the inner force, strong as the muscle of the earth, though you'd tremble and cry and laugh on nothing, nothing at all. It's so clear: breathing, the pulse.

And the dreams; Colin, he would ponder them.

He'd wake in the morning and tell how he'd sifted the soil with his fingers, found a bit of petrified bark, then a fossilized insect all perfect, a little ancient jade figurine of a charging bull. He'd tossed the figure to his father, that impossible rational man who wouldn't touch the naked truth, tossed it to him as proof of his art, his life's work writing. And a horn broke off when his father fumbled, and was lost.

He'd struggle and struggle, sitting cross-legged naked there on the sleeping-bag in the morning sun coming down through the spruce trees, about what it meant: A profoundest self, found in the very earth, ancestral, the creative source; damaged, thrown thoughtlessly to the arch-enemy of art and the ir-rational. Speak not to the deaf, that is to spend your-self uselessly — limited time, limited strength — speak true and to those who would hear.

and love

But of course, of course, Colino. Have I not said this to you so many times?

And why should he even bother to dream such a dream? So slow, so slow, so far behind, but maybe he has to be, male, to fix in himself and in his art.

Kiss him, bite him; he'll climb down quick enough, just watch.

That's you, Lily, a petal floating dry on the storm-ing sea. Or at times the sea itself.

dewdrop

on his

You had gone with Colin, to your origins, where the myths meet, where the dance entered into your soul.

lily

The Mediterranean. You had touched, there was no turning aside. Constellations that coincide, joy among the furies, unity, the smashing of opposites. The mountains and the villages and the towns, the truth.

Be gentle with me, my Colin, I am so innocent, I trust you so, and I have told you who I am but have you heard me? Wait for me yet a while.

Old men with their little coffees trembling under the blue lights, cards slapping violently on the crowded table in the corner, the water running and running from the twist tap where the wine glasses and the grappa glasses would be washed with a wipe of the finger. The glass door on its metal frame stuck half open letting the Apennine air flow in. Quiet children drawn thin like death, sores on their lips, their swollen knees, moving on ancient errands. Two strangers, apart, at an unsteady table with a marble top, two hot vermouths in their silver holders, two bits of southern lemon rind floating yellow in the dark steaming liquor.

His hands open, palms up, toward you across the table. "They will always be extended to you, Lily; whenever you have need." And as he says this his eyes are on you, so tender. Slowly, slowly, Colin, I'm terrified. And a dog comes in, her teats all hanging down, and you are so afraid, and oh! keep her away!

open

in the

sand

You here, little Lily, how, what sense does it make, where is Valley Hope? Oh Pa! you love him so, as you look at this lemon peel, and he has thrown you away and you have lied so to him, and now, because you cannot have this Colin, because somehow it is against the rules, and it is a too different world, you would go straight to home and would curl up in bed beside your Pa where there are no dogs, teeth snarling,

201

no extended hands on the white marble, no long
unknowns climbing before you.

Yet could you leave those hands, could you leave
him, climbing ever higher on his mountain, beyond
all reach? Why must you?

Your hands, they're so plain and smooth and what
have they touched and what have they done? The
holding off, the no, and the joy of being such a little
girl. Must you give it all away? They have all made
you suffer so, and all you would do is go home, stay
there forever.

A tear drops off your chin and lands on the lemon
peel.

With that tear the first light touch of the village
church bell, then the steady heavy blows throbbing
in the night air, vibrating in the bottom of your lungs.
The bar is silent, breathing stopped, faces all turned
up and out into the dark. Lights drive up the dark
street, stop at the bar. An Army truck.

A fire, in the pine forest, may circle the village,
heading for the grain fields where the June harvest
is piled up to wait for the thresher. Scrambling, racing
cars and trucks. The stubble scratching your ankles,
stumbling in the black across the field. Red light against
the night mist, the terrible roar. And there the wall of
soaring flames, the exploding pines, the heat on your
cheek a mile across the fields still.

Your hand meets Colin's.

Black figures against the flames, the shouts and
Italian curses, the sirens and the trucks rolling like
ships across the furrows and the old man whose job
it is to nightwatch the stacked grain, tears streaming
down his face, shining in the light, held by his cane

may

bud

be

flower

be

fruit

Prometheus

Empedocles

from collapsing on the plowed earth.

The wind changes, sharp, a breath of relief across the land. The fire burns back on itself, consumes itself.

Being shown, being spared.

Next day begins your trip into the mountains, another meeting with demons.

Long roads, dust in the resinous air. A bus labors by, though they'd said you'd gone to the end of the line. An hour further, the road ends in a group of stone houses. Mule trails now, for the woodsmen, for the mountain villages beyond.

The spruce forests, the pastures, the brooks. A dog barking furiously at you, at your heels, yet your fear has lessened. You come up to a woman in black sitting on a stump in the dark forest with her white sheep about her, her dog silenced.

Grazing, against some absurd law and of course of course you'll tell no one, and there's a good short cut up that way and more or less along the ridge to the next village, my village, and you can tell them Giuseppina sent you to them and go with God.

You leave her, yet are with her, and you look back and she's still sitting, knitting, black among the white sleepy sheep, and a sunbeam drops straight like a tree trunk in the thick pollen. She knows.

You'll camp in the spruces by a little pond. He busies so and is so intense, when there seems so little to do, for all you have is on your backs. But it is sweet to have him care for you and boil the rice and the coffee and you are so very tired. Then the fire is embers and the sky is stars through the great trunks leaning in on you in a circle. And you are in his arms, gentle, tender, patient arms, as if you'd always been there.

companion

for the

Night

Sea

crossing

♏

203

This, your first night together. The stars sing to you, the stars sing in you . . . *Pa's low voice, the hurting hand, his trembling — pity on him; San Valentino, the blind tearing in you — hate fading.*

Back and back into the mountains. So proud that your legs are strong and can carry you, striding, where he would. That your shoulders are strong and he'd only growled a little and had such love in his eyes when you gave him the melon you had carried for two days hidden at the bottom of your pack after he had weighed everything to the ounce to spare you.

And often in the distance now you see the great snow peaks before you, he with no concern, you with a trembling in your heart. Finally you are on the edge of the forest and the mountain is quite on top of you. The last village, so remote, so stony and gray, echoing its narrow stepped alleys with donkeys' hooves and the bells on the sheep coming in for the milking. They give you grappa and bread and their cheese and coffee and are offended that you would pay and are so delighted that you can speak their language and no one can remember a foreigner having been there ever before. You sleep in the school, one room. A floor can be so soft when you are tired.

O Ziggurat

Tooth

of the

Earth

Next morning they give you a walking-stick, a shepherd's crook, and bid God be with you.

Thick thick sheep's cream with bread and boiled spring thistles with oil, in a shepherd's hut high on the summer pasture. The morning milking, the shouting, the procession through the stone-walled pen, the squirt squirt in the pails, the dogs bringing in another herd.

The sun's hardly warm yet as you set off again.

204

The pasturage thins and disappears among the rocks. Then the snow, so cool to hold in your mouth, so steep and thank God for the stick. On up to the sky, to the black teeth against the sky.

Where the other side is sheer, a cliff, and you weep because you know you cannot go further and the cliff sucks at you and the wind rushes up from behind and would push you over the edge and the clouds gather and you curl inward, despair. O far far Valley Hope!

And he leaves you, shivering under his jacket too, to find a way, he says. Shivering, deep in your stomach, the cliff a monster, waiting for you, you wedged between his teeth. Teetering in the wind, swaying, the whole rock ridge. Nothing, no one. And even then the earth is smitten with a blow. Prolonged, a convulsion from within, shuddering, heaving you to and fro, to shake you off, and all the creatures clinging so perilously to its stone skin. Three times, and the cracking roar and the rumble of rocks dropping and the sound like sand as you can see the snow sliding in ugly wrinkles where you had walked across so long ago. The bitter taste of vomit stinging in your nose . . . *Stinking still where it caught and dried in the fold of your belt where it doubles over to hold the buckle, vomit down your shirt when Goldie broke her leg and Pa shot her right there in the head, and you'll never never never wear it again. You hate him so . . .* You feel the bones of your fingers where they cling to the rock, rock in its agony.

O Earth

Monster

(I love you
I love you
Pa)

Colin, Colin, have they shaken you loose, have they destroyed you, you, so beautiful and noble and gentle and strong and true, they, the demon forces, the dark side of the sun? Come, come to your Lily, let us be

205

sacrificed together to the black gods. No, no! only come and hold your Lily and let her cry out in her terror.

An age of ages and he is here, dropped down beside you in a pause in the fierce tearing wind.

"It is over," he says, "three times and you can be sure it's over and there's no more need to be afraid for I've found an easy way and first I'll take your pack and I'll be back for you in just a bit and I love you so and am so proud that you are here."

And you, you would laugh or scream with rage or turn white with pity for man, but the wind blows all that away and he is gone. And would he be like that if the earth had quite split open to its heart between us?

Back along the shoulder of the mountain, where the clouds are churning and heavy as if they would crush and overwhelm the poor earth. Blinding white lightning splits open the sky. You can only watch, numb. The white sheets of rain erase the valley. And, quite in an instant, every muscle is rigid, every hair creeps over your frozen skin, you've shot up to a kneeling position, your hands outstretched, and a horrible flash cuts into the ridge beside you. The blue smell of ozone, the smell of your terror.

Jupiter's

fire-ether

chance

destiny

providence

Your breath has turned to stone in your lungs, your eyes see nothing, your thought for Colin stretches thin and taut out across the earth and would seem to disappear.

He is beside you again, you can feel his hard body press to you, his breath on your dead face, his distant words saying nothing. Pressing, releasing, pressing on your breast, the sharp pain of a gasp, the sting of blood in your face.

206

Half carried along those dreadful teeth, the rock dropping straight off now on both sides, mercifully into streaks of clouds. To a chute of stones and tufts of grass and pale sad yellow flowers. In despair and fear, down and down, in great strides, each boot sliding in reckless clatters. Skidding on the long streaks of snow where to break through would surely be to snap a leg.

The rain and the hail breaking on you, in an instant wet through. The water running down under your belt, into your boots, and any move finds new spots of the ice cold. Rain in your eyes so you can hardly see your feet where they reach for footing. Hail to turn black to white, a final white before the night closes in and your trail is the hand of fate.

Quite suddenly you're in the midst of crying huddling sheep. The smell of their droppings, of their pungent shorn skin. A pace or two to the side, in a flash of distant lightning, you see the shepherd squatting under the tent of his conical goatskin cape. Three words for you, warm but that's enough, to show you the path to his valley village. Yet still it's fate, for the dark closes in thick and the rain weighs heavy and the wind would have the way.

Torrents that rip across the path and rush about your shins and fill your boots with ice when they had almost become friends in their sloshing warmth. You have to stop and you call to Colin just ahead, shriek to him in the deafness of the storm. He shields you some from the crush of the wind and rain. To move in your clothes, the agony of the cold and the wet and the storm violating your flesh, clutching you between your legs.

Moon's

death

the

deluge

207

The madness, the exhilaration, throwing yourself
down that mountainside, embracing finally, open to
the furies, bursting in your womb. Your cry of love,
from another world, and even in the storm it echoed
from the cliffs above, the full force of your soul, you
cry to the ancient gods. Ahead Colin turns to you and
in the dark, only inches away, you can see his face
reflect your wild delight.

That is the knowing, my Lily.

Was it that night, the warmth of a shepherd's chick-
pea soup, his wine, his beautiful slow smile, the gentle
scratch of his blankets, the smell of your clothes drying at the hearth, the soft talk of the women in the
other room as they prepared their threads for the
weaving tomorrow, was it that night, lying in the dark
on a mound of sheepskins, the embers slipping away,
the body slipping away, the sound of the rain softening
into the breath of dreams?

*Your wedding day. As is always done, you rise early
and go alone into the forest. You are dressed in skins
of the Easter lamb. Deep in the wood, where there are
no paths and you are led by a sure instinct, you come
upon a small sunny dell. At the far side is a grotto and
at its mouth a pool. You go to the edge of the pool and
there you unclothe yourself, carefully laying the lamb-
skin robe on a boulder of smoothest purest marble.
Your nakedness glows forth.*

*You are to bathe, the wedding bath, in the pool. As
you step to its edge two great green frogs float up to
the surface, lie there watching you. You do not hesi-
tate. Your arms high, then entwining, the tips of your
fingers touch lightly to your golden hair, your hands
slowly down, to your eyes, your cheeks, your lips,*

Sun's

passion

Great
Mother

is

slain

your fingernails caressing the throbbing sides of your throat, your shoulders, your breasts and their hard nipples, your belly, passing so lightly through the curls of hair, your thighs, and, as you bend, your inner knees, and calves, until you grasp your feet, your knees spread wide by your elbows. The frogs have not stirred, not blinked, seeing your secrets.

You step into the water. The frogs make way for you, as do the many many smaller frogs which you now see with pleasure, swimming about you in the water bubbling warm from the depths.

Sheep bells, like brook water playing in the stones and hollows, flow by below and stretch out into the distance. Later, the sun is bright on the white wall and there's murmuring outside. Yet still the frogs are with you . . . *Yes, yes, it was that night* . . . frogs that once would have made you shriek, frogs your friends, your ancient guardians in the waters of the earth, your joining with the sources of the soul.

Your preparation, your anointment? The furious attacking elements, fire and air and earth and water, the multiple opposites. The sun shining on that wall, the peace in every cell of your body.

For weeks you stayed there with the shepherds; their village, clinging to the edge of a great chasm splitting through the mountains, high above the sea. Stone houses with their slate roofs, the church, the little bars, two, rivals across the square, the goats and the sheep and the donkeys crying out and the chickens. The fountain with its dozen jets splashing out, where the women would put their wools to be combed by the water to thick soft textures, where they would come and go so straight and noble with their jugs or their

O

fertile

Frog

on

the

Moon

mountain's

water

washing balanced on their heads.

Colin, at a little table against that sunny wall, writing. Not the story of travel he'd been sent to write, but the poetry of his inner voices, the passion found in his soul. How you would sit there, Lily, hour upon hour, sending him all your strength, your heart tip-toeing to the rustle of his pen, hoping hoping hoping when he was still for so long! That little room was flooded with our passion.

Thin days too, days when there were dissonances scratching in your heart. The wishing away of the empty moment, impatient for the future. The empty space below you, that swaying cliff hanging high behind the village, he so unprepared to go beyond the moment. He withholding, the distant look of pain, the fist he would pound on his table, determination, only to again fade to doubt. Clinging clinging to the moment as a refuge. And you reaching in despair to the future, or then reaching back.

Oh Valley Hope, oh Pa! Why not now? Such love, such joy, and here the slow disconsolate blending of hollow moments. Such protection from the pain, from the truth of another's trouble, and here his torment storming on his brow.

Why did you ever tell Colin of Fort Badly, of Pa's girl and he left us he left us he left us? Like a black cloud and lightning while he was writing there in the morning sun, he turned to ask for toast and a sliver of garlic and the bowl of sheep's milk, turned and you could see the torment and the paper blank, perhaps he said, "You look so like that picture of your father."

And it had begun.

It was, "But I *am* my father."

treasured

in the

Earth

210

He's perfect, the ideal: He's quite imperfect, and he'd leave you for Fort Badly, and he drove you to San Valentino hell, and parents are to be left first before we can return to them, the weaning.

And never never never, Colin, with your horrid theories, and can you ever know a family? and you so abstract.

Love was so uneasy that night, through the tears and the clinging together again, the lamp and the darkness. Our soft breathing, the plane trees through the open window, silvered by the moon, restless in the night wind.

Lily, you're standing outside your home in Valley Hope, the afternoon sun slanting through the poplars where you would fly again. From the barnyard comes a figure, the height and the stride and the features of your father, but wearing a long brown skirt that brushes the earth, a blood-red shirt, a black scarf around the head in the manner of the peasant women. He, or is it she or they? comes forward. Your sisters have been with you, Colin too, but now they leave you to confront this strange figure alone. A sense of doom, of unswerving fate, of shadows.

He stops before you, face to face. A look of sad joy on his dark face, he says, "I am to die, it must be, it is right. You are to do it. Take this knife and you shall drive it into my heart."

You turn away, you would run, you are turned to rock by fear. Yet his strength turns you to him again, his strength puts the knife into your hand, his strength joins with yours and you strike him in the breast.

There is blood on you, there is blood flowing on the bare earth where he lies dead.

wind

in the

soft

poplars

You turn, you walk so surely, to the field here to blood
the south of your house where the sun is always
warmer and the soil is so rich. As the others watch you of my
silently from the porch, you take a cloth sack lying full
and heavy against the roots of the apple tree where Father
you climbed with the birds as a girl. Its loop of cloth
over your shoulders, heavy against your belly and
thighs, you set out over the fresh-plowed field. Your seed
hands reach deep into the sack, into the warm seed,
clover seed. Your arm sweeps the arc of the sower. of my
Your eye is on the earth, though you can hear the
swallows slicing the air, the bees hunting for new Father
flowers, in the sun.

The cycles, Lily, the dying, the enriching, the seeding, the fruit. Your life from his death.

You weep through the remaining night, silent, far from Colin under the goat-hair blanket. By morning you know. The village mailman brings a can of honey, Touch o' Heaven.

Colin had understood before you told him. From the weeping, the honey, then your turning to him. He had wanted this so, to see you released, ready to flower.

Yet he who had held you steady, led you through the elements, given you strength to dream, he was lost in pain.

He talked of his father. Strong, sharp as sun on ice, sure. Sure that life could be measured, that it had limits and aims and successes and failures. The evil of unimportance. Writing from the self an indulgence, petty, harmful.

Go to him, my Colin. Embrace him, love him, and how can he not love you? He must, he must, that's

212

what family means, and if you cannot be accepted by him then I cannot, and without that, without joining your family, I cannot join you.

He would not go: he would not leave you. Where could you go? To Valley Hope without him, or stay in San Francisco where life is convention? And he would not understand how his need was yours, how he too must dream.

my Prince

You woke one night to his bitter sobs, you took him to you, his cheek on your breast, his hand clutching so to your shoulder:

my Frog

"Lily, Lily! My father, he was racing, the stiff-legged race of an old man who would be young. His head was on backwards, looking at the past, at his successes, at the people he'd passed. I came to him in his castle and you were there and his head was to the front now, so tired and weak. I took him to me, I shook him with all my force to make him understand. I embraced him and wept and he finally began to weep too and told me he could not lose me . . .

Hero

to

face

his

"I shall go to him. And you, let me first take you to the desert, to stay with Will, I've told you about him, where the air is pure and life is not death. You'll see. And I shall come to you, soon."

Dragon

He slept again in your arms . . . *Perry, Perry, with your face turned empty to the sky.*

You left that village in the full of a summer day. Embracings, tears, a touch of festive thrill. On the balcony over the bar, the grandmother and the little boy, he digs up his short-pants leg and pees gleefully into the black figures and the dust below. Frowns and roars of delighted anger.

You left, his poems now finished. So beautiful,

when you'd read each day's work he'd handed you, your breath and your heart would stop.

You were carrying so much with you, your loads were so light.

You left, swinging down that mule track, hour after hour. And to the town, another bus, and on. An ocean, a continent, San Francisco, an empty day, and on.

To the desert, your eternal dream of the desert beyond, of the endless expansion, the opening, the secrets revealed. Look out on the purples, racing past Banning and the San Gorgonio, the sage and the mountain shadows, the salt white of the sand far below, the silvers and reds and browns of the nearer hills, the sweet faint scent of the desert drying, blooming in the early spring sun. Rushing through the desert air, on.

Past the blights, the ordeals, the monsters lying in wait to capture you. The Buy a Bit of Beauty, Scenic Acreage Freeway Frontage, Your Retirement Dream, the plastic pizza and cheeseburger slowly turning on their steel pole high over the highway, topped with Frosty Heaven. The Official Pollution Control Stations and the Registered Rest Rooms (Women Love Us), the endless procession of gasoline. Old folks dying lonely in their mobile homes, wandering wandering, with their supermarket carts, looking for some packaged mirage. Hi Desert, Hi! Welcome! The trailers and the campers pushing out the margins, nibbling at what's left.

Past where the smog rolls down, where Perry lies, face turning to the sand, where Lily would breathe no more. On to the promise beyond.

my Virgil

the

circles

214

STOP, where Shell and Chevron stare idiotically idle at each other across the road, their patriotic plastic banners ripping in the wind, gas and green stamps and Win! Win! Win!

Turn off and up into the hills. Turn and turn, off into the desert tracks, lost in the rockpiles, found where the Joshua tree reaches out over the blackbush and the lavender wolfberry, stretches its arms, its pointed leaves, into the retreating sky, its spear over Canaan.

PLEASE ASK PERMISSION TO LOOK AROUND

Through the gate in his fence of Joshua logs. Wait by the table and the bench and the mattresses deep-hollowed to his shape. He'd have heard the car door slam. Wait, Colin, let him greet you under the Joshua tree.

Shuffling on the thin floor, the weathered door swinging, "Well, well, yuh, so it's you come back, and this'd be the Lily girl you wrote of, sit down, sit down, while there's sun enough."

Before it got quite dark and we had had our Cactus Coolers and listened to Will about how Jim McKinney killed three or four up in north California and hit out for the Mexican border and how Sheriff Henry Loven went out and got him, by golly, at the Caesar Mine, and about how the only hope for the world is to divide all the land up into self-sustaining farms, now that hunting has gone, so machines can't ruin us for sure, and the government should spend all that war money getting fresh water from the sea, about being guardians with his big brother of that orchard on the Volga and how their sister would bring them hot food in pails on a yoke and they'd feed their dog in a hole in the ground and watch the so pretty blonde girl who guarded the

the

divine

wilderness

where

I

must

search

alone

215

next orchard. Before it got quite dark my Colin had gone.

Oh! I'll write you write you every day, and won't you?

Far off, flown to discover his father. Whatever he said about always being right here beside you. And behind your smiling kiss as you wished him strength and love and luck were salt seas of tears drowning all consolation.

Turn to details, here, lying undisturbed and un-concerned about you, adopting you, some of you. Colin's old Will, his checked wool cap with its cor-duroy earflaps, his old cardigan, his patched pants taking shape and life from his knotted bent-out knees and his withered buttocks, the fly all torn and safety-pinned, the canvas shoes. His lips sucked in to the gums, his eyes slanted down with the years, his cheeks in loose creases, the two sharp folds of flesh from his chin running down under his pale plaid shirt.

are these

echoes

of his

Inner Voice?

The myriad items of his life ordered in disorder about him, his memories and his needs, the array of familiarity. Each a part of him, of his breath and his touch and the gaze of his liquid blue eyes across the teeming room and out the sagging door and over the collection of his ninety years, up to the Joshua tree, the distant piñons and nolinas and the confusion of granite against the sky.

Details to comfort you, yet your spirit has been torn from you and is far far off. You are a shell, a snail shell dusty in the desert. Will, his lips tight together, his eyes drifting to the past, away, sad in you, and sad there is no reaching out between you — friendship should need no time. Oh! touch him, Lily,

216

open, gain and let gain from your love. Flower in the desert sun.

For this, Colin has brought you here, to old Will, his desert, his time. Your father is behind you, to go to when you will. Here to find with Will the wholeness, the going on, to wait Colin's coming, free too, he must, he must.

You will spring, just tomorrow, to the rough back of your bighorn, swift through the spring perfumes. You will breathe the desert, embrace it, it will hold you to its flesh. As the days pass you will sit again with Will by the Joshua, by the piñon in the setting sun, the moon looping low. At the kitchen table, black albums soaking up the oil light. You will sleep to the voice of the bat, wake to the cry of the hawk, gold pulling from across the draw. Black water; graves scratched by the passing of creatures.

seize!

hold!

savor!

be!

Letters will come from your Colin, troubled still, failing to embrace his father. You will reach out to him, put your cheek to his heart, whisper to him across the distance about the strength of your desert ram.

And his last letter, to his Liliana Touch o' Heaven, Box 367, a year and two days since that night of the Dance of Disorder. You will read it in the dim light, the Joshua wood giving you its last heat, Will sleeping at the back in their old double bed, the desert voices ringing in the night.

My dearest Lily: It is past, for I have dreamt and I have learned. I was imprisoned, deep at the bottom of a rock-walled pit, its opening far above against the sky, and at the edge the small black figure of my father looking down. Escape, the crude steps, the heavy door, the ladder. Yet each is set on fire by the com-

217

mand of that figure above, each escape barred by flames.

Finally I do escape. I turn the flames on my father, to consume a great edifice on which so much of his twisted energy had been spent. I go, stepping over barbed wire, out across the earth, naked, free, on my heart the touch of heaven.

Your Colin.

Those fathers, as they sprang from your inner hearts, as you demanded they be, as they could never be — you have killed them. May they live in truer form. The one; you wanted him as an idol, a perfection, there to receive all the power of his Lily's love and libido. The other, a man of excellence, of power and success; you expected, Colin, that he too would converse with the inner voice, accepting the rebellion, attacked and attacker.

Those were your fictions.

you told
me
fire is
madness
or
force

Voices of the wilderness, speak to Lily

So, Lily, as you lie here in the dark, as the voices of the night, softly in the air, tell you of distance and time and the eternity of moments, what can you take to you?

Reality? but all your reality springs from you. Then need your killing of one reality, your image of your father, be replaced only by another still coming from you? Yes? But if you also admit others' realities, your father's of himself, others' of him, then yours can be both all and almost nothing. Can you let the others in, can you accept as many worlds as dwellers, or only yours?

all squared

and

numbered

Philosophical constructions, snarled about you like the cat's claw that grabs at a fawn; but the intuitions, the feelings, what are they, where are they?

Let the voices speak, the immediate, the now, the here.

But damn the rational! Why must it even threaten? Avoiding avoiding the true examination, deep down, here, in here, this is what counts. You'd hear the voices and grammar gets in the way, rules and theories. Leave poor Lily be!

Let the voices speak.

The breath from the bat's wing, is it joyful? Oh let it be not out for bugs, just flying for the fun. The scrape when it hooks back onto its rafter in the corner. Oh and coffee, grounds boiled over on the Majestic, roasting still on the rusty lid — and you'd be no more orderly than he and enjoy it so — almost sweet like chocolate: back streets of Mediterranean towns, how can the passers-by, the others, not notice and stop and want to stay forever by that grilled window where they're roasting inside? The sigh of embers settling in their ashes, the stovepipe cracking as it begins to cool. Against the sweet soft voice of the owl in the piñon. The coyote calling from the moon.

soft

circles

numberless

From the firewood in the box by the door the tiny chewing of termites; may they be happy for they must burn at the stake. Rustlings under the floorboards as the desert rat picks up crumbs that have fallen through the cracks. A moth's despair against the window glass who'd go back to the stars now these false lights here, gained with such exhaustion, are gone — but why, then, why don't they fly on and on to the shining sky of the night, never to return?

Distant deep breathing, Will in his back bedroom. The bed with the sheets brown with dust, and what does it matter and who's to know and "Got to get these changed but the knees and it's not easy."

no

meaning

His Mana's quilt, the bleeding wallpaper. Always the inside place against the wall, only the inside, to be easier for Mana, back and forth. Her steps, a feverish child, the long robe, stirring his poetry paper on the floor, her slippers on the linoleum. A faint faint chord on the piano. The wind clicking the latch, Will's

all

meaning

trembling key now the sanctity has gone. Robin on tiptoe with his muddy fingers. A tremor in the weathered frame: the wind, or Jack the jackass, rapist, scratching his forehead on the boards, back from the sage . . . *Found him by watching the buzzards and then the flies, bloated.*

A distant motor, they're reaching reaching. Or is it Colin? Coming up through the sand, that rattle in his car they'd never find, a rabbit racing across, the final rise, the motor cut and the lights out and water gurgling in the radiator, hot steamy metal smell, and flying flying into his arms and whirled around and around and words all tumbled together. If it were! if it were! Another voice, or the many voices about him. Joining, to mingle with so many others, with yours. Special, but not alone.

He will come, and you will hold each other and be each other, so warm and pure and naked. And you'll know him, you'll hold him from you just so, to know him. And the other voices will talk to him too, not quite though as they've talked to you, the web of conversation, each his own, each the other. Hold him from you for now you know you cannot be one. Each his own, each voice, and to make another's yours is not to hear, is to deny. The hollow unheard voice. Yes, my Lily, you must drive those knives deep, each the other. Only now can the sowing, the harvesting, the cycling, true, begin. Let him speak to all, and all to him, be heard, hear.

To hear all is to love all, but less than all all all and it is but yourself you hear and love. For man this is not enough. Here, Lily, lying, hard, the thin mattress on the cold floor, each voice measured against you,

to

be

alone

is

to

join

221

accepted or rejected. The coyote: his voice a thin
rope to the sky, tying heaven and earth; his voice
to catch a bullet if you spot him. The shifting embers:
the seed, the trunk, the food of love, the awful chill
of the morning, numb-fingered kindling, roaring, the
warm creeping in delight down your spine; death and
let him do it, he knows how, is used to it. So so so.
The privilege of the moment, the endless duty. Choose
the moment, listen; duty, the excuse to resist and hate.
Listen and all will hear.

I hear

Speak to all

Skeleton fingers of the cottonwood rasping on the eaves of the upper floor. The crackling of frozen BVD's on the galvanized wire out back. Scents of night blooming, a skunk's regard for gray fox.

Your treasure, Will

Rush in, down into your warm old crooked self, my Mana's quilt with the musty smell . . . *Fades fast, the glittering treasure, all colors, studding the inner* Treasure *chamber in the mountain cone, Robin on your shoulder. Look now, son, for it's only once in a life-* won *time* . . . Dry throat scratched up from the breathing, eyes half stuck. Lie still and the aches'll stay away. in the

Scratching on the eaves, you'd a fixed it once, pruned up some. Never matter. Rustlings, movings Mystic about, stirrings upstairs. Kids restless for the first sun to point in over Lady Mountain, run the trap line. Center Come banging down the outside stairs, you out to the milking. Tighten up that garden fence. Vegetables for us, not rabbits.

Snapping on the clothesline, spring freeze, sun'll fix that soon enough, and they'll be flapping with the morning wind and Mana'll have them in for the fraying and they're bleached enough and more. Flapping flapping, the crossed-stick scarecrows cocked over the fields of Kov, Kov on the Volga. Will she be bringing it soon, John, I'm so very hungry? So white with her scrubbing and the desert sun. White when you walked up on the ice behind your first dam, for remembering, Helen holding to your arm to keep from slipping and maybe she'd been thinking too how deep it'd be. For remembering. Her hair's all white too, pinned up tight, you'd know it, under her white knit cap-scarf tied over the black wool jacket. Brown hair, short straight to her shoulders, flapper, her cotton dresses to her ankles, always, all her life . . . *Watch down on me, old Helen* . . . and her tight smile and her happy eyes. Getting sadder, sad and far, up there on the ice with Walter, is that Walter?

Sad, had it been too hard? Had you done that to her, Will? Ride for the wild honey, armfuls of flowers, sunset sitting and the children at their lessons, bedmates you'd not done so bad, snow fights when it came in deep. Hard on her. Little fellows dying. Robin. You getting wrought up, caught in trouble over Milton Hitter.

And Crabble. Had no business, damn him! Five years and only Mana, June for a time, and the cattle going and the weeds coming in, and things needing fixing everywheres. San Quentin. "Harris, you'll come to see me?" Harris, your youngest brother, telegraph operating with the UP, that's all you'd hear from, a fine man, a fine man.

Crabble, stretched out there, flopped out dead, his finger on the trigger, revolver, Colt thirty-eight. Hat gone and his hair hanging down, his glasses from one ear, his shirt soaking in the blood.

See, sheriff, no other tracks but Crabble's. Will, you'd not gone near him after the shooting. Just fixed up the gasoline pump to water the cattle for'd figured

air

flows

soft

through

all

moments

this might keep you away for a spell, and turned yourself in to the Justice of the Peace. You can say all
you'll want that he'd been murdered first and then the
pistol shot once and put in his hand, but there's no
tracks.

STAY OFF PROPERTY, SPEAR, THIS
IS MY LAST WARNING

And all those threats he'd kill you, trying to claim
your piece, get at the water hole, best in the valley.
Temper to boil oil, even when he'd first come, and
you'd not trust him far as you could throw a bull by
the tail. Deputy sheriff over in Los Angeles County,
good man with a thirty-eight. Temper, though, damn
what a temper. Retired to ranching, Merit Crabble,
neighbor. But he'd be liking better water and you've
got it, homestead, all proved up. Cahoots with the
cattle and the railroad interests and the sheriff too.
Got it in for you all right.

liked

it

that way

Waiting for you, knew you'd be coming as you'd
always done. Waiting back of that Joshua, with a log
across so'd you'd have to stop and get out. Comes
toward you, you stepped out of the pickup, blue
Dodge, lets at you as you drop 'cause you knowed
it was coming. Slam into the pickup door and you've
got your rifle, automatic, from the cab 'fore you'd
know it, and you'd not expect another chance,
missing old Will once. Dead shot still, old Will, sixty-
six back in 'forty-three that was, and you'd three
shots in him while he was cocking. He'd not move
again.

Will?

And now the best he is is a piece of stone you'd
chipped out, this root of a hand, hauled it up with
Lily in the jeep to the site, set in concrete.

226

HERE IS WHERE
MERIT CRABBLE
BIT THE DUST
AT THE HAND
OF W F SPEAR
JUNE 3 1943

Five or six others, maybe. Where'd they be now? Nebraska, Montana, Arizona Territory. Where'd they be? You'd not remember. Dead shot and they'd not so much as nicked you. Tail flicking back of that log, closest yet. Now they'd stole your rifles, all inlaid silver and gold, Indian work, just a bit ago, but you've the old one still and you'll have it on them revenooers if they're up here for you.

uncommon

itchy

Will?

Manslaughter, they'd got you on. Justice. The only justice you make yourself. San Quentin looking over the Bay, scenic. Helen Jane, and the weeds'll be coming, the summer and the irrigation, cattle-watering if they haven't stolen them off. The windmill and the fences to fix and the firewood, pumps and the truck and the horses. Dams to build, Canaan.

She danced so pretty, that Mexican girl, with the Riders, down by the Barker dam. Paint her, Will, with her long black skirt and her red red lips and the tambourine. Write her a little poem, down by the river bank. June dancing for her little brother, a tarantella on the table under the piñon. They'd give you paints and paper and even you'd go in to San Francisco, Doctor Gunther he'd said you could, trusty, to get those special fancy writing-pen points at the Weyerhaeuser store.

floating

fading

That is after the thirty days in the fishbowl with all their tests of how smart you are and whether you're

227

a criminal or not and whether you're insane, all them psychiatrists. Gunther, the head psychiatrist, who was the good fellow, for all his language. Didn't treat you at all like a crook.

At first, with all that prison grub, you'd got all stopped up and that medical doctor fellow he'd told you just to eat more and something was bound to give soon, explode like. But you'd not taken much to that and you'd wait the day of the week when Doc Gunther would be there for your interview, he'd give you the laxative pills and bust things loose — you'd hear them at the dispensary all laughing, taking cover when you'd be around, for the explosion. Well, not so bad if'n they'll laugh, even at you.

Read and read you did, in the prison library, and they'd let you take books out. Poetry mostly, and you'd copy it out and copy it again into your script you'd been practicing from the manual, number-five pen point from that Weyerhaeuser store, paper store and such. And make up lines and maybe verses to go together.

freedom

Young's Hotel

prison

walls

Painting, and printing on the silk, the valentines:
To my Dear beloved Wife, comes this Valentine to Greet you once more With the best Human Love! Dad.

And birthday greeting cards and Christmas, Mana, and June if she's still there.

But mostly the penning and the poetry.

I'm Jamie Pope without a friend,
I've laid me here, awate my end.
The buzzards pass by in the sky,
The coyotes, patient, howl goodby.
My thurst is gone, no hunger more,
The cold creeps slowly to my core.

So when you find me I'll have sped,
And you'll say, "Jamie, better dead."
My worthless name please carve in stone.
"In life and death I lie alone."

Willy Spear

What's yours, what's present, past, what's copied from the books? Kind of runs together.

They're coming and coming in their campers and their low-slung cars that drag grease on the high points. Visitors, and sure you'd be hospitable, though the kids of now are mostly so undisciplined, can't let them out of sight, nice folks and maybe they'll come in and they'll want a poem and you'll get their address and maybe be copying one out for them later, depending on the circumstances.

Softer with time, old Will, ninety years, and it's nice, comfortable, to work over the words again, though that kid, he bent the point. Put them in their packages, in the pigeonholes of Mana's desk, thumbed and the fingers get stiffer, and there's not so much room on the page now. Pigeonholes like prison cells.

Sit there, out over the Bay. Watch where the fog piles up, watch where the boats, the big ones, come steaming in, and the sailboats (more when the war'd finished) slicing up the Bay or drifting in the sun. Alcatraz and Treasure Island, the ferries. Over, down at the far end, a clear day, they'd say they could see the Moffett hangars where the blimps were and one got loose, 'forty-two, out of control and scraped the top of a hill way up north, stayed there for a night and then blew free with all the crew and they'd never heard more; to Mars.

fading

floating

forms that

disappear

229

Sit there, out over the Bay. The Missis hauling water and the weeds coming in. They're taking your cattle, Will, stealing, 'cause she can't keep an eye out and no one to help, with the war. Like they'd burned up your mines when they'd took over all but your land for the Park. Government, no respect for the individual. Even good justice don't set right with freedom.

trickle

away

Maybe General Patton, he'd help. Tearing up the desert with his tanks and his soldiers with the wooden guns, thousands. Patton, up by the gypsum camp, Palen Mountains, Little Maria Valley. Sit there on his porch, that house they'd give him, where he'd sit and practice desert war and want to know about this and that about the desert. Maybe he'd help. They sure knew how to do things with their tanks and their banging away at the Joshua trees. Thirty-five men a day they'd kill what with one thing or another, and he'd not care it seemed a grain. Send a soldier or two to help, maybe.

antelope

bones

Paroled, Goody Knight, as if it was some great favor, though you'd learned a lot and if it hadn't been for the weeds, for the cattle, for the Missis all alone, sitting there, over the Bay. And you'd see her . . . *Jenny, Jenny, where'd you be now, your fingers on the keys?*

Paroled, and you'd be getting a pardon when Assemblyman Fein got interested and that statement from Crabble's last wife. Crabble with his nine wives, forced him out of the L.A. sheriff's office for cruelty to prisoners, Crabble who'd break any law that'd get in his way. Trapping quail, ripping up the Indian relics, stealing cattle, shot old Jack your best friend burro and you'd taken the bullet to the sheriff and it didn't fit the rifle Crabble'd given them because he'd hid his own and given them his wife's. She says all that later, and it'd get your parole and pardon, like you'd told them all along if they'd wanted to know the truth. Stealing cattle and you'd see the hides with the W↗ brand on his land. Shooting traps and the fence cut, and chopped down Christmas trees. Lying in wait, the ambushes, setting up a shooting range across the road to the Desert Lady, cahoots with Lodger, deputy sheriff of the county, San Bernardino. Will, who'd set the desert blooming, his lakes, his roads, and found gold a dozen times when the others had gone away. And you'd see from the photos of Crabble lying there, biting the dust, he'd his gun all cocked for the next shot, and the wound showed sure he'd been crouching to hide, ambush, and anyhow there weren't no tracks where you'd be able to do that fixing up to hide a murder. And would Will be one for that kind of fixing?

my

Treasure

Back, and the Missis with her bonnet tied under her chin, and how sweet her smile and the eyes that seem to retreat with the years and you can see the hair is white so white and you'd been remembering it as brown and the long ruffle skirts sitting there on the donkey for the photographer on the beach, the three sisters, young Will with his beard . . . *White, the crackling on the laundry wire, skeleton fingers* . . . and she'd get the beard, and not much later the mustache. Five years, and the road's as dusty and the bumps are the same, no, here the wash'd moved its course a bit, bad rutted. But the desert's dying. Say it for that moment, Will, say it and let it lie. No more the wild hay to your belt buckle; the blackbush is taking over, the weeds are dry and bitter. No more the wild

eyes

that

make

the

rain

231

burros and the cows calling for their calves in the rocks; the sand drifts in, the Russian thistle tumbles in the wind. You'll have said it to yourself, and that's enough, though others, they'll say it on and on. June, leaving, crazy old man. Not Helen, never, stick it out with the wind whistling dry and San Quentin far far off. Believe in it, in the desert, in Will. The kindling all laid, fixings for your favorite stew prepared, and to-morrow'd be good enough to see what's to be done.

Tomorrow. Rush back from that land of treasure, Robin on my shoulder, no thought for the pains in my knees. Here, where the birds have silenced the coyote, where there's light now in my window. Slow, move them slow and maybe they'll ease up and maybe I can leave the canes hanging on the back of Mana's chair. Light enough now, and there's a lot to be doing.

go

back!

Today. Are these kitchen sounds?—ears are heavy, and the buzzing and the sheets are cool to the itching, hearing's heavy, I know, I know. Kitchen sounds, and Mana's not beside me. Four years, though, four years ago her time had come.

Kitchen sounds. Lily, a little round face back of the oil lamp, or with that skip in her walk when I told her we'd be going to the Desert Lady, and she'd kiss me like my cheek wasn't old and rotting and stubbly and the aching gums, kiss me with her heart, not like June, in a hurry to move away. It must be Lily, who'd not stir herself these other mornings, Lily up and clattering and the stove kindled and roaring up the pipe and maybe I can feel the heat already, coming in through the living room. Lily.

now!

now!

O Mana, why do you ache so, the hollow in my chest, your white hair flowing on the pillow that would always be clean then, why does the feel of you here hurt so?

Shivering on the edge of the bed, here, spasm of shivering.

Half dead with the stroke, to Banning, but the smile would come through, her sweet smile, and she'd raise her hand to you. And her time'd come, and she'd say "Good-by, my Desert Lord."

Sobbing so, an old man's tears.

Serrano Palms, their flat new graveyard, what does it have to do with Mana, with you? Mana who had always known she'd rest beside our children and old Will, here. They'd taken her there and you'd been in no kind of shape to say nothing. But you'd talked them 'round, County permit, brought her up here, nice carved, three handles a side, one on each end, lowered with the ropes into the hole you and Warren Hildebrand dug, Reverend Marcus and Mana's poem and yours, and you'd covered her in, and you'd said good-by again.

Hot cakes and the honey we'd found, Helen Jane, your hair so pretty brown like that to your shoulders, your face I'd give it a kiss, and if you skip like that and I can see you through that robe, and I'll toss you on the bed and you'll see, you'll see.

Pull them on, easier sitting on the bed. Shaking shaking so much. Damn! that pain shoots in my knees, canes for legs, cowboy Will. Coffee, real, you can smell the difference, eggs with tomatoes, her own invention, tasty, sitting with the table all set and she's gone and found some flowers, in the Welch's jelly jar. I don't much hear what she's saying, the sound's nice and that's what she wants me to know and I know it.

my then

pulling

pulling

233

Sitting here, even after I've pretty much finished and Lily has the dishes in the sink. Sitting 'cause it's easier, and I've never stopped working in my life, wouldn't be right, look what it does to all these modern folk with nothing to do but mischief and dirtying around, sitting here while that twenty-two, good-for-nothing, can stand on in the corner there forever. Sitting here with the north light coming in on the table and the rocks and the lizards, a grain at a time as he flicks his tail. Robin, how long to fill the olla? With that pulling again at my shoulders, pulling, the gold again drawing me, like another sense, somewhere there by the stamp mill where I'd milled out two and a half million dollars in my time. Like dreaming of things that'll happen after. Like years before it'd happened I'd dreamt of Crabble shooting at me and missing and then I'd got him. Or the hypnos', New Hampshire, and the things it'd do. Like the Indian spirit light that burns nights, special nights, to the west where they'd camped through the ages. They'd laugh at me, the others, even Mana, but not my Lily, no, there are these things, and like I never was afraid and Ma said you was born that way, like I'd wheeled dirt for the Ditch and Dam Company in Nebraska, get dirt behind the dam to stop the leak, on a one-foot plank and it was a sheer drop of twelve hundred.

Yuh, Lily, no one's listened to old Will like you. Soon we'll be going out, see what's pulling at me, poke around, that gold there. Like you with your bighorn back in the rockpiles, and your sleeping under the stars, and all that sand and flowers, the wonders no one sees nowadays. Like that, like feeling something asking for you to come.

my now

filling

Exodus to

the East

all

flows

in

234

The Joshua flower from your Lily

There's a flower opening on that Joshua tree, Will, saw it this morning when I was out. Out before the primroses closed to sleep. Like fairies. The sun's all stars on the frost, the wind's given up, scratched enough for one night, scratching on the eaves.

You cried Bonanza! in your sleep, Will, and I figured you'd struck treasure. Remember? You'll see, there'll be something there to look for today, and maybe it wasn't there at all before. Something's growing, I know it, being born.

And how did you like the eggs I fixed you? You haven't said a thing, what with all those tears in your eyes and that long-way look.

Here's Lily to make you skip.

A sharp scythe and the sun on your neck, old Will

Young, light like the cottonwood seed floating on the air — the tree we'd planted together and she'd watered every summer till it had its roots well down — skipping here on the old linoleum. And the years haven't quite caught me either, though maybe stiffened a bit, slowed some. Like our children in the golden days, as they'd race through the guest cabins — never really used, a resort in the 'twenties, dance pavilion, swimming, horses and hunting, dudes, but it failed, the desert didn't just take to the idea, and maybe Will didn't either. Racing to play tricks on their schoolteacher, to catch a butterfly, to hide from a bit of punishment.

old

is

young

Parents, my brothers; only Willy, Jerry Dan, left. My sister, little Gracie, the last, Nebraska, the little girl in pigtails, a heavy hand on her shoulder from the dusty miller behind and his wife broad as the kitchen table, could that be my mother? And then in Pasadena, the old folks' home, it was the year the Missis died. Gracie, seventy-five and her pigtails gone mostly bald, must run in the family. And she rich too with that lawyer husband from over near Scottsbluff. Ten years younger and she all ready to die, and she did 'fore long.

And brother Harris who came to San Quentin; went right through high school, nineteen twelve; three years was all they could keep me. And John Dan, worked for the Governor in Denver, had a ranch. Mother, she'd died in Pasadena and they'd carried her back to Nebraska and buried her next to miller Dan, good Orthodox to the end. They'd not made me one, nor a Christian, with all their murderous ways. Brahmins'd be superior and I'll be going soon to India, just to see, just to see.

Be ready for changes, working, never a day of nothing, like the old folks' home. Changes, mutations, like geology with its forces and transitions, like some creatures living on into new conditions, the whale which was on land as they tell from the hind legs they've found. And man is nothing special except for the damage he does to all the rest and to himself.

Hector, the oldest, teacher, South Dakota; Latin, art, paintings he did so beautiful, and he so tall and handsome, and if only you'd be like him, Jerry.

And Patience.

And the others, eleven we were and all gone but Will.

Will, me, preparing, with the ranch pulled together and everything here and they can have it if they'll put up a museum or I'll auction it off and anyhow, with the hundred and thirty-five thousand for selling the ranch to Tanker for after I pass on, I'll have enough, when the bank gets itself unsnarled and if I keep them revenooers off, and I'll be getting on.

To the bottles shining on the Elbe, to India, and

undivided

O Mother   .

devour

us

your

children

237

I'd like to be seeing that architecture of Rome, and Siberia, and Kov on the Volga, Patience with the yoke, the windmills.

No hurry, the gold'll be there, it'll wait.

Just carry this over and put it in the old 'dobe where it belongs.

Chips, Crabble's stone. Finished now.

My old truck, burlap sacks over the wheels to protect tires that have crumbled into black dust. The ore bin. The grindstone, bicycle seat to footpedal it, and the trickle can above — slice short, they'll not be a stone bigger'n a cactus pear, a sharp scythe and the sun on your neck and Helen she's bringing a pail of fresh-welled water.

harvest

gathering

The 'dobe, needs a-fixing and plastering up some. Get to it.

Tires and the radiator that froze up, irrigation hose hanging on the rafters, bird's nest built in its loops. That's the cardboard suitcase that got bent when we'd a hurry and tied it too tight to the wagon getting to the hospital. My saddle, only the bare wood tree, with its high old-style bear-trap cantle and the pommel with slick fork for roping. The oak stirrup, ironbound. The best, that fellow who made that tree, ash, and I'll get it made up again into a saddle when I get around to it. Bars sharp-withered for my thoroughbred. Wouldn't fit your flat-back quarter horses of today. Be needing a good saddle soon . . . *Pull him up! pull him up! Come down the rope. Burning hair and flesh, the squeal, and slice the sack, seeds into the bucket to fry tonight. Twelve hundred head. The desert blooming . . .*

up
   the
      years

the
   Shaman's
   Rope

238

Wild willow honey, Lily to Will

Wander, dear Will, look it over. Draw it together, here in your hidden home, all this accumulation of your life, things, so much, I hardly understand, the meaning and the tools, bring forth the riches of the desert and the mountains. It doesn't matter, not to understand: which turnbuckle where, just how those ore cars worked, why the pitchfork teeth are shorter here than there, what's in that paper package all trussed up with bailing wire, which cow kicked in the side of that rusting pail.

In the end it's all yourself. Your paraphernalia. Didn't Gracie likely have hers too, sitting in the old people's home? And your Lily? yes, I've mine, and it's with me wherever I may go, and it's . . .

Tap tapping, the toilet stinks; your Lily of the Valley; lightning and the deluge and the terror of the earth and air; a scout bee heading out into the blue sage; Pa singing softly as the fire dies; Colin at his little table weaving his lovely web; the frogs and the blood and the sowing and the killing to bring life and identity. To be separate and distinct that one may then reach and touch.

to return

is

to

go

on

239

Here Will, a mint, found them in my pocket. Lucky too I had them yesterday, no, the day before, when I got to Willow Hole and it was dry dry and full of dead burs and the bees were so thick in the green willow leaves—water somewhere down below still and there aren't any other willows up that draw—you could hear them from way up around the corner before you came in sight, and the hummingbirds all about. You'll come with me next time, Will, when your knees are back in shape, and I'll show you how it's dried up bad.

Good honey, willow honey, the first of the season. We'll go there and follow the bees to their hive, shall we, Will? And the butterflies, hundreds, working through the willow flowers.

Colin, you'll be coming soon?

our

Honey

the

rebirth

She'll move on light in my valley;
Leev Mail Here Pleas

Come with me, my Helen Jane,
For the bees sure are buzzing about;
They're finished now their winter sleep;
There'll be plenty of honey to scout.

No, no, old Will, no time for honeying, all of them gone now and Helen lying down there by the Joshua tree.

Her window in the sky.

Roll, Walter cat, roll in the dust, once, twice, three times, three days and there'll be rain. Like we need it bad too, bring the desert into flower, full. And I'd knowed there'd be a dry this winter from the range animals, how they've drifted off this year, they can tell and'll move away for a spell.   Mountain Pine

Smell the rattler still? The cage where we'd kept him, and we'd studied him when we gave him rodents we'd trapped, watched how he'd hypnos' them and they'd jump plumb into his mouth for the swallowing. By the greasewood, the creosote bush; that'll come with the civilizing, it knows.

Just take this chisel. No hurry, Lily, no hurry.

throne

of the

rain

cloud

Hammer too, I'll manage. 'Nother stone to ready up.

Kissed me, kissed me, and she moves so light in my valley. They'll do it, others, and giggle, the wreck, and maybe I'll pinch their fanny and the winks and the sly looks. But Lily, there's a touching, a reaching out and a touching, a coming back the years. Her eyes, joining, past and future and on and on, and now there's no more need. Now there's no end, I know it, on and on, she'll move on light in my valley.

Nakwach

Just sit here a spell, Hercules Powder, built their boxes strong, here by the rusting press. The old buck rake, ore cars and the steel drums from the dam works, buckboard and the wagon to Banning.

We'll let that Joshua grow up, Robin boy, always like to have them near.

Sit here a spell. The buzzing and the humming, Willow Hole dried up.

Gold, pulling pulling, golden. All this, gathered in my valley. Back to the years of gold, sleeping happy. Now I may go, Kov, my home, on the Volga. Ready. Lily skipping light in my valley. Pulling pulling. Down at the entrance under the Joshua tree, Mana lying, the Russian thistle rolled up to her stone.

LEEV MAIL HERE PLEAS—SERRANO PALMS STAGE

I, Joshua tree; earth to sky

Gentle pain, working working, down in the soil beneath the warm sand.

Stone standing, tall beside the others, chipped with their signs, their bits of blue like the sky.

Sky to bring the rain, hail cutting, torment to my soul spread spring-time white, my gift unending, to my green that draws sweet air to my soul, that breathes off the sourness. Sky to carry the sun, the juice of life, the message on and on.

To loose the winds, press me, tear at me, dance softly with me, spread me to the desert.

Sky turned dark to bear the moon, the night stirrings, nudgings to my side, the grip on my reaching reaching, pushing tunnels in the sand, droplets of the night.

Stone standing tall.

The presences.

Slowed, drawing in, drawing in. Camps, the soft feet softly, cleaning, leaving as before as again. Here again, the hard feet, slowly slowly, bringing in and bringing in. A preparing, a departing. Joining to the dust.

Here the light so quickly. The presence, sowing. Quickly, lightly. Touching again, touching our valley soul.

Stone, standing tall under the whirling sun, the new sun, the sun strong to every cell. Tooth of the earth, seared with the lightning signs, their fire signs, their hidden clay treasures, their burning gold. Signs, the white signs where the eagle sleeps high high over my reachings. Over us, biting the elements, scoured, wearing, sand to our soil.

Stone standing, joining to the sky.

Author's Note

I have dedicated this revised edition of The Joshua Tree *to my friend Bill Keys.*

I owe Bill a lot: his hospitality when I first met him during my wanderings in the High Mohave Desert and during my several prolonged stays with him, his generous sharing with me of his life's story, his wisdom. Much of the story of Will Spear was drawn from what I learned of Bill.

When I last saw Bill, shortly before he died in 1969 at the age of ninety-two, he told me that he was beginning to work on his autobiography. It never happened.

May The Joshua Tree *be my memorial to a heroic life and a good friend.*

Bill's ranch is empty now, preserved in the Joshua Tree National Monument. Bill lies beside his Mana and his little children, across the draw from the old school house. Behind them is a great red-rock sentinel cliff: "Stone standing, joining to the sky."

Robert Cabot
Langley, Washington
March 1988

Robert Cabot

Robert Cabot has known the American West since the 1930's. While writing *The Joshua Tree* he lived in the Mohave Desert and central and northern California. Born in Boston in 1924, Cabot served as a sergeant in North Africa and Europe in World War II, has an A.B. from Harvard and an LL.B from Yale, and has had several careers: lawyer/economist, diplomat, co-founder of an intentional spiritual community, sponsor and participant in many innovative projects in such fields as citizen diplomacy and the environment, novelist, and free-lance writer. He has worked in many parts of the world and now lives with his wife and three of his six children on Whidbey Island, near Seattle.